ALSO BY LAURIE GELMAN

Class Mom

YOU'VE BEEN VOLUNTEERED

YOU'VE BEEN VOLUNTEERED

A Class Mom Novel

Laurie Gelman

HENRY HOLT AND COMPANY
NEW YORK

Henry Holt and Company
Publishers since 1866
120 Broadway
New York, New York 10271
www.henryholt.com

Henry Holt ® and ® are registered trademarks of
Macmillan Publishing Group, LLC.

Library of Congress Cataloging-in-Publication Data

Names: Gelman, Laurie, author.
Title: You've been volunteered : a class mom novel / by Laurie Gelman.
Other titles: You have been volunteered
Description: First edition. | New York, New York : Henry Holt and Company,
    2019. | Series: A class mom novel ; 2
Identifiers: LCCN 2018050182 | ISBN 9781250301857 (hardcover) |
    9781250222206 (international edition)
Subjects: LCSH: Domestic fiction.
Classification: LCC PS3607.E465 Y68 2019 | DDC 813/.6—dc23
LC record available at https://lccn.loc.gov/2018050182

Our books may be purchased in bulk for promotional, educational, or business
use. Please contact your local bookseller or the Macmillan Corporate and
Premium Sales Department at (800) 221-7945, extension 5442, or by e-mail at
MacmillanSpecialMarkets@macmillan.com.

First Edition 2019

Designed by Meryl Sussman Levavi

Printed in the United States of America

10 9 8 7 6 5 4 3 2 1

This is a work of fiction. All of the characters, organizations, and events portrayed
in this novel either are products of the author's imagination or are used fictitiously.

This book is dedicated to my parents,
Ted and Barbara. They weren't here to see
their daughter write a book, but they never for
a second let me doubt that I could.

A note to the fine folks of Kansas City

I have loved setting my books in your amazing city. I try to be as accurate as possible, but please forgive me when I do take poetic license with some things. This is a work of fiction, and sometimes I need to do it to advance the plot. Thanks for your understanding, and please, no more hate mail!

YOU'VE BEEN VOLUNTEERED

To: Parents of Mrs. Randazzo's Third-Grade Class
From: JDixon
Re: Guess Who's Back?
Date: 8/28

Hello, my fellow third-grade parents!

Guess who's back, back again
Jen is back, tell a friend
Guess who's back, guess who's back
Guess who's back, guess who's back . . .

Thank you, Eminem, for that lovely introduction.

Yes, I'm back despite swearing they would have to drag my cold, dead body back into the PTA.

And I'm just in time for hump year! That dreaded year smack-dab in the middle of K–5. I may need to get a therapy dog, what with all the excitement.

I had a very nice year away from being class mom, thanks for asking, and I think we can all agree that Asami Chang did a great job flying solo last year. The fact that she now refuses to even discuss her experience on the job ever again says more about you than about her.

You've all had me as class mom before, so I'm not going to bore you with the usual stuff, but below are the things you really do need to know:

- *My birthday is still April 18.*
- *I have switched to Smoothie King in an effort to lessen my need to caff up. So, any ex-parte meetings will no longer be held at the Starbucks near school. Oh, and I'm going to be grumpy as hell.*
- *Read the school's @#$% email.*
- *It's still my way or the highway. Nothing has changed.*

Did I miss anything? Oh yes, curriculum night is October 11. I'll be soliciting for food and drinks very soon.

As always, response times will be noted.

See you next Tuesday!

Jen Dixon

PS: Our teacher, Mrs. Randazzo, would like you to answer the following questions about your kiddos and get them back to her ASAP. I personally think it's none of her damn business, but whatever. Her email is wrandazzo@WHT.edu.

Questions:

1. *In what way has your child changed the most in the last year?*
2. *What would constitute a successful third-grade year for your child? What do you most want him/her to learn?*
3. *What out-of-school commitments does your child have? Are you happy with the amount of time that he/she spends on extracurricular activities?*
4. *Is there anything else that I should know about your child?*

1

I stare at my computer screen and ponder my email. Is it too short? Too kind? Too sincere? Normally I wouldn't give a royal rip, but we have a new PTA president starting this year. I haven't met her yet, but she sent out a note saying she wants to be copied on all class parent emails. This fact alone has me at DEFCON 3. Smells like a micro-manager to me. Nina would never have wasted her time on that crap.

Sadly, Nina is no longer PTA president, nor is she living in Kansas City. My best friend in the world now calls Tennessee home. She moved to Memphis with my former trainer, Garth, and her daughter, Chyna, in June, shortly after it was named the fattest city in the U.S. for like the hundredth time. The mayor decided to start a "Cut the Fat" citywide health initiative and Garth was recruited through one of his Wounded Warrior buddies to develop a middle school program. It was an easy move for Nina—she can run her web design business from anywhere, and Chyna was more than happy to start high school in a new city after her less than stellar middle school years, poor baby.

But all their change and excitement has left me without my best friend, my kick-ass trainer, and a great babysitter . . . and everyone knows how hard it is to find a great babysitter. Returning as class mom would be so much easier if Nina was still living here—especially since she was the one who, once again, convinced me to jump back into the thankless cesspool.

"Just do it. You know you miss it," she said on our latest phone call.

"What I miss is you, you big jerk."

And I really do. There is a little hole in my heart and an emptiness in my life that no number of texts or phone calls is able to fill. Truth be told, that's why I agreed to rejoin the class mompalooza. I need something to distract me.

Thank God she didn't move away last year. I wouldn't have gotten through it without her. Our family was thrown for a loop when my mom was diagnosed with breast cancer. It was a rough go for quite a few months and Nina was pretty much the anchor of our care circle. No matter how bad it got, Nina never wavered.

Laura, my sweet second-born, was finishing her last year at KU, but she came home every weekend to cook and clean for my parents. Right before our eyes she went from lazy college kid to domestic goddess. I'm not sure where she learned to make a bed with hospital corners, but I'm thrilled she did.

My oldest daughter, Vivs, moved back to Kansas City from Brooklyn, where she was cohabitating with her architect boyfriend, Raj, and took a job as a nutrition consultant at our local Jenny Craig just to be close to all of us. I nicknamed her the Lone Arranger because she single-handedly scheduled all of my mother's chemo and doctor visits along with a schedule of who would be taking her to said visits. Finally, her bossy firstborn personality was used for good instead of evil.

Max was eerily quiet but very cooperative no matter how many nights he spent with Chyna babysitting him. And my husband, Ron, was—well, he was a man and frustrated because he couldn't just fix the problem.

As for me, I was *not* ready to lose my mother, no way, no how.

But instead of standing strong and defiant, I was a very disappointing tower of Jell-O. Who knew I'd fold like origami when the going got tough? There were lots of tears (on my part) and prayers (on my parents' part), and it was all very bleak and sad until one day my mother, Kay Howard, up and decided that cancer had picked the wrong bitch to mess with. She actually said that, out loud. It was the first time I had ever heard her swear and I learned very quickly it wasn't going to be the last.

With my mom in fight mode, cancer became our punching bag, literally and figuratively. I hung a boxing bag in my basement workout area, aka Ron's Gym and Tan, slapped a picture of a cancerous boob on it, and beat the shit out of the picture every day. It was Garth's idea and it really worked. Not only did my arms get toned, I got out all my frustration, so I was ready to face my mother and her never-ending demands. Not demands for herself, mind you, but for my father. Kay was taking no prisoners, but Ray was struggling with the thought of a life without his darling girl, as he calls her. I always knew my parents loved each other, but I'd never realized how *in* love they still are. Mom was ready every day with a list of things my dad absolutely needed. It usually looked something like this:

The newspaper
A poppyseed bagel from Einstein's
Snapple Peach Tea
That toothpaste that tastes like cherry
At least ten hugs

✦ ✦ ✦

Mom is now done with her chemo, thank God. In the spring she rang the bell at the University of Kansas Cancer Center to signal her final treatment, said goodbye to all her "chemo-sabes," and vowed to keep the fight going. Her hair was a casualty of her war with the big C, but beyond that she is all piss and vinegar, which I believe is fueled by her collection of *Golden Girls* wigs. When she wears Blanche, there is no stopping her.

When the phone rings, I already know it is her calling for our morning check-in.

"Hi, Mom."

"Sweetheart, are you busy?"

"Just writing some emails."

"Oh, good. Write one to your aunt Barbara, will you? I think she only gets spam unless I send her something."

"Happy to." I start typing her email address, Iwasacancangirl @aol.com.

Aunt Barbara is a little eccentric. In fact, she is a family enigma. She is my father's half sister from when my grandmother died and my grandfather remarried. I myself have never met her, but stories about her are legendary. She followed her high school sweetheart to Honolulu when she was seventeen, but he left her for a luau dancer. My grandfather thought she would come home after that, but she surprised everyone by staying and working as a waitress in Wailea. She took a two-year course in secretarial skills and landed a job as the personal assistant to some guy who ultimately became a bigwig at the Bank of Hawaii. She worked for him for something like forty years, she never married, and she lives with six cats. I've yet to determine at what point in her life she was a cancan girl, but there's no rush.

As I said, we've never met, but she was that relative my mom would always make me draw pictures for and get on the phone with to say thank you, which is so awkward when you're a little kid. We've always exchanged Christmas cards and photos, and every year she sends me and my children $10 on our birthdays. My mother tells me it's very generous, considering she's on a fixed income now that she is retired. I asked my mom once why she never visits, and why we don't go see her. I was informed we are not the Rockefellers and can't just jet all over the world on a whim. It's the kind of answer you give a ten-year-old if you don't want them to ask again. I didn't.

"So, what's up for today?"

"Your dad and I have a meeting at the parish to talk to Father Dimon about the pancake breakfast and then we're going to Denny's for lunch. Can you come?"

I happen to enjoy the all-day Grand Slam breakfast at Denny's, but I have a full schedule myself. I tell her as much.

"Okay." She pauses. "I can't remember why I called you."

"To ask me to lunch?"

"No." Another pause.

"To check in?"

"No. Oh what the devil was it? Ray!" she yells to my father. "Why did I call Jennifer?"

I hear mumbling, and then my mother says, "Oh that's right. Have you signed up for the Susan B. Anthony yet?"

"It's the Susan G. Komen, Mom, and no I haven't."

"Jennifer, you're the only one who hasn't."

A twinge of guilt hits me.

"Actually, I was going to do it right after my emails."

"Well good. Remember, our team name is the Holy Rollers."

"Yup. Got it. Have a good lunch. I'll talk to you later."

Gotta love Kay. Once she finished chemo and got her strength back she jumped full-tilt boogie into the Kansas City chapter of the American Cancer Society and they still don't know what the hell hit them. She also started volunteering at the Susan G. Komen foundation, and before I knew what was happening, I was recruited for the Race for the Cure this coming May and charged with raising five hundred dollars. And when I say race, I really mean walk. There *is* a race, but Kay wants us to do the one-mile walk, so we can be together. I may do both, depending on how my winter workouts go.

I have asked a lot of my school friends to participate and Vivs, Nina, and Chyna all signed on immediately and started getting sponsors. I'm the only big lollygagger, because what I truly suck at is asking people for money. I haven't raised one dime yet. Or even signed up.

I *will* get to that, but first, I send Aunt Barbara a recipe I saw on-line for pineapple soup that I thought sounded delicious (what with the cayenne pepper and basil). Then I decide to tackle Mrs. Randazzo's questionnaire. I look it over and can't help but smile. I live to fill out forms like this. I'm going to take old Razzi out for a spin and test her sense of humor.

To: WRandazzo

From: JDixon

Re: Questionnaire

Date: 8/28

Hello, Mrs. Randazzo,

Here is all you need to know about one Max Dixon.

1. In what way has your child changed the most in the last year?

He stopped picking his nose and he finally started pooping in the potty. He makes it there about 74% of the time, which is 6% better than his father, but you'll still need to keep an eye on him.

2. What would constitute a successful third-grade year for your child? What do you most want him/her to learn?

Learning the alphabet once and for all would be a huge win. And he really needs to understand the difference between narcolepsy and necrophilia to avoid any future embarrassment.

3. What out-of-school commitments does your child have? Are you happy with the amount of time that he/she spends on extracurricular activities?

I don't really know what the hell he does after school but he's out of my hair for a good four hours and that's enough . . . unless you know of an after-dinner program. If you do, I'm all ears!

---

4. Is there anything else that I should know about your child?

Max doesn't like to be looked directly in the eye, but don't look away, either. And be careful how you speak to him. The medication has done wonders, but it sometimes wears off too early.

Thanks! See you on curriculum night.

Jen

2

"Max!" I scream from our laundry room in the basement. "Where is my detergent?" No answer.

"*Max!*" I scream even louder. Still no answer, so I run up to the kitchen and can't believe my eyes—Max, on his iPad again, this time with headphones on. I had just told him to put it down and tidy up the mess he made making slime. I really want to kill the person who put that recipe on YouTube.

Against my wishes, Kay and Ray gave Max an iPad on his eighth birthday. Post-cancer, my normally frugal mother has started to make it rain harder than a rapper in a nightclub with a stack of hundreds.

"Blame it on the chemo brain, sweetheart," she has taken to saying. "I've dumped all the rules I used on you, and I'm fucking loving it."

Apparently, she lost her hair *and* her filter.

Max adores his iPad and the thing hasn't been more than five feet away from him since the day he got it. Even if he can't play on it, he wants it beside him. It's like an electronic security blanket.

"I need it," he claims. "It just makes me happy. Deal with it."

That last line came courtesy of all the Nickelodeon shows he's become so fond of. At first, I thought it was wonderful that he was getting away from the baby shows, because honest to God, I couldn't have watched one more minute of *PAW Patrol* or *Bubble Guppies*. But then I realized that the next level up in kids' television is sitcoms about precocious preteens sassing their adult supervisors. These have had a horrible influence on my once sweet little boy.

"Max!" I take his headphones off and glare at him.

"What?"

"I'm sorry, what did you say?"

"I said wh—I mean, Yes?"

"I thought I told you to clean up this mess and put everything back." I gesture to the kitchen, which I would generously describe as tidy-ish.

"I did!"

"Where is my laundry detergent?"

"I finished it." He moves to put his headphones back on, but I grab them.

"Not so fast. Put your iPad down. I've told you to let me know when you're about to use up the detergent. Now I can't do laundry."

He looks at his lap and gives me the one-shoulder shrug.

"Oh, you don't care about having clean clothes?"

"No."

"Well, too bad. Now you have to go to the store with me to get some Tide."

"No!" He stands up and faces me. "*American Ninja Warrior All-Stars* is coming on. I have to see if the California Kids make it to the next round."

"Yes, well, that sounds very important, but you should have thought of it before you used up all my laundry soap."

"Mom, no!" He starts to whine (a habit he still hasn't broken).

"Just get in the van, Max. We can be there and back in twenty minutes." I grab my car fob and stand at the back door tapping my foot. After a ten-second stare-down he stomps past me and mutters three words I have never before heard come out of his mouth.

"I hate you."

It hits me like a hot knife in my gut. I suck in my breath and consider my next words carefully.

"You hate me? Really?" I can feel tears forming and I weigh letting him see how much his comment has hurt me. "You feel the same way about me that I feel about rats?"

"Yes." Max tries to look defiant, but I can tell his resolve is wavering.

"Get in the van," I tell him. "And just because you said that, I'm buying pods instead of liquid. No more slime for you."

✦ ✦ ✦

I can't help but wonder if Max's turn to the dark side has anything to do with Ron not being around as much. He's been spending a lot more time at the Fitting Room, his sporting goods store. About a year ago, he had a little idea to start offering a free yoga class on Saturday mornings at the back of the store in the hopes of increasing traffic. Gisele, one of his summer employees, taught the class, and it took off like Max at bath time. I'm not sure what the bigger draw was—the fact that it was free, or the fact that Gisele has this charisma that makes you want her to touch you. I'm not kidding. Ron and I both have a crush on her.

Soon he had to add a class on Sunday to handle the demand, and now it's up to four times a week and Gisele works for him full-time. Yes, it's true. My jock husband is an out-of-the-closet yogi. He's even studying to become an instructor, so he can teach it himself. He now charges $5 for the class, this little idea has brought a whole different clientele into the store, and Ron is the go-to guy in KC for yoga gear. I never knew there was so much equipment: mats, straps, blocks, blankets, bands, and bolsters. The back of the store now looks like the prop room from the set of *Fifty Shades of Grey*. Do people really need all that stuff? Probably not, but who am I to argue? I hope they nama-stay all day, because Max still has to go to college.

Our trip to the grocery store is quick and quiet. I'm still tied up in knots over the "I hate you" comment, and Max is a world-class sulker. It can be hours before he comes out of his funk. It's so annoying when your kids inherit your worst character traits.

When we get back from the store, I throw one of my new pods in the laundry machine, turn it on, and head upstairs to make dinner. Max is already in front of the TV, watching his show.

After chopping a few veggies and throwing a bottled marinade on the chicken, I sit down at the kitchen-counter office and check my emails.

To: JDixon
From: PTucci
Re: Guess who's back?
Date: 8/28

Hey there!

You can't see it, but I'm doing my happy dance that you are back as class mom! I didn't know you had said yes. Let me know if you need any help.

xo Peetsa

To: JDixon
From: SCobb
Re: Guess who's back?
Date: 8/28

Jennifer—

Welcome back. How is your mother? Did she use the hypoallergenic sheets I sent? You can't be too careful after chemo. Graydon has just come from the doctor and we have confirmed the only allergy he still has is to peanuts, so please make sure our teacher knows to have a peanut-free environment in her classroom.

Shirleen

Yes, it's true. Graydon Cobb is no longer in need of a size 8 husky hazmat suit to get through life. To everyone's delight, he has outgrown most of his allergies. *And* he now carries an EpiPen.

"Graydon's got an EpiPen and he's not afraid to use it," Max announced to me after a play date. I don't mind telling you I found those words both reassuring and terrifying.

To: JDixon
From: JJAikins
Re: Guess who's back?
Date: 8/28

Jen,

Hey lady! What's up? Hope you had a good summer. Can't wait to get the kids back in school! Let's try to meet for lunch and catch up.

JJ xoxo

I always seem to forget that JJ Aikins is in our class. You'd think I'd remember someone I dubbed Mini-Me for the first year I knew her. But after the Kim Fancy kindergarten drama I have rarely heard from her except in class emails. Her mother picks Kit up from school because JJ works full-time at Halls in Crown Center. So, to get a kisses-and-hugs email from her is suspicious, to say the least. What, oh what, could she be after?

To: JDixon
From: ALody
Re: Guess who's back?
Date: 8/28

Jen,

Uh, nice to meet you? Allow me to guess some of those "boring details" that you say you left out of your email. Let's see . . . your medication is no longer working, you were raised in a barn (not uncommon in these parts, I'm told), and you put no stock in the old adage "You never get a second chance to make a first impression." You should really check your class list before you assume that you know everyone and vice versa. We are new to the school and my son, Draper, is in Mrs. Randazzo's class. So, if you wouldn't mind taking the time to tell me some of those useless details you seem to assume everyone knows, I'd appreciate it.

Thank you.
Alison Lody

Wow. First impressions work both ways, lady. How the heck did I miss her name when I copied and pasted the class list? I'd better get this woman schooled in my ways toot sweet and defuse this righteous indignation thing she's got going on.

To: ALody
From: JDixon
Re: Guess who's back?
Date: 8/28

Hi Alison

My apologies! I didn't see your name on the class list that I copied and pasted from the PTA. Just so you know, I play things a bit fast and loose as class mom. You'll get used to me. And trust me, it saves you from having to read a bunch of boring stuff. But I have attached the PTA briefing below that will give you an idea of upcoming events this fall.

Welcome to William Taft and sorry I missed your name.

Jen

That should make her feel better. I'm really the Gandhi of class moms, when you think about it.

I get up to turn on the oven and hear a ping from my computer. To my surprise, it's an email from Mrs. Randazzo. That was quick.

To: JDixon
From: WRandazzo
Re: Questionnaire
Date: 8/28

Dear Jen,

Thank you for your prompt reply. I have a few suggestions for you.

First, please send Max to school with some diapers. There is no physical way I can monitor his bowels and teach him the alphabet at the same time. To paraphrase Regis Philbin, I'm only one woman.

Second, I looked up both necrophilia and narcolepsy and all I can say is potato/potahto. He'll figure it out one way or another.

And finally, instead of an after-school program, why don't you just send him to a homeless shelter? That way you don't have to think about him at all. I can always call you if he doesn't show up for school.

Looking forward to a great year.

Thanks,
Winnie R

Oh my God, the sass! The irreverence! The lack of protocol! I write back immediately.

To: WRandazzo

From: JDixon

Re: Questionnaire

Date: 8/28

Mrs. Randazzo,

So good to have you teaching my offspring again!

xo Jen

Oh, didn't I mention that Vivs and Laura both had Razzi? My bad.

✦ ✦ ✦

I look at the clock and realize Ron should have been home by now. I grab the phone and dial his cell.

"Hey."

"Hey. Where are you? Dinner's in forty minutes."

"Sorry, babe. I got hung up here. I'll be about another hour. Can you keep a plate warm for me?"

"Sure. Try to get home before Max goes to bed."

"Roger that. Love you."

"Love you too."

We really need to talk about the hours Ron has been clocking at the store the past few months. At first, I was afraid he was having an affair—I mean, he was there almost every night! And my mother was fighting cancer! How could he? But I did the drop-by on more than one occasion, and every time I found him sitting at his computer poring over inventory reports and account updates. Lately he's been a little better about getting home for dinner, but he still misses more than he hits. I keep asking him if there's anything to worry about and he assures me there isn't. But my Spidey sense tells me otherwise, so it's time to get out my lasso of truth and force it out of him. And yes, I'm well aware that I'm mixing my Marvel metaphors.

I put the chicken and veggies in the oven, run down and throw the laundry in the dryer, punch the boob on the bag for good measure, and head back upstairs.

With a few minutes to kill, I join Max on the couch and see what's happening in the world of *American Ninja Warrior*.

To my delight, he slides over and hugs me.

"I don't hate you, Mommy," he whispers. "I'm sorry."

"I know," I whisper back. "I'm glad you said sorry. Want to eat dinner in front of the TV?"

I know I shouldn't be rewarding him for his earlier behavior, but I figure, what the hell? I want to see if the California Kids make it through, too.

✦ ✦ ✦

Max is asleep and I'm catching up on my gossip, courtesy of TMZ .com, when Ron finally walks in the back door, looking exhausted. His khakis are rumpled and his white polo shirt has a coffee stain on it.

"Hey. Sorry." He nods to the plate on the table. "Thanks for this." Sitting down, he attacks the chicken and veggies like he hasn't eaten all day. I don't even bother to ask him if he wants it heated up.

"How was your day?" I join him at the table.

"Fine," he says through a mouthful of food, and I'm glad Max isn't here to witness this lapse in manners. Ron shakes his head. "Crazy day."

"Crazy good?" I start my fishing expedition.

Ron shrugs and shovels another forkful into his mouth. I don't say anything, but I raise my eyebrows and don't even blink. It takes a few moments for him to realize that I mean business tonight. He takes a big gulp of water and wipes his mouth.

"This is really good." He smiles.

"Crazy good?" I repeat without shifting my eyes from his face.

"Yes, crazy good. Anything else you want to know?"

"Just everything." I shrug. "Babe, what's up? The yoga stuff can't still be why you're working late every night."

"It's not." Ron wipes his mouth again and sighs. "I've wanted to tell you about it, but I really wanted to think it through first."

"Think what through? Can I help?"

He smiles. "You can. I just know you will have a very strong opinion."

"Does it have anything to do with me and Max? I mean, will we be affected by it?"

"Indirectly, yes, but it mostly has to do with the store."

I'm not going to lie. I'm more than a little relieved to hear that it isn't me. But then another worry sets in.

"What about the store? Are we in trouble?" My heart starts to beat a little faster.

Ron leans back in his chair and stretches his arms behind him. I can't help but admire this man I love. He's always had a good body, but I have to say the yoga has really done wonders for his BMI. My fifty-four-year-old hubby has the body of a forty-year-old . . . a *hot* forty-year-old. I look down at my own saggy vessel and sigh.

He considers me with his tired eyes and leans forward. I notice his black hair is finally showing some gray around the temples. At least he still has most of it.

"For the past few months, I've been looking at the possibility of opening a few yoga studios."

"Really? That's huge. Where? Like, another city, or here in KC?"

"I'm thinking about studios in Branson, Topeka, and Lawrence plus one here in town."

"Why so many all at once? Shouldn't you start small?"

"I already did with classes at the back of the store. I've been doing some research and it seems there is a real market for more of a modern-style yoga studio . . . clean lines, light and minimalistic. If I get the right locations, I really think they'll take off. And we'll brand them with great merchandise and a soothing ambiance. A place you go for yoga, but hang out for the tranquility. Maybe even offer meditation classes."

I'm genuinely impressed. "Can we afford it? I mean, is the store doing that well?"

"We're doing fine, but expanding is going to mean a big loan and even more time at work. There's a lot to consider."

I take a deep breath. "It's exciting."

"I think so, too. But we're really going to have to cut back on our spending for the next few years. I mean way back."

I don't consider us big spenders at all. I mean, my favorite store is Target.

"Where do you want to trim the fat?" I really can't think of where we *over*spend.

Ron yawns. "Well, I'm happy you're off caffeine. We save almost four hundred dollars a month now that you've stopped going to Star-bucks."

"That is total bullshit," I say as I do the math in my head. Two trips to coffee heaven a day times six dollars each time—what with the obligatory snack and all—and I'm ashamed to realize I was spend-ing that much. Ron's eyes challenge me to disagree.

"Well, I don't do that anymore, so . . . you're welcome. Where else do I overspend?"

"Since you asked, I think we could save a few bucks not buying designer brands."

"What designer brands?" I demand, hoping he doesn't bring up the Prada boots I splurged on when Max was born.

"You always buy things like Tide and Cascade instead of generic brands. That can add up."

The fact that Ron considers Tide a designer brand is pretty amus-ing, but I go along with him.

"Okay, so store brands from now on, got it." I'm already prepar-ing for the complaining he will do when I switch out his precious Charmin for generic TP. "What else?"

"You could start clipping coupons."

I cringe. I'd rather give myself an enema.

"Or, you know, you could clip them for me, and I will use them." I think that's a good compromise.

Ron yawns again. "Okay. Can we talk about this tomorrow? I'm bagged."

"Sure," I grumble as I put his empty plate in the dishwasher and refill his water glass. Then something occurs to me.

"Hey, how long have you been seriously thinking about this?"

"Probably three months." He gets up and takes the water from me.

I feel a little twinge in my stomach. "Why haven't you talked to me before?"

He sighs. "I don't know. I think maybe if I didn't tell you then I wouldn't have to go through with it, you know? While it was my secret, I didn't have to commit."

"And now that I know?"

He gives me his best Ron Dixon grin. "Full steam ahead, baby."

We head up the stairs. When he is this exhausted I normally offer up sex, because I know he'll decline but I'll still get points for initiating. I also want to know so much more about his franchise plans.

But I have to let this poor man get some sleep.

3

To: JDixon
From: SPike
Date: 9/7
Re: PTA rules regarding emails.

Hi Jen,

My name is Sylvie Pike and I am the new president of the PTA. I know we haven't met yet and I apologize for that; however, you did miss the PTA introductory breakfast on August 25th and that's where I touched base with all the other class parents. (I say "parents" instead of "moms" because we have a couple of dads this year too!)

I just wanted to make sure you got my message about including me on your list when you send emails to your class. It's the easiest way for me to make sure the PTA message is being properly communicated. Rumor has it there has already been a bit of a lapse on your watch. So please, always keep me in the loop with your emails to your class.

Looking forward to a great year.

Sylvie Pike

President, PTA William H. Taft Elementary School

Ouch! I wince. It's only the third day of school and I'm already getting smacked by the PTA prez. That has to be a record for me. I probably should have gone to that introductory breakfast but truthfully, I hate those things. I'm not good at small talk and I always seem to say the wrong thing to the wrong person. Like two years ago when I asked Gilly Walker when she was due. How could I have known her bump was actually a result of not having pooped in nine days? I felt terrible.

Ron comes by the kitchen-counter office and rubs my shoulders.

"Hey, gorgeous," he growls sexily in my ear. I know what he's after and I shoot him down immediately.

"Nope. Not a chance. Too much to do today."

He frowns. "You're no fun."

"Tell me something I don't know. Why are you still home, anyway?"

"Dentist at ten."

"Have you been flossing?"

"I did today."

"Well, that should fool him."

I look at the clock and see it's 9:30. Ron is obviously looking for a little jeans-around-the-ankles action. Clearly, we will be cutting corners in more than just our spending. But if I'm being honest, I should take it when I can get it. Ron's been so tired lately, he's practically asleep before he hits the pillow. Last night I timed him, and he went from awake to snoring in seven seconds.

I do the math in my head and figure a quickie is probably doable, so I turn and give him my sexiest smile.

"Soooo . . . you'd like to drill my cavity before you go? Is that what you're saying?"

The look of confusion on his face makes me want to laugh out loud, but instead I kiss him and whisper, "Make it quick, doctor."

✦ ✦ ✦

Running after sex isn't ideal for a vagina of my age and mileage, but I wanted to get a workout in before noon. Between my mother's illness and Garth moving away, my exercise has been about as regular as my perimenopausal periods. It really pisses me off that it takes so much damn time to get into shape and no time at all to fall out of it.

Today, I really need to pound out my frustrations before my lunch meeting with Sylvie Pike.

When she asked me at drop-off this morning if I was free for a lunch powwow (her word, not mine), I wasn't quick enough to think of an excuse. The no-caffeine thing has really put a damper on my ability to think of credible lies on the fly.

Sylvie is one of those mothers whom I have noticed over the years but, because our kids aren't in the same grade, never actually talked to. Sadly, I've just described my relationship with 90 percent of the parents at William Taft.

I have to admit I've always been a little curious about Sylvie. She has an interesting style. She dresses in loose-fitting, flowing clothes so it's hard to tell what her body type is, and she wears her extremely long dark hair loose down her back. I initially pegged her as one of those moms who brings homemade granola for a snack, but her emails suggest a very organized rule enforcer without much of a sense of humor. Is there such a thing as a type A hippie?

We're meeting at Chili's at 12:30 for a get-to-know-you lunch. After a shower and quick blow-dry I don the mom uniform of jeans and white T-shirt and head to the kitchen. I'm going with the boyfriend fit these days because I need the extra room. I didn't realize that turning fifty came with so many unexpected delights, among them an extra ten pounds that no amount of cardio is going to get rid of. My doctor told me to start eating from a bread plate instead of a dinner plate to manage my portions, and to stop drinking wine. He's no longer my doctor.

I jump in the minivan (my fourth!). This time we've gone with a white Chrysler Pacifica. I can't say I don't miss my Honda Odyssey, but this new one is pretty damn amazing. It has a ton of room, a huge cargo area in the back, a tricked-out entertainment system—and, get this . . . a built-in vacuum! Max actually likes to clean up his own mess. I let him do it once a week as a *special treat* (wink). Tom Sawyer's got nothing on me.

My phone rings as I'm driving to Chili's and I push the button on the steering wheel to answer.

"Jen's Nail and Tan."

"You really need some new material," says my oldest daughter dryly.

"What's up, pretty? Slow day at Jenny Craig?"

"Actually no. I have sixteen people here for a weigh-in, but I just wanted to remind you that we're Skyping with Laura tonight at six."

"Yup. I know. Do you want to come for dinner?"

"Well, I was hoping you'd come to me. I'm trying to make it to a six forty-five screening at the Tivoli."

"What are you seeing?"

"Uh, it's a Russian film about an insane fencer. It won a prize at the International Moustache Film Festival. Want to come?"

Silence.

"Mom?" Vivs sounds concerned.

"I'm sorry, I fell asleep after you said, 'Russian film.' I can't, darn it. It's actually mustache-*waxing* night."

"Why do I bother?" she asks the ether.

"See you at six, sweetie!"

It's been really fun having Vivs live in the same city again, even though it's just temporary. She wants to rejoin Raj in Brooklyn as soon as she can, but I love that she put her life on hold and came home to help with my mother.

I had expected Laura to do the same after college, but she surprised all of us by announcing she was going to London with her boyfriend, Travis. Apparently, his band, Sucker Punch, had booked a tour of what I'm sure are the worst dives imaginable in the UK and Europe, and she went along to support them. I'm not going to lie, my reaction was split between disappointment and envy. I just hoped she would use birth control, unlike her mother. The last thing I want is for either of my girls to have to carry the burden I did. Not that either of them could. As sophisticated and capable as they are, neither could handle a baby the way I did.

Laura's been gone all summer and we've barely heard from her. A couple of days ago, she texted on our family chat that she wanted to Skype. I'm a little scared, but mostly excited to see her tonight and hear how things are going.

I pull into Chili's half-full parking lot, next to one of those cars that is so small it looks like my minivan pooped it out, and head into the restaurant.

I like Chili's because it has something on the menu for everyone. You can eat healthily or not. The challenge is always to force yourself to order a salad with protein and *not* the chicken crispers and fries.

I spy Sylvie sitting at a booth, furiously typing on her laptop. Her hair is pushed back off her face with the help of a pair of gold-rimmed aviators and she's wearing a purple peasant blouse. She is somewhere in her mid-forties; she has what my gran would call great bone structure, and beautiful, large blue-gray eyes that widen when she sees me walking toward her.

"Am I late?" I look at my phone to confirm I am not.

"Not at all. I got here half an hour ago. It's like a mini vacation to sit here by myself."

I nod as I sit across from her.

"I know how you feel. I took a flight to visit my friend in Memphis and it was like a day at the spa."

"I'll have to try that one. I don't remember the last time I flew without a child."

"How many do you have?"

"Five."

"Oh my God" is all I can think of to say.

I'm stunned. I mean, I love my kids, but I drew the line at two. And then I erased that line and drew it at three. But the U.S. Treasury hasn't printed the money you'd have to pay me to have more than three.

Sylvie laughs at the obvious horror on my face.

"Yes, well, God did have a little something to do with it. We're Catholic, so our only birth control is the rhythm method."

"I can see how well that worked for you."

"Actually, it probably did. Matt and I got married right after high school. By my calculation, we could have had, like, ten kids by now."

Well, that's the cup-half-full way of thinking about it. Sylvie Pike is quickly becoming the most interesting person I have met in a long time. How did I not know her before this? Oh, yeah, I don't like to mingle.

"Do they all go to William Taft?"

She shakes her head. "Only two. I have two in high school and one in middle school."

"And you have time to be PTA president?"

She laughs. "I do! I don't work, so what else am I going to do with my day?"

I can think of several things, but I'm not going to burst her bubble. I'm suddenly feeling like quite the underachiever.

"I'll never know how Nina did it. She made it seem so easy."

Sylvie nods in agreement. "I know. She was my hero. Best PTA president we ever had. You guys were really good friends, right?"

"Still are. I miss her a lot."

Our waitress, Candy (according to her name tag), comes by with a glass of water for me, and a Coke for Sylvie.

"Can I get you something to drink?" she asks me in a squeaky voice.

"I'm good with water, thanks. Sylvie, do you know what you want?"

She glances at the menu.

"Yeah, I'll have the chicken fajitas."

"And I'll have the California turkey club sandwich with salad, no fries."

"You got it." Candy picks up our menus and scoots away.

There's an awkward silence and we sip our drinks. Sylvie breaks it by getting down to business. No more chitchat.

"So, Jen, I'm glad we could meet, because I want to talk to you about spearheading a special project for the school this year."

Well, this is unexpected. I thought I was going to get a talking-to about the responsibilities of being a class parent. I give her my curious-but-not-in-a-good-way look.

"Really? Why me?"

"Well, I keep hearing what a fun and efficient class mom you are. You didn't CC me on your first email to your class, but I got hold of a copy and you're pretty funny."

Pretty funny? I must be slipping.

"Thanks, I think. What's the project?"

"Well, you know Marge DeJones retired as our crossing guard, right?"

Marge DeJones was, like, 104 years old and was about as effective at stopping cars as a down pillow. But she was beloved by all the kids, so the school kept her on and just hoped everyone would get across the street without incident.

"I heard. Oh, God, you're not asking me to replace her, are you?"

"No, of course not. Her granddaughter is filling in for the month of September. What I want is for you to spearhead a new safety patrol program for fifth-graders and parents."

Sylvie obviously mistakes my stunned silence for curiosity, so she keeps going.

"A bunch of schools in the area are doing this. I've visited a few and it seems like a really positive experience."

For who? I think, but do not say. For some reason my wit and sarcasm are nowhere to be found. I mean, she must be joking if she thinks I'm the person to launch a program like this. It would mean dealing with OPCs! (Other People's Children!) Plus, I barely have a handle on my own class-mom kingdom.

"Wouldn't you be better off asking one of the fifth-grade parents? I mean, they know the parent body so much better than I do." I silently commend myself for coming up with such a logical rebuttal on the fly.

"Truthfully, fifth grade is a really busy year for the parents. They do an overnight trip to Branson, and they also have that huge science project, not to mention the French festival and graduation."

"So, they all said no." I believe in calling a spade a spade.

Sylvie has the decency to look sheepish. "They all said no."

At this moment of truth, Candy swoops in with our lunch. Sylvie's fajitas are sizzling, and the smoke is blowing directly on me and basically guaranteeing I'll be smelling like a Mexican restaurant for the rest of the day.

"Enjoy!" she sings and beats a hasty retreat.

I take a bite of my sandwich and consider Sylvie. I like her style. She really does have the crappiest job at the school. Nina always made it look effortless, but the truth is the PTA president can't afford to be a bitch to anyone. She takes a lot of abuse and the only response she can make is "Thank you, sir, may I have another?" I wouldn't do it for the world.

I take a deep breath and wish like hell I'd ordered French fries.

"Tell me what-all is involved," I say without any enthusiasm at all.

Sylvie's eyes widen, and she breaks into a smile so big I can see chicken bits stuck in her teeth.

"It's really nothing. Just make up a schedule for the parents and make sure they show up for their assigned day. We need someone before and after school every day just to make sure the kids are doing their job."

"So, you need parents to patrol the patrollers?"

"Exactly."

Once again Sylvie mistakes my silence for encouragement.

"So, is this a yes?"

"I don't know. I'm pretty busy—"

"And you know what they say," she interrupts, "give a job to the busiest person and it will get done."

"And you're sure it's basically just making up a schedule for the parents?"

She nods. "And they have to say yes, because participation is mandatory."

Honest to God, I can't think of a good excuse to say no. This has been quite the crafty ambush. I'm going back on caffeine tomorrow.

"I have one condition. I'll do it if I don't have to copy you on my class emails."

I can almost see her weighing the consequences of having a rogue class mom versus having no safety patrol organizer.

She nods, and her relief is obvious. "Deal. Thank you so much. Phew! You had me on the ropes there for a minute. But Nina said you'd probably do it."

I just smile, take a sip of water, and mentally start drafting a hate text to Nina.

"And I can just get your class emails from someone else." She shrugs and smiles.

I finish my lunch knowing full well that I have been bested. Well played, Sylvie Pike.

✦ ✦ ✦

"And she expects me to make sure the parents all participate!"

Ron, Max, and I are on our way to Vivs's place and I'm venting about my newest job. Luckily Max has his headphones on and is oblivious to my bitching.

"Did you use a coupon when you paid?" Ron asks me as my phone rings. It's Nina, so I put her on speaker.

"Well, aren't you just the gift that keeps on giving?" is how I greet her.

"Oh, stop. If I were there, you'd do it for me."

"I wouldn't be so sure about that," I counter, but she's probably right. "Jesus, safety patrol, really?"

"You're doing a good thing. Marge DeJones is up in heaven smiling at you."

"She's not dead. She's just retired. And if she's smiling, it's because she doesn't have to do frickin' safety patrol anymore."

"Thanks a lot, Nina!" Ron yells toward my phone.

"Oh, you're mad at me too?"

"Yes. We are a united front on this," I answer for him.

"I told her she could have said no!" Ron booms.

"Stop yelling, babe. She can hear you." The noise is getting to me for some reason. "How's Chyna? How's her new school?"

"Jury's still out. It seems okay. She just made the volleyball team so I'm hoping she makes some friends from that."

Chyna has always been one of those kids who do better with adults than with people their own age. She is an old soul and her vocabulary is insane. In middle school she had a really rough time. The boys were intimidated by her, and the girls threw her shade for showing off with her *big words*.

"Remind her to dumb it down and pretend she's an idiot," I advise Nina. "Nobody likes a smarty-pants."

"Yes. Good advice. Thank you, O wise one," says Nina's disembodied voice.

"What's up with Garth?"

"He's okay. Working really hard. Middle-schoolers are such a pain in the ass. And these kids really don't want to work out!"

"He'll turn 'em around," Ron assures her.

"I know he will. But getting there is going to be a bitch."

We have pulled up to Vivs's apartment complex, so I tell Nina we have to go.

"Miss you tons. Give Chyna and Garth hugs from us."

"Miss you too. Let me know how safety patrol works out."

"Thanks for reminding me why I'm mad at you!" I hit End and turn off the car, which makes Max's movie stop.

"Hey! What the hell?"

"What the what?" I turn and glare at him.

Ron is stunned. "What did you say?"

Max looks at his lap. "What the heck," he mumbles.

"We don't talk like that, Max," Ron admonishes him.

"Mom does."

"Well, you're not Mom." Ron looks pointedly at me. We've had a few discussions about my language over the years, and I can tell we're going to have another one later tonight.

"Let's go, Max." I wave him out of the minivan and lock it up.

✦ ✦ ✦

"Mad Max! Whazzup, brotha?" Vivs says when she opens the door.

Max storms past her.

Vivs's eyebrows go up, but I wave her off. She nods knowingly.

"Can we get this going? I really need to be out by six thirty."

I walk into Vivs's apartment already knowing I'm not going to see anything new. She chose to live in a studio when she moved back here last year instead of coming home. She said she didn't want to get too comfortable in KC because her main goal was to get back to New York as soon as possible. The weird thing is, I told her two months ago that my mother was going to be fine and we had it covered, but she still hasn't left.

Her apartment is as minimalist as she is. Just a few pieces of furniture including a red leather sofa bed that I have never actually seen folded up as a sofa, a desk, and two not very comfortable chairs. The plain white walls sport black-and-white prints of famous New York City buildings. One of them is the photo of workers sitting on a crossbeam having lunch during construction of the RCA building.

I get sick to my stomach every time I look at it, but I can't seem to stop looking at it! It would definitely be something to talk to my shrink about if I had one.

"When was the last time you talked to her?" I ask Vivs as we gather around the laptop on her desk.

"Umm . . . it's been a few weeks. You?"

"Longer than that. I text mostly."

"Me too. Do we know where she is?"

"Last I heard they were in Luxembourg."

Vivs smirks. "I heard the only reason they got booked in Europe at all is because someone thought the band's name was Soccer Punch."

Vivs has taken to insulting Sucker Punch every chance she gets. I'm not sure what her motivation is, but she comes up with some pretty funny stuff. Before I can tell her to put a sock in it, the computer rings and Laura pops up on the screen with her beautiful blond hair shaved to a buzz cut and a stud in her nose. Oh, God, here we go.

"Now you know how your mother felt," Ron murmurs in my ear while the girls scream, "Hi!," to each other. I ignore him.

Turns out I don't have to be the bad guy, because Vivs gets right to it.

"What the hell did you do to your hair? It looks terrible."

"Mom!" Laura whines.

"Okay, okay, let's all settle down. We'll talk about the hair in a minute. How are you, my girl? Where are you?"

"We're in Paris. It's so amazing here!"

"Are you using your French?" I ask hopefully. Laura took three years of the Romance language in high school.

"Not much. But it's okay, because everyone speaks English."

"What's the weather like?" Leave it to Ron to get to the nitty-gritty.

"It's nice. Kind of like KC. Getting chilly at night."

"Hi, Sissy!" Max pops out from behind me.

"Buddy! What's up? How's third grade?"

"It's okay. What happened to your hair?"

"I cut it. Do you like it?"

"Umm . . . I like my teacher."

"He has Razzi," I offer.

Vivs and Laura have the exact same reaction.

"What?"

"Mom, you didn't tell me that," Vivs gripes.

"Max, you are so lucky. She was our favorite teacher. Does she still wear that goofy hat?" For reasons unknown, Mrs. Randazzo has always worn a pink fishing hat, complete with lures.

Max laughs. "Yeah. It's so funny." He turns and goes back to playing with his fidget spinner.

"How's Travis?" Vivs asks, and I can tell she's trying to move things along.

"I'm not really sure," Laura says after a pause.

"Why, is he sick?" I ask.

"I really don't know."

"Did you guys break up?"

"Kind of."

"Was it your hair?" Vivs asks knowingly.

"No! It wasn't my hair. Jeez."

"Vivs, stop," I tell her. Then to Laura, "What happened?"

She sighs. "I can't really get into it right now, but he left the band."

"He left? Where did he go?"

Laura shrugs. "Maybe home. I really don't know."

I'm frustrated by her lack of knowledge and concern.

"Well, if he's gone then why are you still there?" I want to know. "Are you coming home? Is that why you wanted to Skype?"

She grins and rubs her nose. That's Laura's tell for when she doesn't want to answer a question. This time when she rubs, she flinches and I'm guessing the stud she put in makes it uncomfortable.

"Not exactly." She giggles and looks away from the screen. Just then I hear a voice say, "Just tell them."

"Who's that?" I ask.

"It's Jeen." She turns her phone around to show us the lead singer of Sucker Punch making himself comfortable on the bed.

"Hi, Jeen," we all say, and I snicker because it sounds like we're saying, "Hygiene."

"Hey guys." Jeen waves as Laura takes her phone and joins him on the bed. I don't think I like where this is going. Thank God for Vivs, who once again gets right to the point.

"Oh my God, are you guys together?"

They both laugh as I yell, "What?"

"When did this happen?" Vivs seems pleased for some reason.

"It just sort of happened." Laura shrugs. She's now reclining on the bed beside her new boyfriend.

Vivs looks at me. "I totally called this when you and Travis first started dating. Remember, Mom?"

"And that's why Travis left?" I ignore my older daughter's question.

"Yeah. Well, we were having a tough time for the last month. He just got so possessive with me. I mean, I couldn't even talk to Jeen without him going nuts."

"Gee, I wonder why?" Vivs's voice drips sarcasm.

Jeen gives a nervous laugh. "Okay, well, I'm going to let you guys talk. Hey, Mrs. Dixon, can you say hi to my aunt if you see her?"

I think I squeak out a "Sure" as the reality of those two dating hits me. *I could end up related to Asami.* I'm a little light-headed.

Once Jeen leaves the frame, I say to Laura, "Okay, spill it."

"Spill what? I told you it just happened." Laura shrugs.

"So you dumped Travis to be with Jeen. Nice."

"Mom, it's not the end of the world to break up with someone and start seeing someone else." Vivs jumps to her sister's defense.

No shit, I want to tell her. I was the queen of that scene in my glory days. You don't end up with two kids in three years from two different guys without seeing a few bedsheets, if you know what I mean.

"I know it isn't. But she's kind of pulled a Yoko Ono, and that's not cool." As always, my heart is with the band.

"What's a yoko ono?" Laura asks.

Ron, who has been silent through most of this, lets out a barking laugh. "No, she hasn't! And Sucker Punch is hardly the Beatles."

Vivs gets up from the computer and starts putting on her coat.

"Look, I have a movie to see, so I'm going to take off. Laura, I'm happy if you're happy, and I still hate the hair. Nose ring is pretty lit, though."

"Thanks. I'll text you tomorrow."

Vivs gives me a quick hug. "Stay as long as you want. The door locks automatically when you leave. Bye, Ron." She hugs him quickly and high-fives Max on her way out the door.

We are left in silence, staring at Laura on the computer screen. I sigh.

"Well, I hope you didn't hurt Travis too much."

"He was okay. We just grew apart. Mom, please don't be sucky about this."

I give Ron an exasperated look and shrug.

"Fine. Now let's talk about that hair."

Fifteen minutes later we are on our way to Pizza Hut for dinner. It was supposed to be Minsky's, but since we are cutting costs, we're taking it down a notch. Plus, Ron has a coupon. Normally I'd bemoan not getting to eat the best pizza in KC, but I'm too busy brooding about the Skype session with Laura to care. Not only did I not get a good answer on her hair ("It kept getting caught in my purse strap") or why she got a nose stud ("I really don't remember. I must have been drunk") but she also didn't seem to have any idea what their plans are. While I stew, Max is watching a movie and Ron is whistling along to the radio.

"Why am I the only one having a hard time with this?" I ask him.

"With what?"

"With her hair and her nose stud *and* her breakup with Travis *and* her general laissez-faire attitude about her plans."

Ron smirks.

"Probably because she reminds you of you."

"Ha! She's going to have to see a lot more action before she can be compared to me."

Ron sighs.

"Thank you, honey. I always appreciate a reminder of your exploits before you met me."

"Seriously though, I can't remember being that . . . that . . ."

"That what? Young? Unburdened? Trust me, you were. To go by the stories you've needlessly shared with me over the years, you were the original easy-breezy girl."

I chew on this for a minute. "God, I just wish she'd found a better band."

I'm tired so I close my eyes for the rest of the ride to dinner. I only open them once when I feel Ron hit that damn pothole on 112th. I'm a little fuzzy, but I think I see someone who resembles Vivs walking down the street arm in arm with a man. We're past them before I can get a good look. I'm probably wrong, but I call her cell anyway just to check in. It goes to voicemail.

4

To: Grades K–5 Parents
From: JDixon
Re: Safety Patrol
Date: 9/10

Greetings, Losers!

And when I call you losers, it's only because I am the winner! I am the parent who has been chosen to spearhead the new fifth-grade safety patrol program at our school. Booyah!

For those of you who don't know me, my name is Jen Dixon. I'm the mother of a third-grader at this fine learning establishment and I am excited to get this show on the road.

While Marge DeJones's granddaughter has been doing a great job filling in helping our kiddos cross the street safely, it's time we let our fifth-graders take the helm (or the stop sign) and show what responsible young people they have become . . . we hope.

The kids' schedule has already been set, but parents will need to help supervise, mornings from 7:30 to 8:30 and afternoons from 2:30 to 3:30.

> *I will post the schedule as soon as I have made it. Please check to see if and when you have been assigned. If you have a conflict and can't make your day, it is up to you to find a replacement. Do not—I repeat, do not—email me. You will only get a poop emoji in reply.*
>
> *Perks of the job include all the hot chocolate you can drink, a bird's-eye view of how kids really behave, and the school's undying gratitude.*
>
> *No, don't thank me, thank YOU!*
>
> *Over and out.*
>
> *Jen Dixon*

✦ ✦ ✦

I'm genuinely curious about how many initial complaint emails I'm going to get. We have 180 school days, so I need at least 179 parents. With 572 students, you wouldn't think I'd have a problem, but I know my customers, and this is going to be a hard sell. May the odds be ever in my favor!

As I turn to unload the dishwasher, my phone rings and I see it's the school calling. This is always the worst moment. In the time between seeing it's the school and picking up the phone, you die a million times with the fear that something has happened to your child. I take a deep breath and answer quickly.

"Hello?"

"Hi, Jen, it's Winnie Randazzo. Max is fine."

Thank God for teachers like Winnie who understand that those are the first words you need to hear.

"Hi. What's up?" My heart is still beating like a jackrabbit's.

"Can you come in and pick up Max from the classroom after school today?"

"Sure. Why?"

"Nothing scary. We just need to have a little talk."

You can add that to the list of things you don't want to hear from a teacher.

"I'll be there at three," I say, knowing that asking more questions will get me nowhere.

"See you then." Razzi hangs up quickly and I'm left to spend the next three hours wondering what the hell is going on.

I turn back to the dishwasher and notice a pile of coupons on the counter. Ron's daily offering. Oh yay, cans of asparagus are three for one. Now all I have to do is find someone in my house who will eat canned asparagus.

I have a sudden need to pound the pavement, so I grab my headphones and my cell, slip on my favorite Nike sneakers, and head out the back door.

While Tom Petty blasts in my ears, I start to run my usual route but quickly find myself detouring toward Ron's store, the Fitting Room. It's about three miles from our house—a little more than I'm used to running, but I'm pretty confident I can make it. Then I can get someone from the store to drive me home.

Right in the middle of "Last Dance with Mary Jane," my phone rings. It's Nina, thank God. I had left her a message earlier.

"Hi," I puff as I slow to a walk.

"What's wrong? Why are you out of breath?"

"Sorry, I'm running."

"So, what's up?" She's all business today.

"Well, in a nutshell, Laura is whoring her way around Europe, Ron is forcing me to use coupons, and I've been called into the school about Max."

"What's going on with Max?" She goes for the least salacious one first.

"I don't know. Razzi called this morning and asked me to pick him up in the classroom this afternoon."

"And she didn't say why? Like maybe he won an award or something?"

"Yeah, I doubt that's what it is. He's being such a smart-ass lately, but I thought it was only at home. Maybe he mouthed off to her."

Nina chuckles. "Well, that won't end well for him. She takes absolutely no shit from eight-year-olds."

"I guess I'll find out in a couple of hours."

"Why is Ron making you use coupons?"

"We're cutting back on our spending because of the franchising. He has to take a big loan."

"Huh. And what's wrong with using coupons? I do it all the time. You can save a lot."

"I know, I know, I just always forget to bring them and they're hardly ever for anything I actually use." I know I sound spoiled and petty. Nina's ready to move on.

"And what's this BS about Laura whoring her way around Europe? I thought that was your thing."

"I may have oversold that one. She broke up with Travis and is now dating Jeen."

"The Asian guy? He's cute."

"Not the point," I grumble. "She dumped Travis and he left the band."

"Did they find someone to replace him?"

"Again, Neens, not the point. She's jumping from one musician to another."

"And *you're* judging her? That's rich."

"I'm not judging her, I'm concerned for her."

"Does she seem okay? Have you talked to her?"

"Oh, she's fine. Not a care in the world."

"Then you should be fine, too. When is she coming home?"

"Not any time soon. I guess the band is extending their tour."

"Has she asked you for money yet?"

"Not yet."

"Huh. I don't have a lot of answers for you, girl. Sounds like you need to have a talk with her, though."

"Yeah, I know. I just needed to vent first."

"You know who might have a thing or two to say about this?"

"Who?"

"Your mother."

"*My* mother? You're kidding, right?"

"Think about it. She's already lived through this whole thing . . . with you."

"Yeah, but Kay had no friggin' idea what I was up to. Remember it was before cell phones and Skype. She was lucky if I had the money to call her once a month."

"Well, I'm sure she worried about you."

"I'm sure she did, but as far as both my parents knew I was hanging with a girlfriend and visiting museums. Ignorance was bliss for them."

"I doubt they were oblivious. You should talk to her."

"I'll think about it," I say as a way to get off this topic. "How are you guys doing?"

"Nothing quite that interesting going on here. I picked up a few clients at Chyna's curriculum night."

Her news reminds me that I haven't sent out my curriculum-night email yet. Oh joy, something else to worry about.

"Listen, I've got to run. I know it feels like a lot to deal with, but just take a breath and take it one problem at a time."

Just hearing my best friend tell me to breathe makes me calm. "I will. Thanks."

"And let me know what happens with Max. Love you."

"Love you too."

I hang up feeling much better, but then suddenly worse when I realize that I'm exactly halfway between home and the store and I have absolutely no interest in running anymore. Or even walking. My heel is starting to hurt—a leftover injury from my last half marathon. I call Ron's cell. Then I remember he has a big meeting with a rep from the yoga clothing line Spiritual Gangster, so I call my mother. She picks up on the first ring.

"Hello, sweetheart."

"Hi, Mom, are you busy?"

"No. I just put some applesauce muffins in the oven so I have a good fifteen minutes to chat before I have to take them out. How's that running training going?"

"It's good but actually, I need a ride. Can you come and pick me up?"

"What's wrong with your car?"

"I'm not home. I'm at the corner of Main and Elm, right near the park entrance. I was running but I had to stop."

"Well, I'm not surprised. That running is a bitch."

Kay Howard 2.0 strikes again!

"Yes, it really can be. Will you come and get me?" I repeat.

"Well, I just put some blueberry, I mean applesauce muffins in the oven, so you'll have to wait until they come out."

"I know, you told me. Can't Dad take them out? I really need to get home."

"I'm not sure your father would know what to do, sweetheart. He's never been very handy in the kitchen."

I close my eyes and pray for patience. "Okay. Well, as soon as you take the muffins out . . ."

"I'll pop right over to get you. Where did you say you were?"

"Main and Elm, by the park." I calculate the odds of my mother getting here without having to call and ask me again where I am.

"Okay, sweetheart, see you in a jiff."

I hang up and take a seat on a bench near the entrance to the park.

With a good thirty minutes on my hands I decide to check my emails. Besides the usual spate of spam, I have updates from my bank and the AARP. Oh yes, I'm a member. Your membership card arrives the day you turn fifty, which I think is a real dick move on their part. But I have to admit some of the discounts they offer are pretty good.

Noticeably absent from my email is even one response about safety patrol, except from Sylvie Pike.

To: JDixon
From: SPike
Re: Your safety patrol email
Date: 9/10

Jen,

Good email. But "Greetings, Losers" is a little harsh. I wouldn't use it again.

Thanks,
Sylvie

I'm insulted! She obviously doesn't know that I rarely use the same material twice. My mom still hasn't shown up, so I text Vivs. She has been ghosting me since I left a message asking if she was walking with a guy on 112th the other night. I decide to go with something tantalizing.

✦ ✦ ✦

Hey . . . Max is in trouble at school.

It takes a minute and then bingo.

What did he do?
Don't know yet. Razzi asked me to pick him up in the classroom today.

I wait, but she doesn't respond. Oh well, at least I know she's alive. I try Ron to kill a little more time. This time he picks up.

"What's up?" he answers. What did people do before caller ID?

"Hey, how was your meeting?"

"Really good. Their stuff is perfect for us. Simple but edgy."

"That's great! I just wanted to let you know I got a call from Max's teacher and I have to pick him up from the classroom after school."

"Is that a bad thing?" I always forget this is Ron's first trip to the rodeo.

"Well, it's not usually good, but I'm hoping for the best."

"Want me to come?"

"No. I'll handle it. I just wanted to give you a heads-up."

"Okay. Well, thanks. It's always nice to have something else to worry about."

"Why should I have all the fun? Hey, are you home for dinner tonight?"

"Definitely."

"Woo-hoo! I'll attempt to make something really good."

"Oh, don't go changing just for me."

"You like canned asparagus, right?"

"Ha ha."

"Love you."

"Love you too."

As I hang up, my phone rings immediately. It's my mother, of course.

"Hi, Mom."

"I'm on my way, sweetheart! Where did you say you were, again?"

✦ ✦ ✦

Kay picks me up in her new blue Hyundai Santa Fe—a gift from my father when she finished her chemo. When I open the car door, she is blasting the soundtrack from *Hamilton* and singing along to "My Shot."

"Hi!" I yell, and she turns the music down.

"Hi, sweetheart. Sorry I kept you waiting."

"That's okay. Sorry I dragged you out of the house."

"It actually worked out well. I have to go to the grocery store any-way. Gilda rang the bell last week and we're having a celebration dinner for her."

The depth of my mother's kindness always amazes me. She has kept in touch with every person she met while she went through chemo and every time someone rings the bell, she has a little party for them.

"I don't remember Gilda."

"You probably didn't meet her." Kay shoulder checks and pulls into the traffic flow. "She came after I left, but I met her when I was taking Claire Hewitt for her treatments a few weeks ago. She wears the most stylish scarves on her head."

"You're so good, Mom," I tell her. Nina's words from earlier start playing in my head: *You know who might have a thing or two to say about this.*

"Can I ask you something?"

"Sure."

"What was it like for you when I was in Europe?"

I can tell she's surprised by the question.

"What was it *like*? It was hell."

"No, really."

"Yes, really! Your father and I were worried sick about you."

"You never said anything!"

"What could I say? You were a grown woman."

"No, I wasn't, I was barely twenty-two!"

"Is this about Laura?"

I don't say anything, so she continues.

"I know your generation has trouble cutting the apron strings, sweetheart, but back then, twenty-two was all grown up. We worried about you, sure, but we'd already raised you. Our job was done. We knew we'd brought up a strong, smart girl. And you did too. You did a great job with both your girls."

I correct her: "*We* did a great job."

She nods. "It's okay to worry, but try not to drive yourself nuts."

She's right, of course. I need to let both my daughters live their own lives and make their own mistakes. Definitely something to work on . . . along with my swearing and my pessimism. Shit, I'll never get to all that.

I look over at Kay and study her profile. The chemo definitely took its toll. Her hair has grown in a few inches, but it is very brittle, where before it was silky. She is much thinner than she was pre-cancer, and that weight loss shows in her face. Her pale skin is sagging around her jawline and her eyes have sunk into her skull. I choke up a bit as I realize that youthful seventy-five-year-old Kay Howard is no more. She is still energetic for her age, but my mom is getting old. Both my parents are. I promise myself to spend more time with them.

"Why are you looking at me? Did I grow a second nose?" she asks.

"Nope. Just thinking how beautiful you are inside and out."

Her eyes cut to me for a second and she frowns. "Have you been drinking?"

✦ ✦ ✦

After my mom drops me off, I have about an hour before school pickup. So, I shower off the sweat I never built up, don the mom uniform, and grab a quick yogurt from the fridge. While I'm scarfing it down, I fire up the iMac at the kitchen-counter office and check my emails again.

Yes! Replies from many of the parents in Max's class fill my inbox.

To: JDixon
From: RBrown
Re: Safety Patrol
Date: 9/10

Hi Jen,

This is the funniest email yet! I love your sense of humor so much.
   Did you send one for curriculum night? I want to bring something.

   See you later,
   Ravi xo

I frown at the computer. I know Ravi hasn't always understood my sense of humor, but the email I sent was pretty humor free.

To: JDixon
From: AChang
Re: Safety Patrol
Date: 9/10

Jennifer,

I'm going to go ahead and assume this is another one of your weird jokes. If it is, it's a good one.

Have you heard from Laura? Any idea how Jeen is doing? His mother hasn't heard from him in a while.

Asami

Clearly Asami has not heard the breaking news about Jeen and Laura. Can't wait to see her at pickup and ruin her day. It will be fun to watch her try to hide her reaction, which I'm sure will be pure horror.

To: JDixon
From: ALody
Re: Safety Patrol
Date: 9/10

Jen,

Isn't there some woman who does the safety patrol? Will this put her out of a job? I need further explanation, please.

Thank you,
Alison

I'm super looking forward to meeting this woman face-to-face. If it happens to be on the same day as my bikini wax and mammogram, it will be as close as one gets to a perfect day.

To: JDixon
From: JJAikins
Re: Safety Patrol
Date: 9/10

Hi,

Are you doing this *and* being class mom? Wow. Any idea what the plans are for curriculum night? And we never got a chance to catch up! Let's make a date.

JJ xo

Yes, I've got to put that on my to-do list.

To: JDixon
From: ABurgess
Re: Safety Patrol
Date: 9/10

Hey there, Supermom! Is there anything you don't do? Don and I were both safety patrollers in grade school. This is going to be fun.

Anything we can bring for curriculum night?

So glad you are class mom again!

Love,
Ali

Argh! I have got to get that damn curriculum-night email out. It's only a few weeks away. I'm glad to see that Ali took Don Burgess's (he's such a fox!) name. My high school crush and his wonderful baby-mama finally got married last spring after what I heard was a lot of begging and promising on Don's part. Believe it or not, Ron and I were invited to the wedding, and it wasn't at all difficult to see Suchafox commit to love another woman for the rest of his life. That was just dust in my eyes.

I have to leave to get Max, so I grab my key fob and jump in the minivan. The clock on the dashboard tells me I will have to break a few laws to get myself to school on time.

As I'm pulling onto Hayward Avenue, I wave to Marge DeJones's granddaughter, who is already ushering kids across the street. Shit. I really am late. So much for ruining Asami's day with the Laura-and-Jeen news.

I park, dash past a bunch of moms while chanting, "I'm late I'm late I'm late," and make my way to room 402 on the second floor of William H. Taft Elementary.

Razzi is sitting at her desk and Max is in a chair directly across from her. The classroom is cheerful but practical. All the bulletin boards have either colorful maps, lists of rules, or work from the students. The desks are in straight rows all facing the front. Razzi is definitely old-school.

"Hi."

"Mommy!" Max jumps up and races to me.

"Hey, kiddo." I hug him.

"Hi, Jen. So good to see you." Razzi gives me a big smile and walks toward me.

"You too, Winnie." I hug her. "How is George?" Her husband teaches economics at Johnson County Community College.

"He's great. Retiring at the end of this year, if you can believe it."

"Are you thinking about joining him?" Not for nothing, but Razzi's been around since the Nixon administration.

"I'm thinking about it. I'm just worried George and I will wind up driving each other crazy."

I laugh. Max seems mystified by this whole exchange. *Yes, teachers are people, too,* I want to say to him.

"So, what's up?" I direct the question to Max. He shrugs. Razzi raises an eyebrow in his direction.

"Max, do you want to show your mother?"

He shrugs.

"They were playing tag football today and Max got a touchdown."

"You did?" He nods. I'm a little shocked. Max is decidedly not the athletic kind. "Did you hurt someone?"

"No."

I look to his teacher for clarification.

"Would you please show your mother what you did after you made the touchdown?"

Max proceeds to shake his hips side to side. He can't keep a grin from creeping onto his face. Once again, I look to Razzi for clarity.

"Come on, Max, do what you did today. It was so fun!"

Needing no more encouragement, he jumps up and down once then starts doing hard pelvic thrusts and moving his arms. He looks like a member of a boy band trying to make his audience of adolescent girls go wild with desire.

Mrs. Randazzo claps her hands and laughs. I give her a curious smile. I mean, it's cute, but kind of inappropriate for an eight-year-old. I look at my son who has a big grin on his face.

"Where did you learn to do that?" I'm genuinely curious.

"I saw it on Nickelodeon."

Of course, he did. "Okay, well . . ." I look at Razzi, because I'm really not sure why I'm here.

"I just wanted you to see how creative and free-spirited Max is at school! Maybe you should sign him up for dance lessons."

At this suggestion all traces of a smile leave Max's face. I think I'm on to Razzi's game.

"Well, we'll definitely look into it," I tell her.

"I just think all that creative physical energy might need an outlet a little more suitable than school."

"I couldn't agree more. Ready to go, buddy?" I ask my suddenly sullen son.

"Yeah." He grabs his backpack and beelines it to the door. I look back as I follow him out, and Razzi gives me an almost imperceptible smirk.

5

To: Ms. Randazzo's Class
From: JDixon
Re: Taking Care of (Curriculum Night) Business
Date: 9/24

Hey, Party People!

Hope the first couple of weeks have been tolerable. I don't know about
you, but I'm finding the third-grade homework a bit challenging. Did
anyone else have to go look up what an estuary is?

On the bright side, in only a few weeks that Fyre Festival known as
curriculum night will be upon us. What? You want to see who isn't aging
well? Who's still married? Who's barely tolerating my emails? Well then,
to quote Bette Davis as Margo Channing in All About Eve, "Fasten your
seat belts. It's going to be a bumpy night."

Normally I would leave a list of things we will need, and have you
email me what you want to bring. However, I hear tell we are using some
newfangled techno thingamajig called SignUpGenius. So, if you click on
the link below, it will take you to a magical place where you can sign up

and I don't have to assign things. Not sure how you guys feel about this, but I'm delighted!

See you at 6 p.m. sharp on October 11th in room 402, aka Ms. Randazzo's class.

Jen

http://www.signupgenius.com/go/30e0f4fa4a82ba2fd0-randazzo
PS They wouldn't let me include wine on the sign-up sheet, so I'll take it upon myself to bring many, many bottles. Cheers!
PPS I can still check response times on this sign-up thing so don't get lazy.

✦ ✦ ✦

"Bam," I say as I hit Send. Done. Glad I got that monkey off my back. Today I've decided to be superefficient and resolve all unfinished business, kind of like Michael Corleone does at the end of *The Godfather*, but with less bloodshed . . . maybe.

I glance at the clock. It says 8:15. "Max, are you ready?" I yell toward the stairs.

He comes loping down, wearing his school uniform, a windbreaker, and his favorite baseball cap with the Fitting Room logo on it. Gone are the days of Max the fancy dresser. He started to tone down his style late last year and now he looks like every other eight-year-old boy. He won't admit it, but I think peer pressure played a big part in the decision.

"Looking good. Do you have your homework in your bag?"

"Mom, for the gajillionth time *yes*!" He heads toward the back door.

"Okay, sorry! I just don't want to get another emergency 'I forgot my . . . whatever' call."

Max has been in a mood ever since the touchdown dance incident. I made him reenact it for Ron, who played along about the dance lessons until Max promised to keep his moves to himself. We then had a discussion about inappropriate gestures and why football players and pop stars are allowed to do them, but eight-year-old boys are not.

"I can't wait till I'm nine" seemed to be Max's takeaway from the talk.

I follow him out the back door and into the minivan. Mid-September and there's a little nip in the air, so I turn up the heat after I turn the ignition. Max immediately reaches for his earphones in the middle console, but I wave him off with a look. He slams his body back into his seat and does up his seat belt.

"So, who are you hanging with at school?" I try my hand at conversation as we get on our way.

"Draper."

I knit my brow. "Who's that?"

Max shrugs. "Draper Lody. He's new. He's really cool."

Lody, right. The lovely Alison's son.

"What makes him so cool?"

Max shrugs again. "He brings cool stuff to school sometimes."

"Like what?"

Max kicks the seat in front of him and sighs. "I don't know. Just cool stuff."

"What did he bring yesterday?"

"I don't remember. Oh wait, it was this thing called Mennen Speed Stick."

That's cool? I think but do not say.

"He brought deodorant to school? What did he do with it?"

I see Max blush a deep red in my rearview mirror. "I can't tell you. It's a secret. Just for guys."

I frown. "Did he put it on his underarms?"

Max cackles. "Nope. Not even close."

While I'm trying to crack the mystery of what Draper Lody does with his Mennen Speed Stick, I see Marge DeJones's granddaughter at her post. She looks to be in her mid-twenties, but it's hard to tell with the curlers in her blond hair. She is sporting a very eye-catching neon pink sweater under her safety vest. I wave as I drive by and she gives me a smile. She is surprisingly pale for someone who works outside twice a day. I turn into the school parking lot and Max jumps out practically before the van has stopped.

"Hey! Be careful!"

"Bye, Mom!" he yells.

"Bye!" I yell back. I choose to believe that he has forgotten that I am actually staying at school today. I have my first meeting with my safety patrollers. We are gathering in the gym at 8:30 with Sylvie Pike and one of the fifth-grade teachers. Apparently, we are going to "walk the route" from the school to the sidewalk and alert them to any dangers they may encounter.

As I head toward the gym, I call Ron. "Can I ask you a question as a guy?"

"I'm flattered."

"Where would you put deodorant, other than your underarms?"

Ron laughs. "Do I want to know why you're asking me?"

"Probably not. But seriously, where?"

"Umm . . . Well, I'm not proud of this, but I used to put it on my balls."

I freeze midstride. I don't know what to react to first: the fact that the man I married put deodorant on his balls or the possibility that this is what Max was talking about.

"Hello?"

"I'll call you later." I hang up to the sound of my husband's laughter.

When I walk into the gym, wishing like hell for a venti latte, I see I'm the last to arrive. Why is everyone always early? About ten kids are running around the gym chasing each other, making the noise of a hundred, and Sylvie Pike is standing talking to Mr. Green, one of the fifth-grade homeroom teachers. He always reminds me of the little kid from the movie *Up,* but all grown up. He is famously known as the most popular teacher at William Taft, probably because he is so cute and single. I walk over to join them.

"Am I late?"

"Hey, Jen. Not at all. Do you know Scott Green?"

"Only by reputation. Jen Dixon." I smile and shake his hand.

"None of it's true." He smiles back. "Thank you so much for taking this on."

"I'd say it's my pleasure, but why start with a lie?" I laugh so he doesn't know I'm not kidding.

"The kids' new vests arrived, thank goodness." Sylvie leads me toward the back of the gym. "Can you imagine those kids having to wear Marge's old vest?" The visual is pretty comical. Let's just say Marge is a roomy gal.

Mr. Green lets out an ear-piercing whistle to get the fifth-graders' attention and we all converge on the utility room, which I guess now doubles as Safety Patrol Command Central. One counter has been cleared of sports bric-a-brac and now holds two bright orange vests neatly folded, two hand-held stop signs that look as though they've been smashed on the ground in frustration once or twice, and an old walkie-talkie sitting in an ancient charger. There is also an electric kettle and a basket full of Swiss Miss hot chocolate packets. Taped to the wall above the kettle is a schedule with what I'm guessing are the kids' names plus a bunch of blank spaces for names of the parents who will supervise that day.

"Fifth grade, look sharp," Mr. Green says with authority, and miraculously all chatter ceases immediately. I'm duly impressed.

He continues. "This is Mrs. Dixon. She will be here every day to make sure you get your vests on and get out to your post on time."

I'll do what now? Clearly no one has briefed the *Up* kid that my role is that of supervisor, not daily participant. I decide to set the record straight.

"Well, either I will be here, or another parent will. But we're just going to keep watch. You guys have the real job." I wonder how sincere I sound.

"Can you please introduce yourselves to Mrs. Dixon?"

No one comes forward, of course. No fifth-grader wants to be the first to do something as embarrassing as saying their name out loud.

Mr. Green sighs. "Aaron?"

A lanky boy with shoulder-length hair and braces raises his hand. "Yeah, hi, I'm Aaron." He can barely look at me.

The boy beside him is half his size and his pants are too big for him. "I'm Jonah." I'm reminded what a painfully awkward age this is for boys.

The dam having been effectively burst, they all take their turn introducing themselves. There are three boys, Carlo being the third, and seven girls including two Chloes (one with shockingly big boobs for an eleven-year-old), a Hanna, an Abby, a Keira, a Mia, and an Isabella. The girls all look at least five years older than the boys—even Aaron, who has the height—and act as though they are auditioning for *America's Next Top Model*.

"Can we try the vests on?" one of the Chloes asks.

"Sure!" Sylvie Pike seems thrilled by the request. They all rush toward the counter at once and I think it's going to be a bloodbath, but Mr. Green stops them in their tracks with two words: "Red light."

They all freeze. I have got to get me some of what he has.

"One at a time. Alphabetical order by first name."

"No fair!" says one of the girls . . . definitely not Abby.

While they try the vests on two at a time, Sylvie sidles over to me. "Want to try *your* vest on?"

"My vest? I get a vest? Is it pink?"

"Yes, and a walkie-talkie. It's tuned to the security desk in the office, so you can call for help if you need it."

If by "help" she means Stan the custodian, I'd be better off with one of the Chloes. In the four years I've been at William Taft, I don't think I have ever seen Stan stand up.

Sylvie interrupts my thoughts by handing me a bright-orange vest that, let's just say, has seen better days.

I scowl. "You're kidding, right?" I reluctantly put it on and accidentally put my arm through a hole instead of the armhole not once but twice. Seriously, the vest looks like it went three rounds with Edward Scissorhands.

"It's Marge's old one. It's just until we raise money for some new equipment. We need new stop signs, too. You can throw a bake sale if you like."

Before I can even respond to that bombshell, Hanna (I think) approaches me and says, "Mrs. Dixon, you could totally wear an orange jacket underneath that and it would look okay."

Sylvie and I both stare at her for a moment. She's absolutely wrong about that, but she has the sweetest face and smile and I'm instantly charmed.

"Thanks, cutie. I'll try it." I smile back at her. For a moment I'm reminded of Vivs and Laura at that age . . . well, Laura, anyway. She was always so sweet.

"Shall we head out to the street?" Sylvie says to the general population and we all turn toward the rear gym door that leads to the parking lot and beyond. I take a last glance at Safety Patrol Command Central and see Hanna picking up the vests from the floor, folding them neatly, and putting them back on the shelf.

✦ ✦ ✦

Out on the street, Marge DeJones's granddaughter and her pink neon sweater have joined us. I have just learned that her name is Sherlay. Not Shirley, mind you, SherLAY. I don't think it will come as a surprise to anyone that this is my new favorite name. I now have a Sherlay and a Shirleen in my life. Check another one off the bucket list!

"You've gotta be extra careful with the little ones," Sherlay is explaining to the group. "They like to jump out before you put the sign up."

While she continues her demonstration, I look out at the street and take stock of what's around. As many times as I have driven through this intersection, I don't think I have ever really noticed what's here.

The corner of 12th and Hayward is relatively busy. It's a four-way stop and sees quite a bit of action, especially around drop-off and pickup times. Across the street from the school, a small strip mall houses a 7-Eleven, Cathy's Nail Salon, and the offices of someone named Dirk Burke, CPA. Diagonal from where I'm standing, there is a gas station, and across from that a small park with a bench.

I turn my attention back to Sherlay and the grown-up kid from *Up*. They seem to be having a very good time explaining to the kids what's expected of them. As I understand it, there will be two children on duty every morning—one stationed on the park side of the intersection and the other by the gas station. They will stop the already stopping traffic by using their signs and their orange-clad bodies and help the best and brightest of KC cross the street and go on to another great day of learning at William Taft. How's that for lipstick on a pig? In the afternoon they will be stationed on the corner nearest the school and do the whole thing in reverse.

My phone buzzes. It's a text from Peetsa.

Where are you?

Crap! I totally forgot I was going to meet her for breakfast. I signal Sylvie, who is intently listening to Sherlay.

"Sorry, I have to scoot out early. Do we have a launch date for this yet?"

"October sixteenth."

"Not until then?"

"Sherlay wants to do it while the weather is good. Are you sure you have to leave?"

"Yes, I'm sorry. I double-booked myself by accident. Can you let me know if I miss anything?"

"You mean besides Sherlay flirting with Mr. Green?"

My eyes widen. I look over and she does indeed have a little pink in her cheeks and a smitten look on her face.

"She'd up her chances considerably if she lost the curlers," I say as I text Peetsa, *On my way.*

I rush to the parking lot, jump into the minivan, and hightail it to Stu's Diner, aka the place with the signs.

Peetsa is sitting in a booth with a cup of coffee in front of her, looking at her phone.

"Sorry! My safety patrol briefing went longer than I expected."

"That's okay. I didn't order you anything. I wasn't sure if you were still off caffeine."

"Dumbest decision I ever made." I sigh.

Steph, our waitress, calls across the room. "Coffee, hon?" I nearly burst into tears.

"Oh, for God's sake just have some." Peetsa sounds genuinely annoyed. "There isn't a special place in heaven for people who don't drink coffee."

It only takes me a moment to cave. I give her a grateful smile, and nod to Steph. She is over in a flash with one of their jumbo-sized mugs and the coffeepot. The scent of the rich dark brew makes my mouth water. Just one, I promise myself.

"What'll it be, girls?" she asks and pours at the same time.

"Scrambled eggs and a toasted bagel," Peetsa orders while I take my first sip of coffee in four months.

"Mmmm. I'm good for now, thanks."

Steph nods and turns to go. "Two new signs if you can find them," she tosses over her shoulder.

This is what I love about Stu's. The walls are covered with hilarious signs from all over the country. I look around for the new ones but instead land on one of my recent favorites.

DRINKING AND DRIVING GO TOGETHER LIKE

PEAS AND GUACAMOLE

"Have you found them yet?" I ask Peetsa, who is staring into her mug.

"Haven't really looked." She doesn't look up.

Something is off.

"What's wrong with you?"

"Nothing worth talking about."

I frown. "Please don't tell me it's Buddy again."

Her eyes fill with tears.

I take her hand across the table, but have to let go almost immediately as Steph slides in with the eggs and bagel. She also has the coffeepot so she refills us both and glides away but not before shooting me a WTF look.

Peetsa has settled into quiet sobs but is nowhere near finished crying. I take her hand again and give her a minute. I also take half her bagel, because seeing a sad friend makes me stress-eat.

About a year ago, Buddy made the colossally idiotic decision to cheat on Peetsa. I say "decision" but I'm not sure that's really the correct term when your dick is doing the thinking.

For reasons unknown, when Buddy turned forty-five he dove headfirst into a midlife crisis. He amped up his workouts, bought some designer jeans, and started listening to EDM, which I now know stands for electronic dance music. At first, I thought Peetsa said he was listening to R.E.M. and I was like, "That's not so bad."

We were all enjoying the new and improved Buddy. He kept initiating these really fun outings to outdoor music festivals and cool restaurants and clubs, and his energy was infectious. He and P. seemed to be having a great time, as usual.

It was Ron who told me about Buddy's newly roving eye. They had gone to a Royals game and imbibed a few too many. I guess Buddy was striking up a conversation with every pretty girl who walked by and making Saint Ron very uncomfortable.

Nothing happened that night, but not long after, Buddy took to "working late" and "meeting a pal for dinner" a little more often than Peetsa liked. She went snooping on his phone and found some pretty suggestive texts from someone named Zuzi. As a veteran of the flirty text myself, I told P. she probably shouldn't worry, but to definitely ask him about it.

After feigning indignation at the invasion of privacy, Buddy ultimately caved and said he'd had a fling with Zuzi after meeting her at a rave. *A rave*????

P. was heartbroken, of course. They immediately went into couples counseling, hoping to iron things out. But instead of helping, it brought up a Pandora's box of other issues in their marriage including money, in-laws, and a few of Buddy's personal habits.

"I thought things were better."

"They were better, but then in our therapy session yesterday he said he doesn't think he can guarantee he won't do it again. How's that for a slap?"

"At least he's being honest," I offer.

"Oh, spare me." Peetsa looks at me like I had suggested pardoning Hitler.

"I know, I know. He's a jackass. I feel so bad for you."

The untouched eggs and half-eaten bagel sit between us like some kind of metaphor for her marriage, half-finished and cold.

"So, what do you do now?"

She shakes her head as her eyes start to well up again. "What can I do?"

"Have you talked to a lawyer?"

She closes her eyes and rubs them. "I really don't want to. How can I do this to the kids?"

"How can *he* do this to the kids. This isn't you." I look at my watch and Peetsa signals for the check. "Can you hang out and talk some more?" I ask her.

"Nah, I've got a bunch of errands to run and I have to pack up some things for Buddy."

"Is he going somewhere?"

"He's going to stay with a friend for a few weeks while we figure things out."

"What friend?"

"Do you remember TJ Stern?"

I shrug.

"You met him at our tiki-torch barbecue this summer. He wore that really bright yellow Hawaiian shirt?"

I frown. "The guy with the scar under his eye?"

"That's him. He and his wife got divorced about eighteen months ago, so Buddy is sleeping on his couch."

"P., I'm so sorry. You so don't deserve this."

She huffs. "Oh, I don't know about that. Maybe I do. You know we hadn't had sex in almost a year."

"How the hell did you manage that?" I really want to know.

"I just wasn't into it. I couldn't get excited about anything."

"Did you try porn?" I ask helpfully just as Steph drops the check and treats me to a look that says *Hell yeah, I love me some porn.*

Peetsa bursts out laughing. It's nice to hear. "Oh my God, only you. No, I didn't try porn. I didn't try anything. I just kept saying no and finally Buddy stopped asking."

She looks at me sheepishly. P. knows my philosophy. I think the key to a happy marriage is sex at least twice a week whether you want it or not, to keep yourselves connected. This goes for both men and women. It's not a popular opinion among the liberated, #metoo women in my life—especially my daughters—but I stand by it.

"I'll get this." I grab the check and leave a generous tip for Steph, knowing full well I'll have to report the extra spending to Ebenezer Ron.

Out in the parking lot we hug goodbye. "Hang in there, girlie. Call me if you need anything."

Peetsa gives me an extra squeeze. "Thanks. There is one thing."

"Name it."

"Can I get out of doing safety patrol?"

This time I'm the one to crack up.

✦ ✦ ✦

As I'm driving up College Boulevard, I realize that I'm very close to Vivs's Jenny Craig branch, so I decide to drop in. I'm not sure what kind of reception I will get. She's still playing hard to get via text, but I figure a face-to-face will help. I pull into the strip mall and park right next to her old blue VW Jetta. It was secondhand when we gave it to her in high school, but she has taken excellent care of it.

Jenny Craig is bustling with activity and I realize I have come during a weigh-in. Since I know Vivs will be busy, I take a seat and check my emails while I wait for the crowd to thin . . . pun intended. I'm buzzing from the much-missed caffeine that is coursing through my system and I need to keep busy.

I don't see any responses from my curriculum-night email and I'm about to start mentally cursing out my class when I remember that we are using SignUpGenius. Chances are I won't hear from anyone unless Shirleen has an issue. I make a mental note to check out the so-called Genius later and see how it's going. I notice quite a few more emails about safety patrol. I have been getting a steady stream for the last few days. Reaction is mixed.

To: JDixon
From: TMilton
Re: Safety Patrol
Date: 9/24

Dear Jen,

What an absolutely great idea to have the students take over safety patrol duties. Bravo! Well done! I'd really love to participate but I don't generally like to do any outdoor activities unless I have to.

But good luck with it!
Tammy Milton, Chloe's mother

Can standing on a corner be considered an outdoor activity?

To: JDixon
From: PJackson
Re: Safety Patrol
Date: 9/24

Jen,

I'm Pam Jackson and I'm happy to help. So would my husband but he's in a wheelchair. So just me I guess.

Thanks,

Pam

"Mom?" Vivs's voice startles me out of my email stupor. I notice the room is almost empty.

"What are you doing here?" She's standing behind the counter and I can't help but notice how great she looks . . . really healthy.

"I just thought I'd stop in to say hi."

"Hi."

"Are you busy?"

"I have a lot of paperwork to do."

"Why are you being so snippy?"

She scowls. "I'm not. I'm busy."

I look around at the now empty office. "I'll only stay a few minutes."

She sighs loudly and gestures for me to follow her back to an area with about six cubicles. She pulls a chair from one of them into hers, so I can sit down. It is sparsely decorated, but on her desk is a picture of our family in my parents' backyard from a few years ago, and pinned to the fabric wall is one of her and Raj at the Empire State Building.

Realizing I'll get more with honey than vinegar, I start with a compliment. "You look great, sweetie." She really does seem to have an extra spring in her step.

"Thanks. I've been doing this boxing class at Fusion Fitness. It's kicking my ass, but I love it."

I give her an admiring nod. "It's really working for you. Hey, we haven't had a chance to talk about the Laura-and-Jeen thing. Pretty crazy, right?"

"I wasn't surprised." She leans back in her chair. "I always thought there was something there."

"I just hope Travis is okay."

Vivs rolls her eyes. "You always worry about the guy. He'll be fine. He was such a baby. He used to sleep half the day away and he made Laura do all his errands. It really bugged me."

This was news to me. "She never told me that." Vivs knows how I feel about lazy men—or lazy people in general.

"Well, she wanted you to like him. And she knew you'd never let her go to Europe if you thought he wasn't treating her well."

"She was right about that. Was he mean to her?"

"No." Vivs takes a swig from her water bottle. "He's just a sloth. She had to take care of everything."

That's called marriage, I say to myself. Aloud, I point out that it's not always a bad thing to be the person in a relationship who takes care of all the little things.

"Mom, she was packing and unpacking his bass at gigs. He was like a toddler."

"And Jeen is better?"

She shrugs. "Well, he's the lead singer. No instrument to deal with."

"Have you talked to Raj?"

The scowl is back.

"A couple of days ago. How's Max doing?"

I regale her with his touchdown dance and she is doubled over laughing. I figure now is as good a time as ever to ask about what I think I saw that night in the car.

"So, was that you I saw walking down 112th?"

She stops laughing. "What do you want me to say, Mom?"

"It's just a question."

"Yes, it was me." Her look is daring me to ask more.

"And you were walking with your arm around a guy." This is more of a confirmation than a question.

"Yes. Please don't ask me anything else."

I can't figure out what her true feelings are underneath this defiant façade. Is she ashamed? Angry? Regretful? I'm about to ignore her request and ask more, but we are interrupted by her boss, Caroline, poking her head around the side of the cubicle. She is a heavyset African American woman with a passion for pastel-colored clothes. She has been wonderful to Vivs this past year and has really taken her under her wing.

"There's a new customer up front, baby girl."

"I've got it." Vivs gets up. That's obviously my cue.

"I'll get going."

"Okay. Thanks for stopping by." She starts walking away.

"Can you come for dinner Sunday?"

"I'll let you know." She waves without turning around.

6

I head home and decide to work out my frustrations about Vivs by punching the boob on my boxing bag for a good half hour. I wonder if she's cheating on Raj. Or maybe Raj cheated on her? And who was that guy? This would all be so much easier if she would just spill her guts to me.

After my workout I realize that I'm running on empty with only that half bagel and coffee in my belly, so I go to the fridge and pull out the fixings for a turkey sandwich. While I'm eating at the kitchen-counter office I finally sign up for the Susan G. Komen once and for all.

After I register as part of the Holy Rollers and pledge to raise $500, I scroll through my emails to see whom I can hit up for a donation. Ron, obviously—his store would probably give me the whole amount if I asked. They're always looking for a tax deduction. But getting the whole sum that way would be cheating, so I keep looking. Most of the women I'm close to are already doing the walk, in support of my mother. So, asking them to sponsor me might be seen as a little much. I happen upon an email from iwasacancangirl@aol .com.

To: JDixon
From: BHoward
Re: Thanks
Date: 9/24

Hi there, Jen,

Thank you so much for the pineapple soup recipe. I'm going to try it as soon as pineapples go on sale at the market.

I'm sending you a picture of Stella and Mrs. Jones. Aren't they just a couple of characters?

Love,
Aunt Barb

I open the attachment and see two of her cats sitting on a dresser, giving the camera a dirty look. I don't know how she lives in a house with so much disdain being launched her way. Also, I wonder just how fixed Aunt Barbara's fixed income really is. Could she spare $20 for her favorite niece whom she has never seen in person? Let's see.

To: BHoward
From: JDixon
Re: A HUGE favor
Date: 9/24

Hi, Aunt Barbara!

Thanks for the picture! The cats are adorable.

I wanted to let you know that my mom and I are participating in the Susan G. Komen Walk to raise money for breast cancer research. I myself am trying to raise $500 and I was hoping you might be able to sponsor me for $20. I know it's a lot to ask . . . even $10 would be great.

It's obviously a cause that is close to my heart and I'd appreciate anything you can give. I've included the link below in case you can help me out.

I'll leave you with a quote from your favorite author.

Love,

Jen

"When you feel someone else's pain and joy as powerfully as if it were your own, then you know you really loved them."—**Ann Brashares**

+ + +

Fingers crossed, I think, as I cruise through my emails looking for other possible donors. But unless Pottery Barn is willing to pony up for a really good customer, I don't have a lot of options. Clearly, I need more pen pals. While I'm considering a GoFundMe page, my phone rings.

"Jen's Massage Parlor."

My husband chuckles. "Don't I wish. . . . Listen, can you get someone to watch Max Friday night?"

"Probably. What's up?"

"I just had a visit from the CEO of Sports Barn."

"Eww," I say before I can stop myself. Sports Barn is one of those massive sporting goods chains and the arch nemesis of local businesses like ours.

"Yes eww, but he and his wife want to take us out for dinner Friday."

"Why would we want to do that?"

Ron sighs. "Because he's rich and he's a titan in my business and he may be able to help me with the franchising. Should I go without you?"

"No way. Where are we going?"

"Café Provence."

"Ooh la la! Fancy."

"Only the best for my wife."

"Especially when someone else is paying." I laugh.

"Exactly."

"See you later, babe."

"Don't forget to book a sitter!"

I hang up and immediately dial my mother.

✦ ✦ ✦

As I walk from the parking lot to the school to pick up Max, I see the usual suspects hanging out. Ravi Brown and Peetsa wave me over.

"What's up, girls?" I ask, and give Peetsa's hand an extra squeeze.

"Just gossiping," Ravi says. "Do you know that woman over there?" She points to someone having an extremely animated conversation with Shirleen Cobb. I squint and see a short, mousy-looking waif with dirty-blond hair. Shirleen towers over her.

"No idea who she is. Why?"

"She drives a Tesla."

"Really? Wow." That's fancy even for Overland Park.

Asami joins our circle. "What are you looking at?"

"Do you know that woman talking to Shirleen?"

Asami looks over. "Of course I do."

We all wait for her to continue.

"She's in our class, for goodness' sake. None of you know her?"

Suddenly I know exactly who she is.

"Alison Lody."

Asami looks at me. "So, you do know her."

"Only through email."

"Wait, is her son Draper?" Peetsa asks.

"Yes," Asami and I both answer.

"Zach got in trouble last week because of that kid."

"What happened?"

"Draper brought crutches to school and said he sprained his ankle. Zach accidentally kicked his crutch and made him fall."

I cough to mask my guffaw.

"How do you accidentally kick a crutch?" Asami asks.

"Well, I don't know how accidental it actually was. I guess at recess Draper was torturing the boys with how cool his crutches were, but he wouldn't let anybody try them. So Zach 'accidentally'"—she makes air quotes—"kicked one crutch and Draper fell down. He told Mrs. Randazzo, and Zach got detention *and* had to write an apology letter."

"Well, I mean, if he kicked a kid with crutches . . ." Ravi says tentatively.

"Yes, but the next day guess what? No crutches. Not even a pretend limp."

"He was faking it? What an asshole." Not the nicest thing I've ever called an eight-year-old, but if the shoe fits . . .

"Wait, is he the boy who brought a skeleton hand to school?" Ravi asks.

Peetsa nods. "And deodorant."

As the school bell rings, I add, "Max says he brings something cool to school every day."

Eyebrows go up all around the circle. I think we're all wondering how superteacher Winnie Randazzo lets him get away with this. It occurs to me that she might not even know.

We all turn our attention to the flock of kids pouring out of the school.

Max runs up to me, waving his vocabulary test.

"I got a hundred percent!" He's rightfully proud of himself. I worked the flash cards with him for three nights.

"Way to go, buddy." I hug him. "How was the rest of your day?"

"Good. Draper brought a Barbie to school. It was so funny."

I look at my group, but everyone is dealing with their own child, so I steer Max toward the parking lot.

"A Barbie, huh? What did he do with it?"

Max starts to giggle.

"What's so funny?"

"I can't tell you what he did with it. It's only for guys in the club."

"The club?"

"Yeah, Draper started a secret club."

Not a secret anymore, I think. *Now it's just a club.*

"What do you guys do in the secret club?"

"We look at stuff that Draper brings in."

"Who else is in the club?"

"All the boys in my class except Graydon."

"Why not Graydon?"

"He says Graydon's weird because he can't eat nuts."

I smile, thinking about the can of whoop-ass Shirleen will open on Alison Lody if she finds out her son is being excluded. Maybe that's what they were talking about at school.

I open the minivan doors and we get in.

"Well, you shouldn't be a part of a club that doesn't let everyone in."

"But I want to be a part of the club."

"Then tell Draper he has to let Graydon in. There's nothing weird about having allergies. How would you feel if you were the only one not allowed to join?"

"Not good." Max looks at his hands.

I decide to change the subject.

"Guess where you're sleeping Friday night?"

Max looks up, excited. "Draper's?"

"Nope."

"Zach T.'s?"

"Nope."

"Zach B.'s?"

This could go on for a while.

"No, you're sleeping at Nana and Poppy's."

"Yay! All-night iPad!"

✦ ✦ ✦

Friday night on the way to the restaurant Ron gives me the 411 on the couple we are dining with. According to Google, Rolly Schrader is a sixty-one-year-old self-made man from Idaho. Sports Barn started as one store in Boise selling used sports equipment. That was thirty years ago. He now has eighty-two stores in thirty-two states and is known for having the best prices on the biggest selection of sporting goods. And to his credit he has stayed true to his roots: he still sells used equipment at some stores. He has been married three times and has seven children and five grandchildren. The current Mrs. Schrader is the lovely Janine, fifty-four, a former Ice Capades performer who met Rolly when she was buying a mini trampoline at his Denver store.

"And tell me again why he was in your store the other day?" I ask my husband.

"He's in town on business and wandered in looking for a sports bra for his wife. I had no idea who he was, but he kept complimenting me on my yoga section. You know, it's the whole back wall now."

I did know that, having already been told thirteen times and counting.

"Well, it's nice of them to take us to dinner," I say with very little enthusiasm. I barely have time to dine with people I know, let alone people I don't.

Ron reaches over and rubs my bare leg. I've gone with a little black dress and my black high heels tonight, and I can tell he likes it.

"You'll be fine. I think it will be fun. Rolly is a good person for me to know."

"And when you say he might be able to help with the franchise, do you mean financially?"

"We'll see. It's a hell of a lot more expensive than I thought. If we're lucky, he may want to invest."

We have left the minivan at home tonight in favor of the love of Ron's life—a silver BMW 3 series he has named Bruce Willis. Actually, the car's full name is Bruce Mofo Willis (BMW) because the on-board computer sounds just like the actor, though we were assured by the salesman that it isn't him. It was quite an extravagant purchase two years ago and I'm a little surprised that Ron hasn't volunteered to trade it in what with all the belt-tightening he's having us do. But the way he feels about Bruce Willis, something tells me it will be the last thing to go. After we park, he looks back at the car three times before we walk through the door of the restaurant. I don't have the heart to ask him to downgrade . . . yet.

Café Provence is quite possibly the nicest French restaurant you will ever find in a strip mall. It is our *special* special-occasion place, not to be confused with J. Gilbert's, our merely special-occasion place. We haven't been here since my father's seventy-fifth birthday three years ago.

The décor is mid-century bistro, with crisp white linens and flowers on every table. The walls are adorned with landscape paintings that I assume are of the French countryside.

Rolly and Janine are already seated at a booth with a bottle of wine in front of them. I silently thank God for the alcohol that will help me through this awkward social outing. Rolly stands up as we approach the table. If I say he looks like a Rolly, would that be enough of a description for you? No? Well, picture a silver fox from the chest up and an old gym teacher from the chest down.

"Good to see you, Ron." He and Ron shake hands.

"You too. This is my wife, Jen." He motions to me and I wave.

"And this is Janine." Rolly points to a very pretty woman with bleached blond hair and a dynamite set of fake boobs. She smiles at us and raises her wineglass. *I'm with you, sister.*

Ron and I sit beside each other and make small talk with the Schraders about the weather (unseasonably warm!) and the price of gas (too high!). How men always know the price of gas is beyond me. Honest to God, I don't think I've ever looked.

After we order our dinner, Rolly and Ron start a conversation with each other across the table, leaving me to dazzle Janine with my snappy repartee.

"Where do you guys live?" I ask, already knowing that they have a huge house in Boise.

"Right now, we're in Boise, but I'm trying to convince Rolly to spend the winter in Florida."

"That would be nice, but would it even be possible? I mean, how hands-on is he with the business?"

"Very. That's the problem. I just hate Boise winters so much." She shudders and takes a long sip of wine. I join her. We are enjoying a Bordeaux that is so delicious I have to remind myself that I agreed to drive home.

"Do you have any children?" I ask her.

"No, I never bit that bullet. You?"

"Yes, I bit it three times. Two girls and a boy."

"That's nice," Janine says, looking around the restaurant. She doesn't seem overly interested in my offspring, so I try another topic.

"You look great. Do you work out?"

She visibly perks up.

"Yes, I do spin class three times a week and Pilates on the weekends. How about you?"

"I run, and I box." I'm fibbing a little on the boxing, but just happy we're having an actual conversation.

"Have you ever tried spinning?"

What the hell is it about people who spin? You'd think they have found the nirvana of exercise. All they ever want to do is take you to their spin class because it will change your life.

"No, I never have, but I hear it's fun."

"Not just fun." She leans toward me. "*Life-changing.*"

Oh, Jesus, here we go. I watch her mouth move as she blabs on about indoor cycling, but I use the time to eavesdrop on what the men are talking about. Rolly seems to be extolling the virtues of expanding your business. I reluctantly switch my focus back to Janine.

"Not only do I sweat more than I ever have in my life, I transform in every class. It's like I shed a layer of skin."

"Like a lizard?" I offer, knowing full well it's the wrong thing to say.

Janine gives me what I think is a hurt look. "You really should try it before you knock it." I can tell she's using a lot of self-control to stay polite.

"I'm sorry. You're right. I should. It just seems so hard and the people who do it are so fit. I don't think I could make it through a class." It's the best olive branch I can offer her.

"Well, you just go at your own pace at first. Sit in the back and just do what you can."

"You've sold me. I'm definitely going to check it out." I cross my fingers under the table, because it's not really a lie when you do that, right?

"I'm going to a class tomorrow morning. You should come."

Shit.

"Umm . . . what time?"

"There's one at nine thirty and another at ten thirty. I'm doing both."

That's nothing to brag about, I think. "Well, sure, I can do nine thirty. Where is it?"

"Fusion Fitness. Do you know it?"

"I actually do know it. My daughter works out there."

"Great! They have the best classes in Kansas City. Believe me, I've tried them all."

I believe her.

"Come a bit early so we can make sure you have the right settings on your bike."

I'm already regretting it.

✦ ✦ ✦

On the way home Ron and I do a postmortem on the dinner.

"Food was great. I love their duck."

"I know. And that warm goat cheese salad was so good. Too much wine for you guys, though."

Ron groans. "I know. I'm going to be hurting tomorrow. But what did you think of them?"

"They seem decent. I mostly talked to Janine."

"Yeah, sorry about that. Rolly and I just sort of fell into shop talk."

"About whose shop?"

"He was asking me about the store and I told him I was thinking of franchising. He had lots to say about it."

"I can imagine. Did he give you any advice?"

"No, he mostly just told me about his experiences. He's had an interesting run of it."

I can't decide if I want to know more. Turns out it doesn't matter, because Ron asks me what Janine and I talked about.

"Spinning."

"What about it?"

"Everything about it! I'm meeting her for a class tomorrow morning."

Ron gives me a mystified look.

"Why would you ever agree to that?"

"Just trying to keep you on Rolly's good side. Plus, as it turns out the class is at Fusion, so at least it's close by."

"Well, I hope you like it. People say it's life-changing."

I don't bother to respond.

7

To: Grades K–5 Parents
From: JDixon
Re: Safety Patrol
Date: 10/8

Hello Fellow Patrol Patrollers!

I hope you are all gearing up for what promises to be an excruciating
experience.

I have attached the first schedule, which starts a week from
today and will take us through December. If you don't see your name
on the schedule, don't worry. It will probably show up in the new year.
And the Old Farmer's Almanac is predicting the snowiest January this
century!

Morning supervisors, please arrive no later than 7:30 a.m. and
head straight to Safety Patrol Command Central (the utility room at
the back of the gym) to meet the patrollers and don your vest. Your
role is supervisory. Watch the kids and only step in when you have to.
Your tour of duty ends at 8:30 a.m. Afternoon supervisors, you are on

> *from 2:30 till 3:30. Please make sure the equipment is returned to Command Central and the kids clean up their inevitable hot chocolate mess.*
>
> *As I have mentioned before, if you have any issues with the date for which you are scheduled, please take it upon yourself to find someone to switch with you. I will not be that someone.*
>
> *Always a pleasure!*
>
> *Jen*

I know damn well that last line is wishful thinking.

I take another loving sip of coffee and don't feel one bit ashamed of my defeat in the battle against caffeine. Everyone is happier, especially Max and Ron. My husband is thrilled that I mostly make it at home and when I do get it on the go, I've swapped Starbucks for Dunkin Donuts. The roast isn't as dark and I don't like the cups, but whatever. We're all making sacrifices.

On this sunny Monday morning, the boys are celebrating this Veterans Day by going to watch the ROTC performances at the Sprint Campus. I, however, am just realizing that I only have twenty minutes to get to my spin class. Yes, I said spin class. You are talking to the converted. No one is more surprised than I am.

Janine and I did indeed meet at Fusion the morning after our dinner at Café Provence. I'm not going to lie, I had a bit of a 'tude walking in there. The man/boy behind the counter forced a pair of the gym's spin shoes on me, explaining that I had to wear them in order to take the class. I thought putting on a pair of shoes that at least a thousand feet had previously perspired in was the grossest thing I would do that day, but I was wrong. That lovely moment came when the spin room doors opened, and a swarm of disgustingly sweaty people came pouring out along with a waft of what smelled like a mixture of BO and vagina. I nearly threw up.

Janine basically cock-walked me to my bike at the back of the room and hovered while I set up my seat height and handlebars. The room was already like 100 degrees and I really wasn't sure how long I would last, what with the smell and the wall-to-wall mirrors that allowed me no place to hide.

A tall, solid-looking gal strode to the instructor bike, calling out salutations to people as she went along.

"That's Carmen," Janine whispered reverently.

Carmen easily clipped her shoes into her pedals, swept her shoulder-length red hair into a ponytail, put her microphone headset on, and said "Hey, peeps! Happy Saturday. Glad you showed up to sweat out the alcohol from last night."

There were whoops and cheers from the twenty-plus riders in the room. *What a bunch of morons,* I muttered to myself. Turns out it was the last negative thought I had that day, because Carmen dimmed the lights and started the music.

Suddenly the room was filled with the unmistakable guitar licks of INXS's "New Sensation," and from that moment on I felt like I had died and gone to heaven. Every song Carmen played was from the soundtrack of my life. She went from rock to pop to hip-hop to a Broadway show tune and it all sounded amazing on the room's pimped-out sound system. I didn't have a hope in hell of keeping up with the class, what with the standing up and sitting down and doing ab crunches, but the music made me want to stay and at least try. At one point I looked over at Janine and she was running off the saddle and singing her heart out to "Livin' on a Prayer." As Bon Jovi belted out, "Take my hand, we'll make it I swear," she grabbed my hand and yanked it in the air. I started singing too, and I didn't even feel embarrassed. It was so liberating.

Before I knew it, we were stretching to the Dixie Chicks' version of "Landslide" and the forty-five-minute class was over. Everyone was clapping for Carmen, so I wholeheartedly joined in. I was dripping with sweat and I'm sure I smelled like the dickens.

"Oh, my God!" I said to Janine as we were walking out. "That was amazing! I loved it. Thank you so much for bringing me! Her music was insane."

Janine was gracious enough not to say, "I told you so," but it was written all over her face.

Since then I have gone three more times. Fusion Fitness was having a recruiting special, so I joined and got the first three months free. Ron wasn't thrilled that I'd joined a gym during belt-tightening season and was even less happy when I told him I needed my own pair of cycling shoes. But I reminded him it was a good way to bond with Janine. And besides, he could get the shoes wholesale, and they really do make for a more efficient ride. And since the only smelly feet to have touched them are mine, I don't gag when I put them on.

Carmen is my go-to girl, but if she isn't teaching I'll try other instructors. Before she went back to Boise, Janine gave me a list of teachers she thought I'd enjoy. I don't know if I'll ever see her again, but I will certainly never forget the third Mrs. Schrader. I owe her big-time.

My phone buzzes as I buckle myself into the minivan. It's a text from Laura.

Hi Mom! We're in Amsterdam. What's the name of that theme park you told me and Vivs about?

It takes me a minute to realize she is talking about Efteling, a fairytale-themed amusement park I went to way back when I was "touring" (ahem) with INXS. I must never have told her the *whole* story of what happened there, otherwise it would be the last place she'd want to go.

That was the day I learned the hard way to always listen to my body. The band had a day off between gigs, so the crew decided to have some fun and go to the amusement park. I was feeling funky that morning. I couldn't put my finger on it, but I just wasn't myself. ("Then who are you?" Michael Hutchence asked me when I told him.

He was such a cut-up.) I really didn't want to miss a fun day with the band, so I took some Tylenol with my coffee and sucked it up. When we got to the park I was told I just had to try *poffertjes*, which are Dutch mini pancakes. By that time, I had moved on from feeling funky and was *starving*, so I scarfed down six of them. You can see where this is going, right? During the first steep drop on the rickety wooden roller coaster, I puked my guts out and then fainted. I woke up on a stretcher on my way to the Efteling first-aid post. I wanted to get up and walk but Butchie, one of the roadies who was with me and the only one of us who spoke Dutch, insisted that I let them examine me. The medic found nothing wrong with me, but a blood test with the band's doctor later that day gave me the shock of my life—I was pregnant.

It's called Efteling. Are you going to go?
Ya. We have some downtime and there's only so much weed you can smoke! (kidding).
Very funny. The Van Gogh Museum is great too, and Anne Frank's house. And go to the Heineken Beer Museum.
Chill, Mom. We're only here for a couple of days. The band has a gig in Utrecht on Saturday. Thanks for the info.
You're welcome, sweetie. Let's talk soon.

I don't get an answer to that suggestion, so I pull out of the driveway and hightail it to Carmen's 9:30 class.

✦ ✦ ✦

Forty-five sweaty minutes later, I emerge from spin class still humming the last song she played—"Paradise by the Dashboard Light," by Meat Loaf—and checking my phone for messages when I run headlong into someone coming out of the men's locker room.

"Oh God, I'm so sorry," I say, and I really am. I hate when people are looking at their phones instead of where they are going.

"No problem. My fault, too." He looks at me and smiles. "Hey, I think I know you."

How anyone could recognize me when I look like I've just had a bucket of water thrown on me is beyond comprehension, but I give him a once-over to see if he rings any bells.

Just as I notice the scar under his eye, he says, "You're friends with Buddy and Peetsa, right?"

He's the divorced friend that Buddy is staying with.

"I'm TJ. We met at one of their barbecues."

"Yes, of course. How are you?"

"I'm good, thanks. You?"

He's not bad-looking and he fills out his gym clothes quite nicely. I'm trying to remember how old he is. At least forty-five, but he certainly doesn't look it, even with his salt-and-pepper hair.

"I'm a sweaty mess, but otherwise fine. Buddy is staying with you, isn't he?"

"Yeah." He laughs. "I haven't had a guy roommate since college."

"How is he doing?"

TJ shrugs. "Not bad, considering. I really hope they can work it out."

"I do too." Suddenly I feel uncomfortable talking about my close friend's private life with a stranger.

"Well, enjoy your workout," I say and head toward the women's locker room.

"Thanks. Nice bumping into you."

Awkward, I sing to myself as I head home.

✦ ✦ ✦

After a shower, I decide to check SignUpGenius to make sure everything on the list of goodies for this Thursday's curriculum night has been spoken for. I don't know if I'm more surprised or pissed off that only two things have been checked—the Browns are bringing cheese, and the Changs are bringing water. Jesus, Jackie Westman hasn't even signed up for cups, and that's her go-to thing! Clearly a reminder email is needed. Do they think I've gone soft now that I'm doing safety patrol?

To: Parents
From: JDixon
Re: Are we on a group diet?
Date: October 8th

People!

I just checked the SignUpGenius thingy and I was shocked (shocked!) to see that only two families have signed up to bring something this Thursday night. (Thank you, Browns and Changs.)

What the heck is going on? I'm pretty sure we can't survive two hours together on cheese and water alone. I really thought I had you all trained better than this. Clearly my year off has made you lazy.

Please, please get those fingers tapping and sign up to bring something. I promised you wine, didn't I? That should be incentive enough.

I'd say thank you, but really, what for?

Jen

I'm making a cup of tea half an hour later when Max and Ron come stomping in the back door.

"Mom! Bruce Willis goes so fast!" is how Max greets me.

I raise my eyebrow at my husband. "Really? How fast?"

Ron gives me a look like he doesn't know what Max is talking about.

"I don't know but we passed so many cars. It was cool." Max's cheeks are pink from being outside all morning, and his eyes are shining.

Ron changes the subject: "Anyone hungry for lunch?"

I scrunch up my nose. "Why don't I make grilled-cheese sandwiches?"

"I'm going to go try on my Halloween costume." Max dashes up the stairs.

"Again?" Ron yells after him.

"Forever," I whisper and start heating the pan for the grilled cheese.

Max's costume this year was quite the drama. He of course wanted to be an American Ninja Warrior, but they don't really wear anything specific, mainly just tight workout clothes. Most of the men don't even wear tops. But a few of them do stand out style-wise, so we decided he would dress like Drew Drechsel, who calls himself the real-life Ninja. Ron had Drechsel's signature orange T-shirt duplicated, and we paired it with black pants. The tricky part was finding a headband the same shade of orange as the shirt. We finally just bought a white one and I spent a very long afternoon dyeing it to Max's satisfaction.

This all happened back in August, the time of year when all overindulgent parents let their children get their Halloween costumes. I usually make Max wait until at least mid-September just in case he changes his mind. But we were feeling guilty about all the time we had spent away from him while my mother was sick so, voilà, a summer Halloween costume that he has worn almost every day since.

"How was spin?" Ron asks while his head is in the fridge.

"Excellent as usual." I bump him out of my way and grab cheese and bread.

"Carmen?"

"Yup. I love her so much."

"Sounds like you might leave me for her."

"I probably will, right after you leave me for Bruce Willis."

Ron nods. "Well, I may have to. I mean, how much beer can *you* carry?"

8

To: Safety Patrol People
From: JDixon
Re: Plot twist!
Date: 10/16

Good morning WHTSPP (William H. Taft Safety Patrol People)!

Breaking news from Command Central. It seems Sherlay DeJones is having separation anxiety from her duties at the corner of 12th and Hayward. In what can only be described as a shocking plot twist, she has asked that she be allowed to stay on and supervise the safety patrollers for the morning shift only. After my initial thought of "In God's name, why?" I realized this is good news for all of us. It means even fewer of you will be called upon to serve. How great is that?

If you've read the schedule, you'll know I have put myself down for the first three days, so I can troubleshoot any issues. On top of street-crossing violations, I will also be on the lookout for littering, loitering, lollygagging, and larceny. Nothing's going down on my watch. I encourage all of you to adopt the same attitude.

> *Wish me luck today!*
>
> *It's my honor to serve and protect,*
>
> *Jen*

With that out of the way, I realize I have some unexpected time on my hands. Sherlay DeJones's eleventh-hour switchback, coupled with Ron taking Max to school, has given me the morning free, and I'm thrilled. I might even get a run in.

I sit back in my kitchen-counter-office chair and debate calling Vivs. Things have been tense between us since I stopped by her work that day. She has shut down every attempt I've made to ask about her personal life and now she's just avoiding me outright. Ron's advice is to give her some space and she will come back when she needs something. For once, I listen to him.

Moving on, I consider sending a note to my class parents. I haven't written anything since the curriculum-night fiasco and I decide I'm still not ready to.

Let me just say this, technology sucks. That SignUpGenius thingy that was supposed to save me time and trouble turned out to be a cosmic joke . . . on me . . . because (and it kills me to admit this) I didn't really understand how it worked. I didn't realize that I was getting email updates from the thingy until after curriculum night, when I found them in my spam folder. Stupid signup thingy. If I'd seen those emails before I would have realized there was a glitch.

As a result, nine people brought mini quiches and one brought cups. Add that to what was already signed up for, we had water, cheese (no crackers), nine dozen mini quiches (no plates or napkins), and wine. Which would have been fine, except that the microwave in Razzi's classroom wasn't working so I had to run to the teachers' lounge every five minutes to heat some quiches up.

Because of all that, I missed most of the socializing and barely caught the end of Razzi's speech about what the kids were going to be doing this year. Normally I wouldn't care but I had actually been looking forward to seeing some of the parents (apparently hell *has* frozen over) and catching up on the gossip. Ron tried to fill me in, but men are generally clueless when it comes to the subtext of an innocent comment. For example, gorgeous Jean-Luc Baton told him that he and Mary Jo renewed their wedding vows not once but twice this summer. Ron took that at face value, but every woman knows a vow renewal is the same as yelling, "Our marriage is in trouble!," unless it's a twenty-fifth anniversary or something. But a renewal in year nine is just a cry for help. I told him as much on the car ride home.

"So if I asked you to renew our vows, you wouldn't?"

"Nope. I meant it the first time."

My computer pings and I see an email from Aunt Barbara. Jeez, it's really late in Hawaii. What the heck is she doing up?

To: JDixon
From: BHoward
Re: A favor
Date: 10/16

Dear Jennifer,

I will be happy to donate twenty dollars for your walk. What a wonderful thing to do for your mother. You have inspired me! I'm going to find a local Susan G. Komen Walk here and raise money too!

Love,
Aunt Barb

Yes! Thank you, Aunt Barbara. Only $480 to go.

It's nine a.m., so I pick up the phone for my daily call to my mother. My dad answers on the sixth ring.

"Hello?" He's practically shouting into the receiver.

"Hey, Dad. What's wrong?"

"Nothing, why? What have you heard?"

"I'm just checking in."

"Wait, here's your mother." I can hear shuffling and muffled voices.

"Yes, sweetheart?" My mom sounds out of breath.

"Mom, what's going on?" I'm starting to get a bit concerned.

"Nothing's going on, Jennifer. What can I do for you?"

"I'm just checking in," I say again. "Did I interrupt something?"

"No, of course not. Your dad and I were just . . . relaxing. We're fine and we don't need anything. Can I call you later?"

"Uh, sure."

"Okay then. Bye."

She hangs up and I'm left staring at my phone. What the hell was that all about? If I didn't know better, I'd think I had interrupted them having sex. Wait, *do* I know better? Were my parents having a nooner . . . at nine in the morning? The thought of them still having sex, at their age, makes me a bit queasy. I mean, jeez, when do we get to call it a day on stuff like that? If I'm still giving blowjobs twenty years from now I'm going to be very put out.

I reach for my phone and text Vivs what just happened. I update her about ten times a day and rarely get a reply. I know I'm being annoying, but I want my bitchy daughter back. This person who ignores me is really getting on my nerves. I also ask her for the sixth time if Raj is coming for Thanksgiving. I know it's more than a month away, but I'm trying to get ahead of the game this year. I realize it's part of getting older—I can't just throw it all together last minute anymore. I need to plan. Soon I'll be taking a trick out of my mother's book by making the mashed potatoes in October and freezing them, so I have one less thing to worry about.

With this to meditate on, I tidy up the house, do two loads of laundry, and take a short run. After a shower and lunch, I'm ready for my first afternoon of safety patrol. I arrive at the school at 2:15, wearing my usual mom uniform and the new black Lululemon jacket I got for my birthday that I'm convinced I love more than is socially acceptable.

It's a crisp, bright fall day and I'm sipping on a generic latte and humming an old Billy Joel song as I head to the gym. My phone buzzes: it's a one-word reply from Vivs.

Yes.

I'm glad. If I see them together, maybe I can figure out what's going on.

I open the gym door to a bunch of what I'm guessing are first-graders playing four-square. I scoot along the wall and head to Safety Patrol Command Central.

My first two patrollers, Hanna and Aaron, have arrived; much to my surprise, Sylvie Pike is there, too. Jesus, how early do I have to be to show up before her?

"There she is!" Sylvie exclaims and waves me over. Her orange blouse and black peasant skirt give her a decidedly Halloween vibe.

"Am I late?" I'm definitely not.

"Not at all," Sylvie assures me. "I just wanted to wish you luck on your first day."

And make sure I'm doing everything to your satisfaction, I think.

"Hi, Hanna; hi, Aaron. Are you guys excited?"

Hanna nods her head and says, "I'm psyched," while Aaron gives me the old one-shoulder shrug to let me know he heard me but is too cool to say anything. They both have their orange vests on already, and their stop signs in their hands.

"Get together for a picture." Sylvie pulls out her phone to take the shot. They awkwardly stand together with embarrassed grins but truthfully, they could be on a safety patrol poster, they are both so cute.

"Okay, time to get out there," Sylvie announces, and I can't help but wonder why she didn't just do this job herself. The kids walk out the door and as I follow them Sylvie helpfully reminds me to take my vest, too. I grab it along with the walkie-talkie and put it on as I make my way across the parking lot to the corner of 12th and Hayward.

Hanna and Aaron must have sprinted, because they are already at their assigned corners and looking sharp. I scan the area and see a few cars in the strip mall parking lot and a man sitting on the bench in front of the park across the street. All seems fine, so when the bell rings for school to let out I feel we are ready for anything.

I'm not sure where to stand to strike my desired balance between "on the job" and "not really here," so I decide to hang back and observe. As the first wave of kids and parents gets to the corner, I'm not at all surprised to see what an electrified bunch they are. When kids get out of school, it's like pulling the pin on a grenade. All their pent-up energy comes exploding out the doors in the form of running and yelling and bumping into one another. And the mothers are busy talking, so they're no help. I'm suddenly very concerned for the fifth-graders who are supposed to contain this rodeo. No wonder Sherlay took the morning shift. Not even Max could manufacture this kind of energy in the morning, except maybe on a Saturday.

"What are you wearing?" The voice of my son startles me out of my thoughts.

"Oh, hi, sweetie. It's my safety patrol vest. Do you like it?"

"No. You look stupid."

"Gee, thanks. And for that, you can go sit under that tree and don't move until I'm done."

"But you asked me!" Max is confused, and I can't blame him. We haven't yet taught him the art or value of the little white lie.

I turn back to the corner and see that despite the waves of anarchy that keep approaching the intersection, my patrollers have everything under control. I wander up to Hanna and ask how it's going.

"Great. It's pretty easy after the first bunch of kids." And she's right. The first two or three crossings were a dog's breakfast but after the rush, and for the next twenty minutes, kids come in dribs and drabs. By 3:30 Aaron is amusing himself by playing his stop sign like a guitar.

Sylvie Pike weirdly pops out from behind a bush at this point to let us know it's okay to go in. Does she think I don't own a watch . . . or a cell phone? And was she there the whole time?

As we walk back to Safety Patrol Command Central, with Max grudgingly in tow, Sylvie asks me how it went.

"Well, nobody died, so I'd call it a win."

"That's not funny," Sylvie says, and I remind myself that snarky isn't always the way to go.

"I thought it went really well," I assure her. In fact, I have to give myself snaps for pulling the whole thing off so seamlessly. I'm glad I said yes to this task. I don't know what I was worried about.

9

To: Safety Patrol People
From: JDixon
Date: 11/26
Re: Today's debacle

Greetings—

I'm sure by now you've all heard what happened at safety patrol today so let me just state the obvious: this cannot happen again. Please consult your schedule and your child's, and if there is a conflict, make arrangements to have your shift covered by another parent. Sending your cleaning lady is not an option. Also, if your child is sick, please have them reach out to a patrol friend. I'm hoping today was a once-in-a-lifetime incident.

And for those wondering, Draper Lody's nose was not broken, as previously reported, but there was an impressive amount of blood.

Onward,

Jen

And that's what I get for giving myself snaps. I should have known the shit would hit the fan at some point. What is it about long weekends like Thanksgiving that makes the best-laid plans get shot to hell?

I get up from my kitchen-counter office and grab a coconut water from the fridge. Max is allegedly doing his math homework at the kitchen table, but it's hard for me to tell since he covers his work with his arm. I can't decide how to punish him for his part in today's fiasco. I know he didn't mean any harm, but my God, did he have to get the homeless guy involved?

Here's what happened. This afternoon while I was waiting with Ravi and Shirleen for our kids to get out of school, they proceeded to give me shit because I hadn't sent out a class email since early November.

"I mean, Jennifer, we depend on you to let us know what is going on in that classroom," Shirleen informed me.

"Not to mention I depend on you for a good laugh," Ravi added with a smile. "At least every two weeks."

Shirleen's sniff told me she didn't agree. "Do we have any field trips coming up?"

"Not that I know of." I was going to share with them that I thought Razzi was getting a bit lazy in her old age. But when I looked past Shirleen's shoulder toward the street I noticed the safety patrollers weren't at their posts. I looked at my phone. It was 2:55.

"I'll be right back," I said to them and ran to the gym to check Command Central. The vests and stop signs were sitting in their baskets. I looked at the schedule on the wall and saw that it was Hanna and Aaron's week again. Where the hell were they?

Just then a middle-aged woman with graying blond hair pulled in a tight bun appeared at the door out of breath.

"Oh, thank God. Are you the parent on duty today?" I ask while searching my mind for the name of the person who was scheduled.

"Please, eez dis safety program?" Her thick Slavic accent surprised me.

"Yes! Glad you made it. Hanna and Aaron haven't shown up for some reason."

"I do patrol for Hanna. She sick with cold."

I blinked a few times to make sure I wasn't dreaming.

"You're here to do safety patrol for Hanna?"

"Yes, and Mrs. Ali. I clean for them." I had no time to absorb what this woman was saying to me because at that moment the bell rang. *Shit.* I was torn in six different directions. I immediately texted Ravi to tell Max to meet me at the safety patrol corner, grabbed the two stop signs and vests, and told the woman to follow me.

"What's your name?" I yelled back to her as we sprinted through the parking lot.

"Martika," she puffed, trying to keep up with me.

"And Mrs. Ali sent you?" The name rings no bells.

"Yes. She was helping Mrs. Pam."

Mrs. Pam? "Pam Mitchell?" The name of the patrol parent on the schedule finally came to me.

"Yes," Martika grunted.

We got to the corner just as the first wave of people swarmed the area.

"Hold on. Okay. Just let me get my vest on," I said with authority as I tossed Martika the other vest and a stop sign. Luckily, we were both able to barely fit into the kids' vests. I then stuck out my sign to stop the already stopping traffic.

"Like this," I told her, stepping onto the street in front of the cars and helping my charges cross safely.

"Mom, what are you doing?" Max was standing a few feet away with a boy I didn't know.

"Hi, sweetie. I'm doing safety patrol. Just hang out and wait for me okay?"

"Can Draper and I have a play date at our place?"

"Uh, sure." I was helping another group to cross the street and making sure Martika was holding her own, so I only gave them a passing glance. "Is it okay with his mom?" Draper nodded.

For the next twenty minutes I was engrossed in the task of helping people cross the street, all the while trying to put together the events that had brought me here. Neither Hanna nor Aaron had shown up for safety patrol; neither did Pam Mitchell, and neither did her substitute, Mrs. Ali, who sent her cleaning lady instead. I couldn't have written a weirder scenario.

As the steady stream of people turned to a drip, I thanked Martika for her help and told her to just leave her vest and sign on the grass. I took a deep breath and turned to talk to Max. But he wasn't at his usual tree. My eyes darted all around the schoolyard and parking lot. No sign of him. My heart started to pound. I turned to look across the street and finally spotted him. He and Draper were sitting on the bench beside the park *talking to a man*!

Before I could stop myself, I screamed his name at the top of my lungs.

"Max!"

He looked over and waved.

"Get over here *now*!" My voice sounded shrill and panicked.

He and Draper said a few more words to the man and then crossed the street back over to me.

"What do you think you're doing?" I asked him. I had no doubt I was embarrassing the crap out of him.

"We were just talking to Mitch."

"Oh really? And who is Mitch?"

He pointed across the street. "He's that guy. He lives in the park."

I was about to launch into a speech about not talking to strangers when I heard a resounding thwack. Draper had picked up Martika's abandoned stop sign and was hitting anything he could find, using the sign like a baseball bat.

"Excuse me, Draper. Please put that sign down."

"Why?" Draper asked while swatting a half-full juice box he had picked up by the curb.

"Because it isn't yours and that's not what you use it for."

Now this next part is a little weird. You kind of had to see it to believe it. Basically, Draper sauntered toward me to hand me the sign. As he was passing near Max, he batted the sign in my son's face as if he was going to hit him, like a "Made you flinch!" move. Unfortunately, my Ninja-loving son is not familiar with the fake-out, so he put his hands up and not only stopped the sign but pushed it back so hard it slammed Draper in the nose.

"*Ow!* Fuck!"

Nice mouth on the kid! He dropped the sign and put his hands to his face while I reached into my jacket pocket and thanked my lucky stars I had put a fresh Kleenex pack in there. I asked a stunned Max what the heck he was thinking while I pulled Draper's hands away from his face so I could assess the damage.

"I thought he was going to hit me" was all he said.

I concluded that Draper's nose was not broken. But he was crying, so there were tears and snot mixed in with a lot of blood. Ugh. This is gross enough when it's your own kid. With someone else's kid, it's just disgusting.

"I want my mom," Draper sobbed.

"I know, kiddo. I'll call her. Do you know your mom's phone number?"

I dialed the number he gave me through his sobs and while it was ringing I noticed that we had drawn quite a crowd of rubberneckers, including Mitch, the guy who lives in the park. I found myself wishing that Sylvie Pike would jump out of the bushes.

"Hello?" Alison picked up on the second ring.

"Hi, Alison? This is Jen Dixon. I'm here at school with Draper. He's fine, but he has a bloody nose and you might want to pick him up."

"How did he get a bloody nose?" she asked with more calmness than I could have mustered if the roles were reversed. "He said he was having a play date at your house."

"He is . . . was. They were waiting for me to finish safety patrol."

I hear a sigh at the other end of the line. "Can you bring him home? My daughter is sick, and I can't leave her right now."

"Of course. What's your address?"

She told me, and I typed it into a message bubble on my phone.

When I hung up, one of the gawkers wondered if I needed any help. I recognized her as a safety patrol parent, so I asked if she could take the signs and vests back to Command Central. I wanted to get Draper home ASAP. I walked both boys to the parking lot and didn't notice I was being followed until we got to the car. A glance over my shoulder showed me that homeless Mitch was limping about ten feet behind us. The hairs on my neck stood up.

I'm not going to lie. Homeless people make me uncomfortable. I'm well aware this is not one of my more attractive qualities, but I can't seem to help it. Plus, this guy had just followed me to the car. My danger radar was on high alert.

"Excuse me, ma'am."

Shit!

As I opened the van for the boys, I scanned the parking lot and was relieved to see a few adults and students still milling around. Feeling a little more secure, I turned to get my first real look at him.

Mitch was about five ten, with dark, weather-beaten skin and sad brown eyes. He was wearing jeans, a down jacket, and what looked like very old black sneakers.

"Yes, sir? How can I help you?" I asked in my no-nonsense voice. I had already put my car keys between my fingers in case he attacked me.

"You dropped this on the grass." He held out my phone.

Three things popped into my head immediately.

1. *I'm such an asshole.*
2. *Eww, Mitch is touching my phone and God knows where his hands have been.*
3. *Do I have any small bills to give him?*

"Oh! Thank you," I sputtered, took the phone from him, and scurried back to the van.

"You're Kay's daughter, right?" he asked my back. I turned and gave him what I'm sure was a freaked-out look. He smiled.

"I know your mom from the church and I've seen you a few times." *A very few times,* I think to myself. Church and I are on an as-needed basis.

I still hadn't said anything, so he continued.

"Your mother is a really nice lady. I'm glad she's feeling better."

"Um, I have to go," I stammered, realizing I had forgotten about the child gushing blood in my back seat. "Thank you for my phone." I got in the car and drove away as quickly as I could.

"Isn't Mitch nice, Mom?"

"Mm-hmm" was all I could get out. I couldn't think about Mitch, what with Draper still quietly whimpering and holding a huge wad of Kleenex to his nose.

"I said sorry to Draper," Max informed me. "He said it's okay." In the world of eight-year-olds, they were already at bygones. I wished mothers were that easy.

We pulled into the driveway of an extremely large Tudor-style house with a silver Tesla parked by the garage. Wow. Alison Lody is Alison Loaded! As I rolled to a stop, Draper jumped out of the back seat and ran to the front door yelling, *"Mom!"* and sobbing anew.

"Stay here," I said to Max as I hauled myself out of the minivan and walked to the door. Draper had already run inside, and I found him in his mother's arms. I only had a second to take in the glamorous foyer I'd stepped into. I saw a lot of marble and gold leaf and a huge staircase. It was like I'd stumbled onto the set of *Dynasty*—the eighties version. The only thing missing was Alison with shoulder pads and a perm. As it was, she had tight jeans, a crisp white shirt, and a blue cardigan on her petite body. What I like to call rich-people casual.

"Hi, Alison. I'm so sorry about this."

"What happened?" she demanded more than asked.

"Max hit me with a stop sign," Draper helpfully informed her.

Alison looked at me in stunned silence.

"Well, technically yes, that's true but it was an accident," I started to explain, but she cut me off.

"You know what? It doesn't matter. Thank you for bringing him home." With one arm around her son, she used the other to gesture toward the front door.

I had no idea what to do. I couldn't tell if she was pissed off or just really easy-breezy about bloody noses. As I headed to the door I heard a sweet voice say, "Mrs. Dixon?" I turned around and at the top of the sweeping staircase stood Hanna, my favorite safety patroller, in a fluffy pink robe. At that point the pieces snapped together like Lincoln Logs. Martika works for Mrs. Ali aka Alison (*click*) and was filling in as a patroller for Hanna and Mrs. Ali (*click*) because Mrs. Ali was helping out Mrs. Pam (Pam *Mitchell*, who was supposed to be on duty today: *click*).

"Hi, Hanna." I tried to keep my voice neutral. Hanna *Lody*. Wow. Was she adopted?

"I'm sorry I didn't make it to safety patrol today."

"That's okay, sweetie. Feel better. Hey, do you know where Aaron was?" I realized I had yet to solve that little mystery.

"He got back from Arizona today."

"Hanna, go back to bed, please," Alison said crisply. She turned to me. "Thank you again for bringing Draper home."

"Well, um . . . thank you for trying to help out Pam. That was nice of you."

"I don't even know her. She called me out of the blue. Don't let me keep you." She pointed to the door again.

She couldn't have been making it any plainer that she wished me gone, so I headed to the minivan where Max was, I'm sure, waiting to find out how much trouble he was in. We had a silent ride home, and when we got there I suggested he get right to his homework.

So as I watch my son do just that, I'm wishing my coconut water had a little rum in it. Max tests the waters of my anger by asking what we are having for dinner.

"Leftovers," I say as I open the fridge.

"Again?" I can tell he's trying not to whine, but he wouldn't be out of line if he did. Thanks to the two-turkey fiasco this past weekend, I'm sure we'll be eating it until Christmas.

✦ ✦ ✦

Thanksgiving was a lot of work. I hosted ten for dinner, plus I had Nina, Garth, and Chyna staying with us the whole weekend. My parents were there, of course, and Raj came with Vivs, which meant I was doing double duty cooking dinner and trying to figure out what was going on with them. I really missed Laura (who was still in Europe) for obvious reasons but also because she is the biggest help with meal prep and the best gravy maker. I was forced to serve my mother's salt-infused concoction and it tainted everything it touched. Nina said she could hardly notice, but she, like everyone else, was chugging a lot of water.

God, it was good to see Nina. I knew I missed her, but I had no idea how much until I had a daily dose of her for ninety-six blissful hours.

Vivs and Raj seemed to be having a hard time readjusting to each other. I guess distance doesn't always make the heart grow fonder; sometimes it just makes it less tolerant. Their relationship has never been smooth sailing, but this particular weekend it was a white squall. Vivs was on Raj for everything he did and didn't do. And she definitely couldn't let it go that he took it upon himself to have a fully cooked twenty-pound turkey delivered from a local deli without telling anyone, including me, who had already cooked a twenty-pound turkey. It was a sweet gesture, but it created a tryptophan nightmare.

"He's driving me nuts," she told Nina and me while we were washing the last of the dishes from dinner.

"How is he driving you nuts?"

"I don't know. He's just always there . . . breathing."

I banged a pot on the counter. "Oh, no. Not *breathing*!" Nina cracked up.

"Mom, stop. I never realized what a loud breather he is. And chewer! Did you hear how loud he was chewing at dinner?"

I look to Nina for help.

"You know . . ." she began, then took a sip of wine. "Usually if your partner's personal habits are starting to bug you, it means you need some time apart. But all you two get is time apart. You should be all over each other."

"Like Nana and Poppy!" Vivs neatly pivots the topic away from herself. "Oh my God, what is going on with them?"

My parents had indeed been exceptionally affectionate with each other all evening, which only added fuel to my coitus-interruptus theory. I told them about my weird phone call the other day and Vivs couldn't stop cringing.

"Where does this little beauty go?" Nina held up the gravy boat from hell, which Ron's ex-wife, Cindy, gave us as a wedding gift. It's a porcelain turkey where the neck is the handle and the gravy comes out the butt.

"In the special place of honor with the rest of our priceless treasures." I gesture toward the linen closet in the hallway just outside the kitchen. "Behind the old towels." I turned to my daughter. "Nina's right, you know. You need to figure out where your hostility's coming from. Because if his *chewing* bothers you now, in ten years you won't be able to breathe the same air as him."

I'm not sure if they figured anything out, but Raj left two days early. Vivs claims they haven't broken up.

✦ ✦ ✦

"How about I make turkey tacos?" I ask Max.

"Okay." He shrugs without lifting his head from the table.

My computer pings while I'm cooking. I glance over and what to my wondering eyes should appear but an email from Sylvie Pike. Oh, joy.

> To: JDixon
> From: SPike
> Re: Safety Patrol
> Date: 11/27
>
> Hi,
>
> Are you free for a quick powwow tomorrow morning after drop-off? I'll meet you at 8:15 in the safety patrol room at the back of the gym.
>
> > Thanks,
> > Sylvie

Hmmm . . . now, that sounds like a command performance. I email her back that I will be there. Jesus, is it really only Monday?

10

To: Mrs. Randazzo's Class
From: JDixon
Re: Remember me?
Date: 12/03

Hello, Fellow Parents!

It has come to my attention that I have been neglectful in my communications with you guys and I apologize. But I have had a shiny new toy to play with called safety patrol and it's been keeping me very busy.

Exciting news from Mrs. Randazzo! She has finally decided on a field trip for our offspring. About time, am I right? I thought they'd never leave the classroom. To reinforce all they have learned about Native Americans this fall, the class is going to the Shawnee Indian Mission in Fairway on December 14th from 10 a.m. to 11:30. I don't have a lot of details right now, but I'm guessing there will be some beading involved.

After the debacle that was the SignUpGenius (all the notifications ended up in my spam folder, so I never saw them), I'm going back to *doing it old school. So, if you are interested in chaperoning this super fun trip, please email me back. As always, early birds get the yummiest worms, so type fast. We'll need three parents.*

While I have you, I want to give you a heads-up about the class holiday party—December 21st in room 402, right after the Christmas concert. I'll be soliciting for refreshments next week. As for Razzi's holiday gift, we (and by we, I mean I) have decided to give her a giant white coffee mug that all the kids will write messages on. Shirleen Cobb has offered to fire up her kiln and reenact a scene from the movie Ghost *to get the mug made. When I have it in my hot little hands, I will commandeer the classroom one afternoon to have the kids decorate it.*

Always a pleasure!
Jen Dixon, Safety Patrol Monitor and On-the-Job Class Mom

I'm humming "Sunday Morning" by Maroon 5 as I send my latest offering to my class. Ravi and Shirleen were right: I'd really been delinquent with the class updates. But after my "powwow" with Sylvie Pike, where I was gently told that I needed to "get it together," I have pulled up my socks and gone overboard to stay on top of things, including checking in with the safety patrollers and parents daily to make sure everyone knows to show up. If that's what I have to do to avoid Sylvie's disappointment, I'll do it. Despite the fact that she's a pain in my ass, I like her. I found myself opening up to her about my troubles with Vivs and she was a very sympathetic ear, which was nice. I get the feeling there is a really fun person in there somewhere, just dying to come out. I'm thinking about inviting her out for girls' night with Peetsa . . . maybe in January.

I slam out a group note to Chloe, Carlo, and a kindergarten parent named Christmas Angel O'Toole (she'll be the first to tell you it's on her birth certificate) reminding them they are all on duty tomorrow, before I grab my keys and gym bag and head to spin class.

I'm convinced these classes are the only thing keeping me from resorting to pills and booze. No matter what is going on in my life, I can forget about it for a blissful forty-five minutes while Carmen takes me on yet another musical adventure through my past.

As I'm driving to Fusion, I start thinking about Mitch the homeless guy. I talked to my mother about him during one of our morning phone calls last week.

"Oh sure, I know Mitch," she told me. "He's a regular at the shelter."

"Do you think he's dangerous at all?"

"Why would he be dangerous? He's just homeless, Jennifer, not a criminal. He does odd jobs for us at the church."

"How did he end up on the streets?"

"Why don't you ask him?"

"I don't want to talk to him!"

My mother doesn't even try to mask her frustration.

"Jennifer, you really should try to get over yourself. You've watched your father and me help needy people your whole life. I'm really disappointed that none of it rubbed off on you."

She's right. I did *not* inherit their inexhaustible kindness to people in need. Sometimes I feel like the missing link. It would have been nice to receive that gem in the gene pool instead of freakishly large bunions. But I made a lot of promises to the universe when my mother was sick—mostly about being a better person—and I need to start following through.

And I will, right after Carmen's class.

✦ ✦ ✦

To: JDixon
From: SCobb
Re: Class Trip
Date: 12/04

Jennifer:

I'd be happy to go on this trip. I don't know if I've ever told you, but I'm one-fifteenth Kickapoo. Bud and I take Graydon to the Powwow every year. He loves the funnel cakes.

Shirleen

A red-headed Native American. Wow. You learn something new every day. And Shirleen, on a field trip? This should be good. I wonder if I should go along as well, just to show I'm still relatively on the job, all evidence to the contrary. I'll see how many volunteers I end up getting. Participation usually takes a big nosedive in third grade. Parents just aren't as excited as they were in the cute years, and really, who can blame them?

We had our first snowfall last night and then the temperature plummeted, so this morning's drop-off was what my gran would have called a Turkish bazaar. (Her repertoire of inappropriate phrases is legendary. We thank God quite often that she died before being PC was mandatory. She never would have made it.) Sherlay DeJones looked particularly miserable in her parka and vest. I don't know if she had her curlers in, because her hood was up.

The sound of my email pinging startles me.

To: JDixon

From: ALody

Re: Class Trip

Date: 12/4

Jen,

I'll chaperone this trip.

Alison

She really has a way with words, doesn't she? So, it will be me, Shirleen, and Alison Lody. Wow. Did I piss off a witch?

It's ten a.m., so I call my mother to check in. She answers on the first ring.

"Jennifer, good. I was waiting on your call."

"You can always call me, Mom. Phones work both ways."

"Well, I need you to drive your father to the club for his lunch meeting."

I love how my mother refers to the Kiwanis Club as "the club." It sounds so fancy.

"Sure. What are you up to?"

"Nothing. I just don't want to go out."

"Are you feeling all right?"

"Of course I am. It's just too damn cold."

"Okay! I'll be over at eleven forty-five."

"Oh, sweetheart, on your way could you pick up Dad's prescription at the CVS?"

"Anything else?"

"As long as you're there, I could use some Pronamel and your dad needs Preparation H. He has a hemorrhoid the size of a golf-ball."

"TMI, Mom. See you in a while."

As I hang up I can hear my mother say, "What is TMI?"

✦ ✦ ✦

I'm driving with my dad and conversation is light as usual. My father is a man of few words.

"So, what's new at the Kiwanis Club?"

He shrugs. "Same as always. Helping kids."

"How do you think Mom is doing?"

"Great. More energy than ever."

"And you guys are good?"

"Yup" is the only answer I get, but I see a little blush come to his cheeks.

As we pull up to the club, Dad asks if I want to come in and say hi to "the guys."

"Maybe when I come back and get you. I'll be back around one thirty."

"Okey-dokey. See you then." It takes him three tries to hoist himself out of the car and then he shuffles toward the door. God, I hate watching my parents grow old.

Since I'm out, I decide to pop by the store to see if Ron wants to have lunch with me. I drive into the Fitting Room parking lot and scurry to the door, trying to keep the freezing-cold air from permeating my coat.

I find Ron in the back, at his desk and on the phone. He looks up and smiles as he continues his conversation.

"That sounds good. Let me check with Jen and get back to you. Right. Okay, bye."

"What's up, sugar booger?" I lean down to give him a kiss. "What do you have to check with me about?"

"Rolly and Janine are coming to town next weekend and want to have dinner with us."

"Great!" I sound excited because I actually am. The Schraders have come to town four times in the past couple of months and we always have such a great time with them, albeit a drunken one. I'm not one to judge, but Rolly and Janine can drink like sailors during Fleet Week. The last time we went out we closed down the restaurant playing this crazy drinking game that Janine suggested, called Never Have I Ever. Someone says something they have never done, and you have to take a drink if you have actually done it. We were at Outback Steakhouse (Ron had a coupon) in a back booth and pretty sequestered from the rest of the restaurant. Janine suggested the game just as we were finishing the third bottle of wine. She could have suggested cow tipping at that point and it would have sounded good to me.

The questions started off innocently enough: "Never have I ever jumped out of an airplane" (Ron had to drink on that one) and "Never have I ever dined and dashed." But all too soon the statements got pretty racy. I'm proud to say I drank more than anyone else, proving yet again that I have left very few stones unturned in my life. Thankfully, Janine and Rolly seemed to get a big kick out of promiscuous me.

"Never have I ever had a threesome," Janine said and while I tossed back another sip of wine I was surprised that she hadn't.

"Not even in your slutty Ice Capades years?" I asked dubiously.

She shook her head. "Too many gay men."

"Never have I ever spit instead of swallow." I wink at Janine. She doesn't budge. Wow, respect.

"Never have I ever kissed someone while married to someone else." Rolly's gaze roamed our little circle mischievously.

I looked at Ron, thinking he and I would have a laugh over my almost-kiss with Suchafox a few years ago, but to my great surprise, he took a sip and so did Janine.

"Who have you been kissing?" I was only half kidding.

"When I was married to Cindy," he drawled. Oh, I knew that.

"Your turn, Ron." Janine nudged him. He leaned forward dramatically and looked directly at me.

"Never have I ever . . . farted and blamed my kid."

There was a moment of silence then Rolly and I both took a drink.

"I knew it!" Ron slapped the table and we all had a rollicking drunken laugh over a fart joke. It was a great night.

"I should call Janine and see when she wants to spin."

Ron pushes his chair back from his desk and pats his lap. "Come sit. What are you doing here?"

"Just killing some time before I have to pick up my dad from his Kiwanis meeting." I snuggle into his lap and put my arms around him. I'm reminded of the early months of our relationship, when I'd stop by for a quickie on my lunch break.

Ever since Ron pressed Go on franchising, he has been working even longer hours. Thankfully, he's able to do a lot of it at home, so at least he can have dinner with Max and me. But then he goes into the room once known as our dining room, which now looks like Office Depot threw up in it, and is on his laptop for a good three more hours. I miss my TV partner in crime. I'm like three seasons ahead of him on *Breaking Bad*.

"It'll be nice to see them. I just hope my liver can survive it."

"I didn't know someone was strapping you down and *making* you drink." Ron tickles me.

"Have you moved forward on asking Rolly to invest in the expansion?"

"Not yet. Still priming the pump."

"So, where do you want to go for dinner?"

"I was thinking about that steak-and-seafood place you love."

"Bristol? Really? I didn't know they gave out coupons."

"Very funny. I never used that gift card my staff gave me last Christmas."

"I forgot about that. Okay, good. I'll make a reservation. Hey, can you slip out now and grab a bite with me?"

"It'll have to be drive-through. I'm pretty swamped."

"Taco Bell it is."

✦ ✦ ✦

I'm still munching on my cinnamon twists when I pull into the Kiwanis parking lot again. Inside my dad is sitting on a bench with his two best friends, whom I still call Mr. Collins and Mr. Arrucci. I put on my best daughter face and brace myself for the "My, hasn't she grown up?" comments from these men, who have known me since birth. I'm almost fifty-one, but they always make me feel like a kid again. I kind of like it.

"How was lunch?" I kiss my dad on the cheek.

"Fine. I thought your mother was picking me up."

"Nope. I dropped you off, remember?"

"Oh, right."

We leave Dad's friends to a chorus of "Drive carefully!" and hold on to each other for warmth as we walk to the minivan.

I take my time driving my dad home. When he gets out he says, "Thanks for lunch!" I don't bother correcting him. I make a pit stop at Dunkin Donuts for some hot chocolate before pick up, where I unfortunately encounter one Alison Lody arguing with the girl behind the counter about whether or not she used nonfat milk in her latte. Spreading her joy as usual, I see. I want to tell her a little fat won't kill her, but instead I back out of the shop and decide I'll pick up a Swiss Miss at Command Central.

Chloe and Carlo are bundled up and trudging to their post when I pull into the parking lot.

"Are you guys all set?" I ask them from the comfort of my warm car.

They reply "Yeah" in unison and without much enthusiasm. Christmas Angel, who is right behind them, seems even less happy, if that's possible. On days like this the bloom is most definitely off the safety patrol rose, not that it was ever on.

I zip my coat higher, pull on my hood, and tell myself to butch up. I'm from Kansas, for God's sake. I beeline it into the school, because I want to go over the plans for the school trip with Razzi.

In room 402 I see the kids getting their coats on and lining up at the door. As they file out I grab Max and tell him to wait in the hall for me.

"Hi, Winnie, do you have a minute to talk about the trip?"

She looks up at me. Between the fishing hat and the dirty glasses she looks a bit like a crazy bag lady.

"The trip? Oh, the trip! Yes. Sorry. You say trip and I think 'Bahamas!' Did you call and set it up?"

"No. Was I supposed to?"

"Well, yes. I sent you that email about it."

"The email only told me it was happening, not that I needed to set it up."

"Are you sure?"

"Yes, I'm pretty sure. I'm happy to do it, I just didn't know."

"Well, okay then."

I pause, unsure of what has just been decided.

"Okay, meaning you want me to take care of it?"

"Yes, Jen, please do." She turns and starts writing on the chalkboard.

"Okay then, I will." I don't know what to do next, so I say goodbye and head downstairs to the parking lot with Max dragging his feet behind me. When we get in the car I start it up and immediately whip out my phone to find Winnie's email about the trip, just to confirm that she hadn't asked me to set it up. She hadn't. Great. Another person in my life is losing their mind.

"Sweetie, how was school?"

"Good."

"What did Draper bring today?" This question is now on the daily roster because the answer is always entertaining.

"A shark tooth. Bor-ing."

Wow, a rare miss for Draper.

We ride in silence for a few minutes while I decide how to ask this next question.

"Hey, does Mrs. Randazzo forget things sometimes?"

"Like what?"

"I don't know, anything."

He thinks for a minute.

"She couldn't find any staples one day."

"Huh."

We ride the rest of the way home in silence while I try to figure out if Razzi's losing it, or I am.

11

To: Mrs. Randazzo's Class
From: JDixon
Re: Sweets and Treats after the concert
Date: 12/14
TO BE SUNG TO THE TUNE OF "LET IT SNOW, LET IT SNOW, LET IT SNOW"

Oh, the Christmas party's in a blinky
And we'll need some food and drinky
But since it won't get itself here
Volunteer, volunteer, volunteer!
We'll be meeting in 4-0-2
When the concert songs are through
And since it's that time of year
Volunteer, volunteer, volunteer!
We'll need bagels and cream cheese too
Water, juice, coffee, and Yoo-hoo
Donuts, muffins, and lots of fruit
But nothing that will make the kids toot!

Oh, the children will surely be happy
And Razzi's feet will be a-tappy
But only if you all adhere
And volunteer, volunteer, volunteer!

December 21st, people. Let's get the lead out. I want this off my plate.
Response times will be noted.

Jen

I look at my song parody and wrinkle my nose. Not my best work, but I'm crushed for time. I'm off to the Shawnee Indian Mission with my two besties, Shirleen Cobb and Alison Lody. I have not spoken to Alison since the stop-sign incident. I saw Draper the next day at pickup and he was sporting an impressive black eye. Max said he was fine in school and still reigned over the secret club meeting at recess, where he showed everyone his latest treasure, a pair of very strong reading glasses.

"When I put them on they made me sick to my stomach!" Max raved.

I'm not sure what kind of reception I'm going to get today from the lovely Alison, but I'm hoping for the best.

I pull into the school parking lot and see the kids are just starting to board the school bus. I park and rush over to see Winnie Randazzo bundled up and counting heads.

"I'm here," I announce.

"Oh, good." Winnie gives me a smile. She has swapped out her trademark pink fishing hat for a woolen one with a huge pompom on top. "The other two moms are on the bus already." She leans in close and whispers, "I don't think they like each other very much."

I grimace and climb the steps of the bus after the last two have boarded. Razzi is right behind me. The kids are as loud and rambunctious as you'd expect them to be, what with the thrill of getting out of the classroom and actually going somewhere. Even the most boring museum trip is met with as much excitement as Disneyland . . . at least until they get there.

I notice Max sitting with Mike T. in the third row, so when I pass by, I lean down to kiss his head.

"Mom! Stop." He bats me away like an annoying fly.

"Can I sit with you guys?"

Mike T. wisely says nothing, but Max is happy to inform me that parents sit at the back of the bus.

I'm tempted to force him to scoot over, but Razzi is waiting for me to move so I ruffle his hair as I walk toward my designated area. I see Shirleen and Alison sitting in separate rows and looking at their phones.

"Hi, girls! Thanks for coming today."

"Well, I wouldn't miss it," Shirleen chirps. "I always like to reconnect with my roots." Her coat is undone, and I see she is sporting a colorful beaded vest. I guess I should be thankful she didn't come in a full feather headdress.

I look at Alison, who hasn't looked up from her phone. I decide to sit beside her and let Razzi take the seat next to Shirleen.

"Let's keep the noise down to a dull roar!" she yells at the class. As the bus lurches onto the street, she turns to us.

"Now ladies, when we get there we are going to be touring just the north building and learning the techniques for basket weaving and beadwork that have been passed down through the generations."

Shirleen proudly rubs her vest and nods.

"After an hour, we will hand out a snack and then get the kids back on the bus."

"That's it?" Shirleen says, a bit too loudly. Alison finally looks up from her phone and rolls her eyes.

"What were you expecting? Smoke signals and a scalping demonstration?"

Whoa! Even I can see the inappropriate in that little comment.

"Well, obviously not," Shirleen snaps back. "And I certainly wasn't talking to you. I was talking to Mrs. Randazzo."

Razzi seems fascinated by this exchange and is in no hurry to stop it, so I jump into the unfamiliar role of Voice of Reason. "Guys, the kids can hear you."

This shuts everyone up for a good ten minutes, until I say to Alison, "I'm sorry again about Draper's nose."

"It's fine." She sighs.

"Your daughter is a real sweetheart. I love having her in safety patrol."

She just nods and looks straight ahead. I'm finding this conversation very unsatisfying. Why am I sucking up to this woman? I take out my phone and play Words with Friends until we get to the Mission.

Inside, the kids are separated into two groups. Razzi and Shirleen go with the basket weavers and Alison and I with the beaders. We are directed to stand against the wall and observe. They have set up stations for the kids to try their hand at this ancient Indian craft. Just as I'm thinking this is going to be the longest hour of my life, Alison leans over and whispers, "Thank God I'm with you and not her." I can only assume she's talking about Shirleen.

"She's not that bad once you get to know her." I know better than anyone that Shirleen is an acquired taste.

"She's trying to blame Draper for her son not having any friends."

What happens next can be filed under "When will I ever learn?"

"Well, it may have something to do with the club."

"What club?"

Wishing I could jump in a time machine and go back thirty seconds, I reluctantly answer her. "Um, the secret club that Draper started for boys in the class."

Her look tells me she has no idea what I'm talking about.

"They meet at recess and Draper always brings in something to show everyone."

"He does?" Her eyebrows shoot up. "Like what?"

I shrug. "All different things—deodorant, a cockroach preserved in amber, a skeleton hand, and something he said was to stop a bloody nose, but from Max's description I think it was a tampon."

"What are you even talking about? Who told you this?"

"Max." I shrug.

"Are you sure he isn't making it up?"

Hey, slow your roll, lady. My son is many things, but not a liar.

"Trust me, he doesn't have that good an imagination."

Alison's expression is one of silent fury.

"Why didn't the teacher tell me about it?" she demands.

"I don't think she knows."

"Oh, isn't that convenient." She is keeping her voice low, but her irritation level has skyrocketed. "What is it with you people? We are *new*. We *just* started at this school. I've never felt so unwelcome, and now my son is being blamed for some club and a boy not having friends? We had a play date with that kid, by the way, but he didn't want to do anything. He barely said a word."

"Well, Max told me Draper excluded him from the club." I figure I may as well just wade all the way into the shit show.

"I really don't want to hear any more." Alison turns and walks over to Razzi, says a few words, then walks out. Wow. I thought I'd seen everything, but a parent walking out on a field trip is definitely uncharted waters.

Razzi gives me a curious look, but I just shrug and pretend to watch the beading demonstration. I'm so preoccupied that I barely notice the two groups switching places and before I know it we are handing out cheese and grapes courtesy of an obviously very conscientious snack mom. I'm guessing it's Asami's week.

"Why did she leave?" Shirleen asks me on the bus ride home.

"No idea."

"She told me she wasn't feeling well," Razzi informs us. I'm relieved Alison didn't tell her the truth.

"Winnie, do you know about the boys' secret club in your classroom?"

"It wouldn't be a secret if I knew about it, would it?"

She winks at me.

I'm confused. "So . . . you *do* know?"

"Of course I do. They all huddle together at recess."

Shirleen sniffs. "Everyone except Graydon."

"Really? He didn't want to join?"

"That Draper kid wouldn't let him!"

Razzi looks skeptical, so I tell her that Max told me the same thing.

"Well, I'll handle that," she assures us.

"I'm surprised you let the boys form a club."

"Oh, it's typical behavior for third-graders." She waves me off. "They all love to be in a club. The girls have them, too. But they aren't allowed to exclude anyone. I'll have a talk with Draper."

I glance at Shirleen to see if this has mollified her. It's hard to tell.

To: Mrs. Randazzo's Class
From: JDixon
Re: Holiday Party Goodies
Date: 12/17

Hello, Superstars!

Thank you, one and all, for heeding the call so speedily. I knew you had it in you! The best response time came courtesy of Ali Burgess, who got back to me one minute and fifty-four seconds after I sent the email. It was just the lift I needed in an otherwise bleak day. Merry Christmas to me!

Here's the list. And remember, if you don't see your name, don't panic! There is always next time.

Burgess—Yoo-hoo
Chang—mini bagels
Adams—cream cheese
Baton—water

Alexander—donuts

Dixon—coffee and tea

Wolff—juice

Kaplan—fruit

Zalis—muffins

Remember, December 21st in the classroom after what I'm sure will be a rip-roaring concert of timeless Christmas melodies.

At the party, we will be giving Razzi her mug, which is very big and very colorful. I won't burden you with details of my afternoon in the classroom getting the kids to decorate it. I'll just say I have a much better understanding of why people take drugs.

Stay real,

Jen

I look at the clock and see I have about an hour to get myself all dolled up for dinner at Bristol with Rolly and Janine. And by dolled up, I mean take a shower and possibly put on some lipstick. Mommy's going out tonight!

After showering I do something that is not for the faint of heart. I take a good look at myself naked in the mirror. To quote the great actress Bette Davis, this aging thing "ain't for sissies." I felt pretty good when I turned fifty, but every month since then has seen a slow decline into flabbiness. Regardless of how much time I spend spinning and running and hitting the bag in my basement, I can't lose the layer of fat that surrounds my middle area and my thighs. Not to mention the general looseness of skin around my arms, legs, and neck. Time does indeed march on.

I quickly grab for my robe when I hear Ron's footsteps on the stairs. He hasn't seen me naked in the light for about two years, and I'd like to keep the illusion of youth that clothing provides me just a little bit longer.

While I'm putting on some makeup, Ron dashes in, rips off his clothes, right in front of me, and jumps in the shower. It must be so nice to have no body shame.

He starts singing "Bohemian Rhapsody," his go-to shower song, and before you can say "Scaramouche Scaramouche," he's out and toweled off.

"Have you set up spinning with Janine?"

"Yup. Tomorrow. We're doing a double."

He shakes his head. Ron's a nonbeliever. I took him to a class about a month ago and he hated it, mainly because he couldn't get the hang of it. It was a rare moment of physical superiority that I was able to lord over him for a good week.

He is of course dressed and downstairs before me, but when I finally emerge in my holiday frock he whistles his approval. I've had it for years, but it's a classic—a black lace, cap-sleeved, V-neck dress, cut slim and then flared at the waist. No matter what I look like naked, I still cover up nicely. It's all smoke and mirrors and Spanx, but hey, what isn't?

Max is at my parents' place for the night and Ron has hired an Uber so we don't have to worry about drinking and driving. I'm surprised to see him leaving his best girl (Bruce Willis) home on a Friday night, but I'm not complaining.

Bristol is my favorite seafood place. I know it can be hard to get excited about fish, but they have these mini New England lobster rolls that I actually dream about.

The Uber drops us off at 7:30 sharp and we see Rolly and Janine standing just inside the door. There are hugs all around and we are led to a nice corner booth.

After we order, I'm expecting the men to talk shop, leaving Janine and me to exchange spinning notes; I'm surprised when Rolly turns to me.

"So, Jen, what's up?"

"Nothing much." I shrug. I look across the table and see that Janine and Ron are having their own conversation.

"You were born here, right?" Rolly asks.

I nod. "Born and raised."

"Ever get the itch to leave? Switch things up a bit?" Rolly's eyes are doing a dance between my face and my cleavage. This is new.

"Well, I sowed some wild oats for a few years in Europe." I cross my arms in front of me. "But when I came home, this is where I wanted to be. I love KC."

"Wild oats?" Rolly's silver-gray eyebrows go up, and he smiles. "Tell me more."

He leans in and just like that I'm uncomfortable. I don't share my sordid past with many people. Not that I think Rolly would judge me—something tells me it would make him like me more.

"Oh, you're going to have to ply me with a lot of wine to get that story out of me."

"Waiter!" he yells, and chuckles.

"Let's talk about you. How many grandchildren do you have, again?"

His eyes light up as he tells me about all five of his grandkids, ages twelve down to seven months. They all live in and around Boise and he has everyone to the house for dinner every Sunday.

"It's the best part of my week," he effuses.

"Are you talking about your *grandchildren*?" Janine jumps in. "Babe, that's not very sexy."

I give Janine a quizzical look, but she just takes a sip of wine and winks at me.

"Speaking of sexy, did we tell you guys that we were propositioned by a couple of swingers?" she asks.

"No way!" Ron and I say at the same time. "Oh my God! Tell us every detail!" I add.

Rolly guffaws. "We were in Scottsdale for the Sportsman Show, sitting in the bar at the Marriott talking to this nice couple. We'd had a few drinks and all of a sudden they just asked us."

I'm so intrigued I can barely contain myself.

"What did you do?"

"We told them we'd think about it!" Janine blurts out and then starts hysterically laughing, so we all do. I'm dying to know more, but our lobster rolls arrive and Rolly starts telling a story about the time he caught a lobster with three claws.

✦ ✦ ✦

I'm sweating it out to "I Am Woman," by Helen Reddy, and Janine is beside me singing her heart out. Carmen is doing a big female empowerment ride in honor of her own birthday. I kind of feel bad for the two guys in the class.

I'm glad we're doing a double. After last night's eating and drinking jubilee, I really need to purge some toxins.

Dinner was a lot of fun, and thank God for the Uber, because as per usual when we're with them, we were about as fit to drive as a monkey on cocaine. On the way home, Ron and I were far too drunk to do a proper postmortem on the dinner, and this morning he was still snoring when I snuck out after leaving cereal on the table for Max.

It's seriously some kind of miracle that I'm here at all. Between my hangover and the fact that it's bone-chillingly cold outside, staying in bed was a much more tempting option. But I'm glad I made it, because Carmen's double birthday ride has proved epic.

As Janine and I drift out of class on a wave of smelly steam and the Indigo Girls' "Closer to Fine," I ask her if she has time to hang at the juice bar.

"God, yes, I need some greens in me. I swear my sweat is one hundred proof!"

We both grab bottles of green juice and take a seat in the corner by the window.

"Thanks for dinner last night," she says after we take a few gulps.

"We always have so much fun with you guys."

She nods. "We do, too. We should go on vacation somewhere together."

"That would be insane!" I can't even begin to imagine what a boozy adventure that would be. "Hey, tell me more about those swingers you met."

Janine raises an eyebrow. "Something I should know about you, dirty girl?"

I smirk. "No, I'm just so curious. Nothing like that has ever happened to us. I don't know how I'd react."

"It took us by surprise, that's for sure. I'd do it in a second, but I'd have to get Rolly on board." She gives me an overexaggerated eye roll that makes me wonder if she's kidding or not. I change the subject.

"Rolly has been so great about helping Ron with the expansion. I hope he doesn't mind."

"Please. Rolly doesn't do anything without a reason."

What the hell does that mean? I frown and look past her toward the front door. I'm treated to the sight of Vivs rushing in along with three other people, including Buddy's friend JT.

"Vivs!" I yell a bit too loudly as I wave. "Hi, sweetie!"

"Mom!" She looks up. I've clearly startled her. She checks in then stops by our table. "What are you doing here?"

"Spin class. Vivs, this is Janine Schrader. Janine, this is my older daughter, Vivs."

"Nice to meet you," they say in unison. I notice JT has stopped and is standing with Vivs. My eyes shoot back and forth between the two of them.

"This is JT. We take the same boxing class."

"We know each other," I inform her.

"You do?" She looks at him and he nods.

"Through Peetsa and Buddy. I had no idea you were Jen's daughter, though. Small world, huh?" He laughs awkwardly and won't make eye contact with me.

"Well, have a good class, you guys." I'm trying to give Vivs a look that says, "I'll be wanting to talk to you about this later." But all I get is a wave as they walk toward the locker rooms. I look after them, while several unpleasant thoughts enter my mind.

"You don't look happy," Janine observes.

"Mmmm" is all I can muster.

"She's very pretty." Janine gives me a big smile. "Is that her boyfriend?"

"God, no!" I say adamantly. "Her boyfriend lives in Brooklyn. He's an architect." Who am I trying to convince—me or her? I switch the subject. "What are you guys doing for the holidays?"

"We're taking all Rolly's kids and grandkids to Miami. Kill me now."

"Oh wow. Where are you staying?"

"The Fontainebleau. Ever been there?"

"No, but the name alone makes it sound like heaven."

"Do you guys want to come?"

"To Florida? Yeah, right!"

"I'm serious."

"Well, for one thing, I have a bucketload of people coming to my house for Christmas. Plus, I think the Fontainebleau is too much for our budget."

"Not for long," Janine singsongs.

I tilt my head. "What do you mean?"

She takes a swig of juice. "I mean, after you franchise you'll be swimming in it, right?"

"Hardly. Ron says we're going to be poorer before we're richer."

"Well, you never know." She looks like she knows something I don't.

The green juice has started to work its magic, and thanks to my shy colon syndrome there is no way in the world I can poop at the gym, so I gather my things to indicate I'm heading out.

"So great to see you." I give Janine a big hug.

"You too. I'll email you some ideas about where we could all go on a trip."

"Great!" I say as I sprint for the car. That juice is working faster than usual.

13

The holiday concert and party will forever be my least favorite school event, thanks to the shame of having been fired as class mom three years ago just as the kids were taking the stage to sing. I should be so lucky this year. The safety patrol workload has been a little heavier than I expected, and despite my pleas and promises of poop emojis, I seem to be the go-to fill-in person. It's always the same story. At least once a week I get a last-minute call from the parent on duty claiming that they're sick or they forgot about a dentist appointment, and they can't find anyone else to fill in for them. I'd be dubious about the "I'm sick" claims, but it has been an especially bad flu season. Even Sherlay DeJones hit me up to cover for her one morning. That was a low point.

Ron and I are sitting in the third row with our iPhones ready to catch the magic. I'm always hoping for a moment worthy of *America's Funniest Home Videos,* but in four years at this school the only noteworthy moment happened last year when one of the fifth-graders walked into the Christmas tree.

The concert begins, and each class troops out on stage to sing a classic carol. This year the third grade is regaling us with "I Saw Mommy Kissing Santa Claus," which they can't seem to get through without a lot of giggling and kissing sounds. It's pretty adorable. As soon as they're done, I slip out of the auditorium and head up to room 402 to make sure everything is ready for the party.

I'm surprised and happy to see that Razzi's minimalist classroom has been transformed into a winter wonderland, courtesy of dozens of snowflakes, signed by the kids, hanging from the ceiling, and colorful boxes wrapped to look like presents. I see Max's name on quite a few of the snowflakes and only a couple look like he cut them with a butter knife. Shiny gold garland frames all the windows and little white lights are strung across the teacher's desk. It looks enchanting.

I quickly deck the back table with all the food that has been dropped off and finish just as the class is returning from the concert along with their parents. The noise is deafening, but Razzi quickly gains control.

"All right, settle down. Children, take your seats. Mike T., get away from the donuts."

Peetsa has sidled up to me near the breakfast goodies.

"Where is Ron?" she whispers.

"He went to pick up a box of coffee from Dunkin. I wanted it to be good and hot. Is Buddy coming?"

She shakes her head. "We agreed that it would be awkward. He's picking Mike up after school and they're going to a movie together."

"Jennifer, are there peanuts in these muffins?" It's Shirleen, of course.

"Yes, they're actually peanut muffins. I made them myself."

She glares at me. "What have I told you?"

I look at my shoes. "It's not a joke."

She nods, satisfied, but I'm not done.

"Shirleen, it's our fourth year together. Have I ever let a peanut into the classroom?"

"Well, you can't blame me for asking. You're a little distracted this year."

She's got me there.

"I'll never be so distracted that I forget about Graydon," I assure her.

"Shirleen, the cup you made is amazing," Peetsa chimes in for me.

Shirleen gives us a rare smile.

"Well, I sure had fun getting my wheel out. It's been a while."

Leaving them to talk pottery, I go mingle with the other parents. Hunter's two moms, Kim and Carol Alexander, tell me they are headed to the ski slopes the second they leave this party. They look like they jumped off the pages of an L.L.Bean catalogue. I'm just starting to catch up with Don (Suchafox) and Ali when Razzi takes command of the room by blinking the lights on and off. In a weirdly Pavlovian response, the kids all immediately stop talking and put their hands on their heads. Wow. I may try that at home.

"Happy holidays, everyone! Thank you for coming this morning. I think our kids did a terrific job at the concert."

There are whoops and clapping from the parents.

"I just wanted to say your children are truly a delight and a gift and I can't thank you enough for sharing them with me each and every day."

Wow. I forgot about this sentimental side of Winnie. It's touching.

"A special thanks to our class mom, Jen, for keeping the trains running on time this year." To my surprise, this receives genuine applause and one "Woo-hoo!," from Peetsa. Razzi nods to me and I walk to the front of the classroom.

"Well, thank *you*, Mrs. Randazzo! Our kids absolutely love being in your class. And we have a little something for you, to say Merry Christmas." I open a cabinet and pull out the gift from where I hid it earlier.

Razzi unwraps the box and takes out the mug, which I have to say looks great. Between Shirleen's pottery skills and the kids' color-ful decorations, it's a win. There are oohs and ahhs from everyone and Razzi seems genuinely touched.

"Thank you! Oh, my goodness. I'm going to put this in a very special place." She puts it down on her desk. "Okay, let's eat!" At this, the kids attack the food table like a pack of starving Chihuahuas. Ron walks in with the box of coffee held high over his head so no one accidentally bumps it and ends up with hot French roast on them.

I turn to get some coffee and bump headlong into Alison Lody.

"Alison, hi. How's it going?"

She shrugs. It's like this woman is never happy. Either that or she thinks resting bitch face is the new black.

"Do you have plans for the holidays?" I figure that's a safe enough topic of conversation. I was wrong.

"No. The kids are going to Palm Beach with their father, but I'm staying here."

I'm about to ask if she has other family to spend Christmas with when a spectacular crash pulls everyone's attention to the front of the classroom. I look over and am mortified to see that Max and Draper are standing over the broken pieces of Razzi's Christmas present.

"Oh God, why me?" Alison says under her breath. We both start toward the scene of the crime.

"He did it," Draper informs the room while pointing at Max.

"No, I didn't!" Max sounds outraged at the accusation. "*He* did it."

"Well, it looks like you both had a hand in it," Razzi's voice booms from across the room. "Please pick up the pieces carefully before somebody steps on them."

They both fall to their knees, mumbling to each other while they clean up the mess.

"What happened, boys?" I ask.

Neither says a word to me.

"Draper, tell Mommy what happened."

That's how she talks to her almost nine-year-old? It sounds creepy to me, but to my surprise it's the key that opens Draper's lying pie hole.

"I was just looking at the cup and he tried to grab it from me."

"I was telling him to put it back," Max explains.

You could hear a pin drop in the class. Razzi walks to her desk with a broom in her hand. "Please, everyone, let's not stop the fun." Then she adds, a bit too enthusiastically, "It isn't a party until something is broken." Quietly, to Max and Draper, she continues: "Well, I'd say you're both lucky that this is the last day of school for two weeks. As it is, I'd like one paragraph from each of you explaining why you shouldn't touch things that don't belong to you . . . at least four sentences. Due the day we get back from vacation, understood?"

"Yes," they both say with their heads down.

The class goes back to partying, with the help of some Christmas music and a slide show of the kids playing on a screen at the back of the room. I help myself to a cup of coffee and look around at the cast of characters assembled. It's a nice group, for the most part. Many of them I really don't know that well, but that's my fault.

Sylvie Pike wanders in with her black hair flowing behind her like she has a constant wind machine in her face. It makes for quite an entrance. She gives the room a once-over and heads toward me.

"Nice party, Jen."

"Thanks. Mrs. Randazzo gets credit for the decorations."

She nods. "I want you to start thinking about ways to raise money to get new safety patrol vests for the grown-ups. I've been getting complaints from the parents about having to use the ripped one."

The look I give her says I don't really want to know more.

"It's just, if we make enough money we can think about buying new stop signs, too."

"You're killing me."

She smiles and gives me a one-armed hug. "Perks of the job."

She drifts over to the treats table and I turn my attention to my son. He's been waiting to give me a tour of his work on the walls. Once he has shown me all of his assignments, I start to clean up, hoping it will encourage people to be on their way. Ron takes Max down to the lobby to sift through the lost-and-found, which has been vomited onto two large tables near the school entrance. I'm hoping Max's black mittens turn up.

I'm the last one out of the classroom, so I give Razzi a big hug goodbye.

"Winnie, have a great holiday. And I'm so sorry about the cup. I'll get the kids to make a new one in January."

"Oh, please. Don't even worry about it," she says kindly. "I have a cupboard full of those."

She does? And here I thought we'd come up with something unique and special. "Well, I think it would make the kids feel better if we do."

She shrugs. "Whatever you think. Hey, Merry Christmas, and thanks for all your help."

"You too."

14

To: Safety Patrol Patrollers
From: JDixon
Re: New Year/Old Rules
Date: 1/5

Dear Patrol Parents,

Happy New Year! Hope you all had a great holiday and are well rested and ready for the rigors of the upcoming safety patrol season.

First the good news . . . we are going to get new adult vests in three different sizes. No more wearing shredded plastic! You will now be looking sharp in neon orange that fits you the way it should.

Now the bad news . . . we need to have a bake sale to pay for the vests. Obviously, we will need some baked goods to fulfill the "bake" part of the sale. Only homemade treats are acceptable. Kidding, of course! Bring whatever you want, just keep it nut free.

The sale will take place January 21st in the school lobby at 3 p.m. I'll need volunteers to help me man the tables too. Wow, there are lots of opportunities to start the new year on my good side, so don't hesitate to start baking and volunteering!

Happy days are here again!

Jen

"What are you working on?" Ron asks. We are hanging out in bed waiting for the local news to come on. Well, not really the news—the lottery numbers they announce just *before* the news. Lately we have taken to trying our luck because hey, you never know.

"I'm organizing the bake sale from hell." I attack the keyboard like someone with a vendetta.

"Why is it from hell?"

"Because I have to organize it."

"Why would you volunteer to do that?"

"I didn't. I was volun-told." I continue typing.

"Are you doing the brownies?" He's talking about my trademark sticky, chewy, five-napkin brownies, of course. I haven't made them since the picture day fiasco in Max's kindergarten year.

"I would, but Asami still holds a bit of a grudge and I hate to poke the bear."

Ron yawns and puts his computer on his bedside table. "How is Asami?"

"I'll tell you tomorrow. I'm having coffee with her before pickup."

"Not at Starbucks, I hope." He's fluffing his pillows and burrowing in, which tells me I'll be watching for the lottery numbers on my own.

"No, Sergeant Money Police, we're meeting at Dunkin Donuts."

He nods, satisfied. "Don't forget your coupon."

I stick my tongue out at him. I don't mind telling you, this belt-tightening really sucks. Christmas was pretty thin. Ron and I opted not to exchange gifts, although he did wrap up a desk calendar for me called "Words You Should Know to Sound Smart," in the hope

I'll find other ways, besides profanity, to express myself. Let me just say it was an excrementous gift. Our presents to others were relatively lame, except for Max's of course. I hated it. We are usually very generous, but this year we basically gave the equivalent of a book of coupons for hugs.

We didn't even go out on New Year's Eve, and we ate at home almost every night except for the time we were invited to my mom and dad's. And of course Laura was still away, so when I say it was low-key, I mean we were in the dead zone.

The only significant news from the holidays was that Vivs and Raj broke up again. She assures me it's final this time. She spent a week in Brooklyn and came back to KC with all her belongings. When I asked if she was okay, she blankly asked me why she wouldn't be.

"Why are you guys meeting?" Ron disrupts my mental grousing.

"I've been feeling out of the loop lately and I'm hoping she can fill me in."

"And what makes you think Asami is in the loop?"

"She just is. She knows everything that's going on."

He shakes his head into the pillow.

"It's an illusion."

"What is?"

"The loop. There is no loop."

"What are you talking about?"

"In my experience, the loop doesn't exist. People are just living their lives, and no one person really knows *everything* that is going on."

Since this has never occurred to me, I take a moment to weigh its validity. I decide he isn't in the loop either.

"Lotto numbers!" Ron mumbles from his horizontal position. I had tuned out the television but clearly, *he* hadn't.

I grab my phone and take a picture of the TV screen. I left the tickets in the kitchen, so I'll have to check them when I wake up.

+ + +

I'm shocked and saddened to learn the next morning that we are not instant millionaires. I was so sure. Oh well, there's always next week.

Ron has taken Max to school, so I get an early workout down in Ron's Gym and Tan while also doing a load of laundry. I'm finding it hard to get used to the smell of the most recent generic laundry detergent we are using. It's way too floral. This is my fourth attempt to find something I like. The first two were supposed to be unscented, but for some reason they both made our clothes smell like wet dog. The third one had a hint of cotton candy—the kind you get in the summer at one of those traveling carnivals. Max liked it, but it made me sneeze.

I've decided I need a girls' night out. They have been few and far between since Nina moved, mostly because it's left to me to organize them. I sent Peetsa a text early this morning suggesting this Friday night. I also reached out to Sylvie Pike, because I have a feeling she'll be fun with a little jiggle juice in her system.

After my shower, three texts are waiting for me. One from Peetsa saying Friday is great and asking where we should go, one from Sylvie thanking me profusely for inviting her, and one from Asami confirming our meeting at two o'clock today and asking if we can change the location to the vegan bakery on 39th Street. While I'm typing *Sure,* WhatsApp pops up on my screen and I see Laura is video-calling me. I push Accept.

"Hey! What's App?"

Laura grimaces. I guess I've used that joke once too often. "Hi, Mama."

"Where are you?" It's my standard first question these days.

Laura sighs. "Somewhere in Germany . . . umm, Weimar? It's really cold."

"It's cold here, too. We missed you at Christmas."

"I know, I missed you guys, too." She seems a little down. Her hair has grown out an inch or so and she wears it slicked down on her head. She also looks like she's put on some weight. Her face is definitely more rounded.

"How is Jeen?"

"He's good." She brightens a bit and I'm heartened to see that at least there isn't trouble on that front. "He's so busy. How's Nana?" I guess we're done talking about Jeen.

"She's doing really well. She loves the scarf you sent her." I pause. "So, what's going on, sweetie?"

"I need you to send me some money."

"Boy, are you barking up the wrong tree," I blurt out before I can stop myself.

Laura frowns. "What do you mean?"

I have always told Laura she could ask for money as soon as she needed it, and I meant it. But that was before the dark time—the time of clipping coupons and using generic tampons.

"Sweetie, I'm sorry I haven't told you before, but Ron and I have had to cut way back on our spending because of the franchise expansion."

"I don't need a lot. Just a few thousand euros."

I let out a face fart. "In what world is a few thousand euros not a lot?"

"Mom! I'm not kidding."

"Neither am I. We've had to use most of our savings, Laura. We don't have that kind of money just lying around right now."

Laura sighs. "Should I ask Nana?"

Hmm . . . My mother has been playing pretty fast and loose with her cash since the chemo. It's not a bad idea.

"Well, if you do, make sure to ask both Nana and Poppy together and tell them you'd like it to be a loan."

"Okay."

We are quiet for a moment. Something is not right.

"Can I ask what the money is for?"

She shrugs. "Just living expenses."

"If it's getting tough you can always come home, you know."

"I know." Silence.

"Anything else going on?"

"No. I'm just tired. And I wish I could work here, but we never stay in one place long enough."

She doesn't sound thrilled about this. But then she perks up.

"I'm going to call Nana now. Do you think she's home?"

The clock tells me it's ten after one.

"Your guess is as good as mine. You know Nana."

At this Laura gives me a sad smile.

"Aww sweetie, cheer up! I hate to see you so down."

"I'm okay. I'll talk to you soon." She clicks Disconnect and I'm left to wonder if there's more she isn't telling me.

✦ ✦ ✦

I have never been to the vegan bakery on 39th Street, so when I pull into the parking lot of Mud Pie just before two o'clock, I'm more than a little curious. I was expecting it to be in a strip mall, but it's actually located in a bright yellow house with white trim. There is a small outdoor patio, which obviously isn't open on this cold January day, but I'm guessing it would be a nice place to sit in the summer.

Inside is warm and welcoming. My olfactory sense is in overdrive thanks to all the delicious aromas coming at me. More than half the tables are filled, with people working on computers or having quiet conversations. I spot Asami sitting at a corner table staring out the window. When she sees me, she waves.

"Hi." I slip into the seat beside her and shed my parka like it's the biggest burden I have ever carried. "I didn't know you were vegan."

She gives me a confused look.

"I'm not. But Jennifer, I'm glad you wanted to meet. I have something to talk to you about."

I thought this was *my* meeting but okay. I think I know what's on her mind. Jeen told his family about him and Laura a few weeks after we found out. I will never forget Asami beelining toward me at school pickup, thinking she was going to freak me out with the news—much like I had wanted to do to her when we first heard. She had a look on her face that can only be described as galvanized. When she realized I already knew, it was like I'd thrown up on her favorite shoes. Since then we have barely mentioned it, our theory being that if we don't talk about it, maybe it isn't really happening.

"Okay. Just let me get a cup of coffee."

"Try the cinnamon roll." She waves our server over. I take the suggestion, and she orders tea and a scone.

Asami looks good. It's impossible to know how old she is, because she has looked the same for the four years I have known her. Her skin is as close to perfection as you can get when you're past thirty, and her new bob hairstyle really suits her.

"So, what's on your mind?" I figure if I let her go first, she'll be more generous with her gossip.

"I think it's time for the kids to come home," she says with her characteristic brevity.

"I wholeheartedly agree, but I'm curious why you think so."

"My sister is worried that Jeen is working too hard."

"You know, I just talked to Laura and she said he's really busy. What's he doing?" It's the question I didn't get a chance to ask my daughter.

"Getting work for the band. Their tour was supposed to end in November, but Jeen didn't want to come home. So he spends all his time looking for places that will book them."

Our waitress arrives at this point, so I take a moment to collect my thoughts and take a sip of what turns out to be delicious coffee.

"Any idea how that's going?"

"We don't know, but he called home the other day and asked for more money, which tells us he's not making enough to survive."

I decide not to mention that Laura had just made the same request.

"Did you send him any?"

"I didn't, but of course my sister did, although not much. It was basically enough for a plane ticket home, but she hasn't heard from him since."

I take a bite of my cinnamon roll. Holy crap, is it good. This place is going to be dangerous for me.

"How do you think we can convince them to come back?" I already know the answer.

"Well, I was hoping you could come up with something. You have such a crafty mind."

That's as close as Asami has ever come to giving me a real compliment. Unfortunately, I think she is overestimating my abilities.

"I'm not sure we can make them come home if they don't want to."

"But why don't they want to? I don't understand."

Before I can enlighten her about the sheer euphoria of touring Europe with a rock band, my phone rings. I don't recognize the number.

"Hello?"

"Hi, Jen?"

"Yes." I'm already regretting answering.

"It's JJ. I'm the safety patrol mom for today, but I forgot that Kit has an orthodontist appointment. I'm really sorry."

I let that hang there for a minute. I look at Asami and roll my eyes. Man, this train is never late.

"Hello?"

"I'm here," I say. "Have you tried to get someone to fill in for you?"

"Yes, and no one's available."

"No one? Can your husband take your spot?"

"Yeah, right." JJ laughs. "Seriously, can you cover me?"

I close my eyes and pray for patience. "Well, I guess I can, but you'll have to sign up for another day."

"Great! I owe you. Let's have lunch sometime. Bye."

She hangs up before I can say anything, so I start to pull my things together. Asami is shaking her head at me.

"What?"

"They should have to pay you when you're nice enough to fill in for them."

"Right? I'd be rich." And with those words, an idea begins to form in my—how did Asami put it?—crafty mind.

"I've got to get to school. Here." I offer her a ten, but she waves me off. "It's on me. I'll be five minutes behind you. Keep thinking about getting the kids home."

"Will do." I run outside, jump in the minivan, and peel out of the parking lot. It isn't until I'm halfway to school that I realize I never got to ask Asami for gossip.

15

To: JDixon
From: SCobb
Re: Bake Sale
Date: 01/10

Jennifer,

I'm going to make nut-free, gluten-free, sugar-free, and dairy-free brownies for the bake sale. I'd like them placed on a separate table and well marked. I've been reading about celiac disease and I think Graydon may have it.

Shirleen

Is she kidding? That kid lives on carbs and doesn't miss a day of school. Last month she was convinced he had plantar fasciitis.

To: SCobb
From: JDixon
Re: Bake Sale
Date: 01/06

Shirleen,

Thank you for being so considerate. I will make sure your brownies are put on a table next to the organic produce and water we are selling so as not to get contaminated.

Jen

I smile. I really have grown to love Shirleen. And that thank-you I gave her is sincere. No one else would even think to provide for the immune-challenged kids.

But thoughts about the bake sale are taking a back seat right now, because it's girls' night! Peetsa, Sylvie, and I are going to TGI Friday's to get our freak on. I even have Ron's seal of approval because it's Ladies' Night, so we can drink for free from six p.m. to seven p.m. Woo-hoo!

I drive to the school to check on the safety patrol (all good) and join Peetsa and Ravi at pickup.

"Sorry you can't come tonight," I say to Ravi.

"I know. I'm so disappointed. I hate going to Rob's business dinners. They're so boring."

Ravi's husband works as a salesman at a high-end tire company, and they have to do a client dinner like every two weeks. I feel for her. When I have to go out for dinner with Ron and one of his brand reps, all they do is talk shop.

"Next time we'll make sure you're free." I turn to Peetsa. "Are you psyched?"

She shrugs. "I guess. Hey, maybe I'll meet a guy."

I'm not sure I'd want to meet a guy on Ladies' Night at TGI Friday's but I like her optimism.

The bell rings and the kids come tearing out the school doors like the building is on fire. I don't see Max at first, but then I spot him walking slowly toward me with Razzi. Ruh roh!

"What's up?" I ask.

"He isn't feeling well."

"Oh no! Sweetie, what's wrong?"

I look at Max and his eyes are glassy. As I put my hand to his forehead, Razzi mouths, "One hundred and two." My eyebrows go up.

"He was fine most of the day. He just started feeling poorly about an hour ago."

I nod and thank her.

"Feel better, Max."

He leans into me and I hug him. Not much can keep Max down, but a fever is his Waterloo, as it is for most kids.

"Do you need to cancel tonight?" Peetsa asks.

"I'm not sure. Let me get him home and see what's what."

"Okay, just let me know. It's fine either way."

I thank her and lead Max to the minivan.

✦ ✦ ✦

Once I get my boy settled in his bed and give him some Children's Motrin, he immediately falls asleep. I call Ron and fill him in.

"So . . . should I cancel?" I really have no intention of canceling, but I may as well make him think he's doing me a favor by staying home with his sick child. Ron takes the bait beautifully.

"No way! I'll be home in an hour and I can take care of him. You deserve a girls' night."

"Are you sure? I mean, I hate to leave you . . ." I trail off.

"Please! I've done this before."

Uh, no you haven't, I think. And it's true. Shame on me, but I have never left a sick Max alone with Ron. I think my love for my husband has been well established, but he has this "tough it out" mentality when it comes to Max. And that's fine, except for when he's sick. Ron doesn't have the empathy gene. He's like, "I'm sad you're sick, but really? Are you still sick? It's been two hours already."

But none of that is going to stop me from going out tonight. Max will likely sleep through, and if he does wake up he'll just want some soup and his iPad.

"You're the best," I tell Ron. "I'll see you when you get home."

Upstairs, I check on Max and he is sleeping soundly under his American Ninja Warrior sheets and comforter, so I jump in the shower.

As I finish drying my hair, Ron comes in and kisses my cheek. I have on my favorite pair of jeans, wedge-heeled black boots, and a tight black turtleneck sweater.

"Looking good, Mrs. Dixon." He leans on the counter and gives me a once-over.

"Feeling good, Mr. Dixon." I smile.

"Good enough to go to Vegas?" He smiles back.

"What?"

"I just got a call from Rolly on my way home. He's invited you, me, and Max to go to Vegas over spring break."

"I hope you told him we can't afford it."

"I tried but he said he's having a company incentive retreat there and has extra rooms. He wants to send plane tickets, too."

"That's insane. Why would he want us there?"

Ron shrugs. "Not sure. Maybe he wants to talk about buying me out."

"You want to be *bought out*?" This is news to me. "What happened to him just investing in your expansion?"

He sighs and sits down on the toilet. "I'm just so freakin' tired of worrying about money. If I'd known expanding was going to be such a ring of fire around my butt I would have stuck with my one little store and shut up about it."

I hate to see him like this—borderline defeated. This is not the man I married.

"I know you don't want me to work, but I'm happy to get a job—even part-time." Ron has always prided himself on being the lone provider for us and since I never really had a career, I was happy to be home with Max.

"We're not there yet, but thanks for offering again." He looks at his shoes.

"Vegas might be fun," I posit as I put my lipstick on. "But what would Max do? Play the slots?"

Ron lights up. "No, that's the best part. Guess who is filming in Vegas that weekend?"

"*The Real Housewives of Las Vegas?*"

"*American Ninja Warrior.*"

I gasp. "Seriously? He'll go insane! Well, now we have to go." I start mentally planning what clothes I'm going to bring.

"I think so, too. I'm going to tell Rolly it's a yes."

I look at my phone.

"I've got to run. Do *not* tell Max about this until we know it's set, and then we can do it together. I can't wait to see the look on his face."

"Any instructions for him before you go?" Nurse Ron is on duty.

"If you're lucky, he'll sleep through the night. But if he wakes up, just give him some chicken noodle soup and let him watch TV." I kiss him, leaving a Passion Berry stain on his mouth.

"Got it. Have fun. Don't drink too much."

I roll my eyes. "Please! It's not like Janine is going to be there."

✦ ✦ ✦

"How's Max?" Peetsa asks when she picks me up in her Jeep Cherokee. I can hear Pink's "Who Knew" playing softly on the radio.

"Sleeping, thank goodness." I stomp my feet and clap my gloved hands to get warm. "Fever is down, thanks to the Motrin."

"I haven't heard of anything going around. Do you think it's the flu?"

"He doesn't have any other symptoms." I shrug. I really don't want to talk about it. I might start feeling guilty and make her turn around, so I change the subject.

"Can we do a Buddy update before we see Sylvie?" I know P. doesn't like to talk about her personal life with very many people.

She sighs and turns the radio all the way down. "Well, he's completely moved out. Took the last of his stuff a few days ago. You know he found an apartment, right?"

"No! Where?"

"Downtown near his work."

"So, no more TJ's?"

"Nope. Moved out of the love shack."

"The love shack?"

"That's what Buddy called it, because TJ was always having women over."

I'm not sure why, but that makes my skin crawl. I want to ask if she thinks Buddy had women over too, but I think better of it. "How are the kids doing?"

"It's hard to tell." Peetsa hits the brakes as a cat runs in front of the car. "On the surface they seem fine. Not sure what a shrink would say."

"Probably that you're doing a great job." I pat her leg.

We pull into the parking lot at TGI Friday's and hustle inside the restaurant. This is one nasty cold snap. The only upside is it's too cold to snow.

Friday's is a cheery place to go. With the red leather booths and carnival-like atmosphere, it's almost impossible not to have a good time. Or so I thought.

"Oh my God, it's all women in here." Peetsa doesn't sound happy.

"Well, it *is* Ladies' Night," I remind her. "Maybe the men come later."

We're seated at a small table and order a couple of glasses of water while we wait for Sylvie. My back is to the door so I don't see her until she is upon us.

"Hey, guys. Look who I bumped into in the parking lot."

I look up and see none other than Alison Lody standing by our table. Alison fucking Lody. Instantly, my girls' night is ruined. My yum is yucked. My balloon of happiness is effectively popped.

"I'm meeting someone here." Alison seems embarrassed. "You guys know her—Asami from school."

I have a fake smile plastered on my face, but all I can think is "Okay, where's the hidden camera?" It's the only excuse I can imagine for this unwelcome moment of worlds colliding.

"You guys should join us," Sylvie says, unwittingly signing her own death warrant. Oh, yes, I will kill her later.

"Stop cringing," Peetsa whispers in my ear. Cringing? I thought I was smiling. I take a deep breath and regroup. I need alcohol if I'm going to make this work.

"Let's get a bigger table," I say with a bit too much enthusiasm.

Sylvie grabs the hostess and asks for a table for five. Asami arrives just as we're settling in and peeling off coats and hats and scarves. She looks as surprised by this group collision as I am.

"Good evening, ladies." A tall, dark, and delicious-looking waiter with electric-blue eyes addresses us. I see Peetsa visibly perk up. In fact, he has the undivided attention of the whole table. "My name is Brandon and I will be taking care of you this evening. Can I—"

"Margarita, please." I don't even let him finish.

"Oh, that sounds good. I'll have one too," Sylvie says.

Apparently, it's a lemming party, because everyone goes for the same drink. As Brandon saunters away, our entire table checks out his nice, tight black chinos.

"So how fun is this?" Peetsa addresses the group. They have found a round table for us so there will be no escaping the conversation. Despite my best efforts, I have ended up seated between Asami and Alison.

"Do you do a girls' night all the time?" Peetsa is directing this at

Asami and Alison. I've decided not to open my mouth until I've had some alcohol.

"No. It's our first time. How about you guys?" Asami has a smile on her face. It's like seeing a unicorn.

"Every couple of months Jen and I get together, but it's fun to have more people this time."

Peetsa is obviously forgetting the best part about girls' night, which is *talking about these very people*!

To distract myself until the drinks arrive, I take out my phone and text Ron.

All good?

After a beat, he replies:

Yup

Is Max still sleeping? I continue.

Yup

His brevity is annoying. Luckily our cutie-pie waiter shows up with five margaritas. I drink mine in one gulp and order a second.

"We should order some appetizers," Sylvie suggests.

"Do you know about our ten-dollar endless appetizers?" Brandon inquires with a flash of his perfect teeth. I'm betting he sells a lot more than apps with that smile.

"No, tell us about it." Peetsa returns his smile and turns her ample boobs toward him. Jesus, P., keep it in your pants. But Brandon rolls with it. This isn't his first Ladies' Night.

"You order any appetizer for ten dollars and you get unlimited free refills."

This sounds oddly familiar. It only takes me a moment to realize with a combination of horror and delight that I have a coupon for this! Mine will only be $5. Ron will be so happy.

"Let's each order something and we can share," Sylvie suggests. She just can't stop being the PTA president no matter where she is. But it happens to be a good idea, so we order a carbo-loaded feast filled with all things crispy and deep-fried.

"To girls' night out." Peetsa raises her glass.

"To girls' night out," we all respond. I catch Alison Lody's eye. She looks different. I'm about to ask if she has cut her hair when my phone rings. It's home.

"Hey, what's up?"

"Mommy?" a little voice croaks.

"Max! Sweetie, how are you feeling?"

"Where are you?"

"I'm out for dinner, but Daddy's there."

"Where?"

"He should be in the living room or the kitchen."

"He's not. I'm hungry."

What the hell?

"Hang on, sweetie. I'll find him." I put my hand over my phone and tell Peetsa to call Ron's cell immediately. She does it without question.

"Did you have a good sleep?" I ask my son.

"Yeah. Can you come home?"

Peetsa hands me her phone with a concerned look.

"Where are you?" I ask my husband.

"I'm home." He sounds out of breath. "Where else would I be?"

"Well, Max is awake, and he can't find you."

"I'm in the basement on the treadmill." He now sounds like he's moving. "I had my headphones on. . . . Hey, buddy."

I have one phone up to each ear and I can hear their reunion. I exhale, not realizing I had been holding my breath for the last two minutes.

"Are you okay?" I ask my son.

"Yeah," he sniffs. "When are you coming home?"

"In a little while. Dad's going to make you some soup—right, Dad?"

"I'm on it. How's girls' night?"

"I'll tell you later."

"Okay. Love you."

"You too."

When I hang up I see the whole table is staring at me. The appetizers have arrived, but no one is eating.

"Everything okay?" Peetsa asks.

"Oh! Yeah, sorry. Max woke up and couldn't find Ron because he was in the basement with his headphones on."

The group gives a collective groan. "Only a man would put headphones on when he's looking after a sick kid," Sylvie says.

"You were so calm!" Alison sounds impressed. "I would have been ripping his head off."

I smile and lift my second margarita. "I credit this drink. To tequila, the soother of savage tempers."

As we dig into our chicken wings and potato skins, my phone buzzes with a text.

Where's the soup?

Seriously? I mean, how hard could he have looked?

In the pantry, on the second shelf to the left.

Do you heat it in a pot or the microwave?

Your choice.

Okay thanks. Have fun. We're all good here.

I put my phone down and turn my attention to the table. The drinks have definitely lightened everyone up. We are starting to have some laughs, courtesy of Sylvie Pike, whose lips have been decidedly loosened. Forget Asami. This is the woman in the loop.

Beside me, Asami whispers, "Have you been thinking about our problem?"

"I have, and I really don't want to trick them into coming home. They're in their twenties. Let them figure it out for themselves. Hey, how did you and Alison end up going out together tonight?"

She shrugs. "We've met for coffee a few times and she suggested a night out. She's single, you know."

I nod. "I've always found her a bit . . . standoffish." It's the kindest word I can think of.

"She can be. But we have a lot in common."

I frown. I can't imagine what, except that I disliked each of them the first time I met them.

Young Brandon is back with more fried zucchini and spinach flatbread for us, along with more drinks. I watch Peetsa beckon him to her side.

"How old are you, doll?" she asks him with a come-hither lilt in her voice. I immediately look around the bar to find her a more age-appropriate target for her flirting.

"Twenty-two, ma'am." Ouch. Calling a woman ma'am is the equivalent of giving her a cold shower. He may as well have called her grandma. Peetsa looks mortified.

"Hey, does anyone have an update on Mr. Green and Sherlay?" I want to change the subject pronto.

"They've had two dates," Sylvie offers up with an eye roll. "Both times they went to the movies. She's in love."

"And what about him?" Peetsa asks.

"Jury's still out."

Sylvie continues with some details, but I'm distracted. My phone is buzzing again.

Do you know where the iPad is?

Middle drawer dining room sideboard.

And the extra paper towels?

I know I should ask why, but I don't.

On the shelf above the washing machine.

Okay, thanks. Love you.

And right now I'm only fond of you, I think.

When I reenter the conversation, they have moved on to March break plans. Alison is talking about taking her kids to Aspen.

"That's some pretty swanky skiing," I tell her.

"Well, my ex-husband is paying, so screw him."

"Nice guy, is he?"

Alison and Asami both chuckle. They obviously know something I don't.

"Oh, yeah. He's a real prince. Left me and two kids right after I finished chemo."

"You have cancer?" I say this a bit too loudly. Fortunately, the ambient noise in the room swallows my voice.

"*Had* cancer, I hope," she corrects me.

"What kind?" I almost whisper.

"Cervical."

"I'm so sorry." Maybe it's the alcohol, but I've never said anything with more genuine empathy.

"It's fine. Well, not fine, but it did help me realize what a dick I married." I notice the others are lost in their own conversations, so I feel I can ask some details.

"How are you now?"

"Better."

"When was your last treatment?"

"Coming up on sixteen months ago."

My phone buzzes again but I ignore it.

"I just saw my mom go through it for breast cancer. It flattened her."

She asks me a few questions about Kay's recovery, and then I finally hear her story. Apparently, Trent Lody moved his family to KC from Dallas after landing a senior VP job at the shipping company YRC.

"He bought this huge house that was supposed to make us feel better about leaving Dallas."

I've seen that house. It would have made me feel better.

"I got diagnosed about two months after we moved here. To his credit, he didn't leave until I actually finished the chemo."

"He's such a giver," I deadpan. My phone has buzzed twice more, so I apologize to Alison and take a look.

Where's the Motrin?

Never mind, found it.

How much do I give?

I shake my head and type back, *One teaspoon. Are you sure he needs it?*

I look up at Alison. "I'm so sorry. Max is sick and apparently my husband is brand-new to our household and doesn't know where anything is."

My phone buzzes again.

Where's the thermometer?

Top shelf medicine cabinet in our bathroom.

Are you having fun?

Yes. I really don't get enough texting time with you.

Either I pissed him off or he gets the hint, because I don't hear from him again. I turn back to Alison.

"So he left you. Did you have any idea?"

She shakes her head. "None. But I guess leaving had been his plan all along. I didn't find out until later, but his mistress moved here too."

"Why bother uprooting you at all if he was planning to leave?"

"The kids." Alison shrugged. "He wanted them in the same city. So now I'm stuck here." She looks sheepish. "Sorry. It's a nice place, it's just not home."

I truly feel bad for her, and a little ashamed that I haven't been nicer. My mother's words come back to haunt me. I really do need to get over myself. If someone is being a bitch, chances are they have their reasons. And those reasons aren't always apparent.

"What are you girls talking about?" Peetsa crouches down and sticks her face between our heads. I can tell she won't be driving home tonight.

"I was just about to ask Alison if she wants to join the Holy Rollers at the Susan G. Komen Walk." The look on Peetsa's face is classic. To her credit, even in her drunken state, she manages to swallow her confusion at my sudden attitude change and says, "Definitely!"

I turn back to Alison. "A bunch of us are doing it with my mother," I explain.

"When is it?"

"Last weekend in May."

She only takes a moment to say, "I'd really like that. What do I have to do?"

I explain to her about signing up as a Holy Roller and pledging to raise $500.

"I know it's a lot of money, but—"

"Not a problem. My ex-husband will be happy to help." She smiles for the first time since I've known her.

"This is good," I say and as though we have just made some sort of pact, we shake hands.

I look around the table and see everyone is winding down even though it's only 8:30. That's what happens when you go early to Ladies' Night.

"Should we ask for the check?" Sylvie Pike reads my mind.

We all nod or shrug.

"I took the liberty of asking for separate checks." Jeez, this woman is on top of things. Our man-candy Brandon is busy charming a table of twentysomethings, so she asks a passing busboy to tell him.

With my coupon and the fact that I only imbibed between six and seven when drinks were free, my total is a whopping $5.80. Wow. I really am a cheap date. I pay with cash and leave a very generous tip for our waiter, hoping to make up for the earlier harassment he had to endure.

✦ ✦ ✦

I have dropped a very tipsy Peetsa off at her house and am driving her Jeep to mine after promising to return it in the morning. I'm worried about her, and not just because she's going to have a world-class hangover tomorrow. Separating from Buddy has really taken the wind out of her sails. I feel like it's going to be a while before she is ready to get back out there despite her Whore of Babylon shtick tonight.

Thinking back on the evening, I'm actually glad we ended up as a big group, and I chastise myself for always jumping to the negative before I give something a chance. It's clearly a pattern in my life that needs to be broken, but it won't be easy. I'm sorry, but sometimes the cup *is* half empty and there is no other way of looking at it.

I'll keep working on this, but first I need to go home and give Ron a tour of the house.

To: Safety Patrol Patrollers
From: JDixon
Re: Bake Sale Tomorrow
Date: 01/20

Hello, my little Betty Crockers!

Just a reminder that all bake sale goodies should be dropped off at the back of the gym near Safety Patrol Command Central by noon tomorrow. We should be able to raise a good amount of money as long as the coaches and custodians don't get to them first.

And for goodness' sake, send your kids with money! There will be no more students signing bake sale IOUs that never get repaid. That insanity stops now.

As always,

Jen

I send the email from my kitchen-counter office and head to turn off the timer. A second batch of cupcakes is coming out of the oven and I'm almost done frosting the first.

I'm going with monkey-face cupcakes for my bake sale offering. They are a perennial crowd-pleaser because they both look and taste delicious. But man, are they a pain in the ass to make. You need two different shades of chocolate frosting, a really good piping bag, and M&Ms Minis and Junior Mints for the eyes and ears.

"Is this what you wanted?" Ron asks as he jogs up the stairs from the basement. He is carrying a very large glass jar that once held 5,677 jelly beans and yes, I know that for a fact because I counted every damn one of them when Vivs's senior class tried to raise money for prom with a "Guess How Many Jelly Beans in the Jar" contest.

"Perfect. I knew we had it somewhere." I place it in the sink and fill it with hot soapy water.

"What do you need it for?" Ron dips his finger into the frosting and is rewarded with a slap on his hand.

"It's for the bake sale," I say vaguely. He doesn't need to know the details. "Did you talk to Rolly yet?"

"Yup. We're all set. Vegas, baby!" He starts to cabbage-patch around the kitchen. It's the only dance move he knows.

We've put off telling Max about the trip because, frankly, he's been such a little jerk lately that he doesn't deserve a treat. I know calling my kid names isn't going to win me any parenting awards, but the shoe definitely fits.

He's taken to fighting us on anything he doesn't want to do. One of our worst nights was when I asked him to help clear the dinner table. He informed me that if he had a sister living at home he wouldn't be forced to do this kind of work.

"And what kind of work is that?" I asked him.

"Girls' work."

Ron and I looked at each other with a mixture of surprise and amusement.

"I clear the table and I'm not a girl," Ron informed his son.

"That's because Mom will be mean to you if you don't," Max said matter-of-factly.

I didn't know where this was coming from.

"I'm sorry, what am I missing?" I asked him.

"A heart," Max replied without missing a beat. That was last week—definitely a low point in my parenting life. I'm sure he thought he was being funny, but something tells me these past five days without play dates and dessert have curbed his enthusiasm for comedy.

"When do you want to tell Max?" Ron has left the timing of the reveal up to me since I have been bearing the brunt of his behavior.

"Let's see how he does the rest of the week. I'd like to see a genuine change in his attitude, not just a humbling while he's being punished."

"Okay, but try to let it happen soon."

I nod and turn my focus back to monkey cupcake number 11 of 24. It's going to be a long night. I decide to call Vivs and catch up. Sightings of her have been rare since the holidays, and we barely saw her then.

"Hi, Mom," she answers.

"Hi, sweetie, how are you doing?"

"I'm fine. Do you need something?"

"Nope. Just called to chat. I'm making monkey-face cupcakes for the safety patrol bake sale, if you can believe it."

"I really don't feel like talking right now."

"Oh, come on. I'm stuck in this kitchen and you haven't even told me about Brooklyn."

"I did tell you. Raj and I broke up."

"But you didn't tell me how or what happened afterward."

I'm treated to an annoyed sigh.

"Mom, please. We broke up. For good. That's it."

She seems unnecessarily irritated by my questions, which only makes me want to ask more.

"Was he hurt? Was he surprised? Did he agree or did he try to fight for you?"

"I'm hanging up." Suddenly there's nothing but dial tone in my ear. Vivs has had some epic bad moods in her life, but this has to be some kind of world record for her.

✦ ✦ ✦

Miraculously, the bake sale treats are plentiful and intact when I get to the gym at two o'clock. Two very enthusiastic kindergarten moms (whose names I can't seem to remember, so I call them Beauty Mark and the Other One) have offered to help set up and sell. They even made extra bake sale signs. We carry the treats to the lobby of the school, where the custodial staff has set up two long tables with white plastic tablecloths.

As we are setting things out, Shirleen comes through the front door, huffing and puffing and bearing a tray of what I'm guessing are her gluten-, sugar-, dairy-, and egg-free brownies, otherwise known as bricks.

"Down here, Shirleen," I call to her. "We've cordoned off the end of this table, so nothing contaminates your brownies."

"This will work," she says after giving the table a once-over. I have put up two rows of water between her brownies and the rest of the treats. It's an impressive spread with cookies, muffins, lemon puffs, Mallomars (from the grocery store; no judgment), raspberry tarts, and more cupcakes. Looking at it all laid out, I realize I haven't thought about what I'll do if we have leftovers.

My cupcakes are center stage, and right next to them I place the big jar Ron got for me yesterday. This is the manifestation of an idea that started when Asami told me they should have to pay me to fill in for them at safety patrol. I'm sure she was kidding, but I thought it was genius. I place booklets of raffle tickets and a homemade sign in front of the jar.

RAFFLE

$5 FOR FIVE CHANCES TO

GET OUT OF SAFETY PATROL!

ALL PROCEEDS GO TO
THE SUSAN G. KOMEN FOUNDATION

That's right: I'm selling the opportunity for someone to skip their assigned day of the worst job ever. It's the perfect way for me to raise money for the Holy Rollers. I figure, I'm here at pickup every day anyway; I may as well take the extra forty-five minutes and watch kids help kids cross the street. But I'm going to make it crystal clear that this is it. I will not be answering emergency "I forgot about blah blah blah" phone calls. These five chances are the only way I will ever fill in for someone again . . . unless it's an emergency . . . or I'm not busy.

The bell rings at three and the kids start pouring through the lobby. But instead of running right outside as usual, they are stopped in their tracks by the glorious sights and smells of the bake sale. Their mothers start streaming in the front doors.

"Everything is a dollar," I let them know while pointing at my monkey-face masterpieces (if you don't count the ones that have crossed eyes; I was pretty tired by the last few). Max comes running over to me asking for money.

"I gave you two dollars this morning," I remind him.

"I know, but I lost it."

I'm trying to make change for people and hand out pens to those who want to fill out their raffle tickets. This is exactly why I gave him the money this morning. I knew I'd be busy.

"How did you lose it?"

"I lost a bet."

I stop what I'm doing. "What bet?"

"Draper bet me my bake sale money that I couldn't sit under a table while he knocked three times."

I furrow my brow. "And?"

"And he only knocked twice and didn't come back. Mrs. Randazzo made me get up."

I don't even know what to start with . . . that my son apparently has "Sucker" written on him somewhere, or that he would gamble away his treat money in the first place.

"Well, I'm sorry that happened, but I'm not giving you any more money. I hope you learned a lesson."

Max looks close to tears, so I pull him behind the table with me, give him a hug, and get back to work.

"Hey, stranger!" It's JJ Aikins. "These look amazing. Kit, do you want one?"

Kit shakes her head and walks to the cookie table.

JJ shrugs. "Sorry. I think they look delicious. So, what's up? How have you been?" She attempts to casually sit on the table, and succeeds in sliding it back two feet. I'm handing out raffle tickets and pens and selling cupcakes, so it isn't an ideal time for a chat, but I don't want to be rude. I'm well aware that JJ has suggested three times that we have lunch, and I have never followed up.

"Been good, thanks, you?" I hand change to a fifth-grade mother and put her raffle tickets in the jar.

"Oh, you know, same old, same old." I'm completely mystified that JJ could think this is a good time for me.

"What did you guys do for Christmas vacation?" she asks.

"Stayed home," I answer while I replenish my cupcake plate with the second batch.

"That's it? Don't you guys usually go somewhere?"

At this point, my raffle ticket line is five deep and I need singles for my cash box, so I let JJ know that I will tell her everything over lunch.

"How is next week for you?"

"Tuesday works. Let's go to Starbucks. I love their protein box."

"Sure, sounds great. See you then." I barely look up, but can tell she has moved on. Thank God!

I'm not at all surprised by how many raffle tickets I sell in the first twenty minutes. I knew it would be a hit, but the "Hell yeah" and "Great idea" reactions feel good anyway.

"Is this a joke?" I look up and see Sylvie Pike frowning and eyeing my jar and sign.

"Nope. Not at all."

"You're selling chances to get out of safety patrol."

"Yes, I am." I'm getting uncomfortable now.

"And the money is going to breast cancer research."

Why does she keep stating the things written on my sign?

I hand a book of five tickets to one of Hunter's two moms and wait for Sylvie to rip me a new one for violating some ethics clause in the PTA manual.

"Well, I just think that's brilliant!" she effuses.

"Really? I'm not crossing any lines?"

"Oh, probably." She shrugs. "But we're going to make enough for the vests from the bake sale, so I say go for it."

Now that's what I'm talking about! A drama-free, boundary-pushing school incident! As the great Bob Dylan once said, "The times they are a-changin'."

And as if to prove my point, Alison Lody strolls over, holding Draper by the arm.

"Hi. I heard someone lost a bet today." She looks at Max. He's still pressed to my side and doesn't say anything.

"Mm-hmm." She nods. "Well, Draper has something to say."

Max and I look at a decidedly mortified Draper, who admits the bet wasn't fair and gives Max his money back.

"I saw it on YouTube. This guy has a video of all the bets you can't lose."

"That sounds cool." Max is perking up quickly.

"But not something you do to your friends," Alison chides.

"Mom, can I get a treat now?" Max asks. I'm really not sure what the protocol is for situations like this, so I tell him he can buy one thing. I take the other dollar from his hand. He and Draper run to the next table to check out the Mallomars. All is forgiven, of course.

"Sorry about that. I was giving Draper money just now and he told me how he, quote, 'took a kid for all he had.' He's so much like his father."

I smirk. "You must be so proud."

She looks at the almost empty table between us.

"Sorry I didn't bring anything."

"There's always next time," I assure her.

Her daughter comes walking toward us with a curious look on her face.

"Hi, Mom. Hi, Mrs. Dixon."

"Hi, sweetie," we say at the same time and then laugh awkwardly.

"Hanna, want a cupcake?" I ask her.

"Aww . . . they look too cute to eat," she says before taking a big bite. Once her mouth is full, she asks, "Mom, can we go? I've got to work on my science project."

"Sure. Find your brother." Alison hands me a dollar. "Thanks, Jen."

"See you soon." I watch her walk away and am relieved to no longer feel that gut rot I used to get when I saw her. Little Jen is growing up.

It's slowing down sales-wise and I think about starting to clean up, but then a wave of fifth-graders who were on a field trip rushes through the front door and we're busy all over again. Looks like I won't have to worry about leftovers. Even Shirleen is part of the clean-table club. I'm told her bricks were very tasty and the two kids who actually have celiac disease were grateful to have something to buy.

It's four o'clock when we start packing up the crumb-filled tables. The only leftovers are six oatmeal raisin cookies (big surprise there). My first instinct is to toss them, but instead I wrap them in some extra tinfoil.

We have quite a success on our hands; I realize it's because this is only the second bake sale this year. There are years when you can't swing a cat without hitting a bake sale, and people get tired of them. But this year, the novelty has proven very profitable.

According to Sylvie Pike, the goodies netted $117, which will get us vests and new stop signs. Those of us who are left (me, Beauty Mark, and the Other One) applaud the good news and I'm impressed by the amount until I count my raffle money—$245! Woo-hoo! I'm a fund-raising genius.

"Can one of you come and witness me pulling the five raffle tickets?" I say to my coworkers.

The Other One walks over. "I hope you pull my name," she lets me know. Frankly, I won't know if I do, I want to say to her.

I stick my hand in the jar and roll the papers around.

"Okay, here we go." I pull out five slips, one at a time, and read the names.

"Shanice Tyler. Maggie Grimmer. Bailey Dawson. Sue Akimo. Lily Booth." Not surprisingly, I know none of these women. But I'll be happy to call all of them tonight and give them the good news and put their safety patrol dates into my calendar. That part will be a bit of a buzzkill.

Max and I hightail it out of the school and into the minivan. It's my dad's birthday, so we're having a family dinner tonight. We're meeting everyone at Garozzo's at six o'clock (the dinner hour of choice for the under-ten and over-seventy crowd). As we are pulling out of the parking lot, I spy Homeless Mitch bundled up against the cold, sitting on his park bench. "I can do this," I chant quietly as I pull the car up to the curb beside the small park.

"Stay here," I order Max and jump out with the tinfoil package in my slightly shaking hands.

"How are you today, Mitch?" I ask the large man on the bench, who stands up immediately. He still scares me, but not as much.

"Not bad, thanks. Yourself?" When he smiles, I see his teeth are stained brown and yellow, but at least they're all there.

"We had a bake sale and I brought you some cookies." I hand him the package. His large hands in their ripped mittens shoot out to take it.

"Thank you."

"Do you need anything?" *Who is this woman?* I ask myself.

"No, thanks. I'm going to start making my way over to the shelter pretty soon."

I look at the sky. It's only 4:15, but it's getting dark. "Do you want a lift?" I ask him.

"Umm . . . no, thank you. It's not far."

I'm surprised by his answer, but I don't ask again.

"Okay, well, have fun." I instantly hear how stupid that sounds. *Yes, Mitch, have fun sleeping on a cot in the moldy basement of an old church with thirty other unwashed men and women.*

But he just smiles again. "I will. It's taco Tuesday."

It takes me a moment to realize he's joking. I give a good guffaw and make my way back to the minivan and to Max.

"What did you give Mitch?" he asked as I pulled into traffic.

"Just some leftover cookies. Hey, what did Draper bring today?"

"Nothing."

This answer isn't surprising. In fact, it has become the norm. It seems Draper's mother put the kibosh on his daily show-and-tell antics. The boys club now spends most of its time trading Pokémon cards.

✦ ✦ ✦

We pull up to Garozzo's in Bruce Willis with two minutes to spare. Normally we'd take the minivan, but it's low on gas. I see my parents sitting just inside the door dressed in their Sunday best, which these days is yoga pants and a blouse for my mother, and beige pants and a blue sweater for my dad. They have probably been here since 5:30.

My mom wanted to cook tonight, but I steered her away from that notion, because, frankly, my taste buds have only just returned after her Thanksgiving gravy. We've picked Garozzo's so dad can have his favorite dish—"Vitello Spiedini Sophia Marie." It's veal, rolled with salami, cheese, and pine nuts, grilled, and topped with a marsala sauce. Not my cup of tea, but he loves it.

"Happy birthday, Poppy!" Max jumps onto my father's lap and nearly knocks him off the bench.

"Happy birthday, Dad." I give him a steadying hug. I swear I think he's getting smaller—definitely thinner.

"Jennifer, we were going to send out a search party for you." My mother makes it seem like we are twenty minutes late instead of two minutes early.

I ignore the jab and let my husband smooth things over by telling her how nice she looks.

We settle into a booth and Vivs comes running in with a bouquet of blue and green balloons trailing behind her. I haven't seen her since New Year's Day.

"Sorry I'm late!" she exclaims, even though she isn't, and makes the rounds hugging everyone before she settles across from Max at the end of the table. My eldest looks tired. This is the busiest time of year at Jenny Craig—all those earnest souls who have pledged to lose weight migrate to the clinic in January to take advantage of the New Year New You campaign. She must be exhausted, but she's putting on a good face, that's for sure.

The waitress arrives and asks if we would like anything to drink. Much to my surprise, my mother is first out of the gate asking for a very dry gin martini straight up with olives.

"Wow, Mom! Loudmouth soup? Since when?"

She nods. "It was my New Year's resolution. I have gin every day now. It relaxes me."

Well, that remains to be seen. Until now, Kay's consumption of alcohol has been limited to the occasional glass of wine. It will be interesting to see how a little Beefeater affects her.

Ron orders a bottle of wine for the rest of us and we settle in.

"So, Dad, how does it feel to be seventy-eight?"

"A lot like seventy-seven." We all laugh.

"I think Laura is going to try to FaceTime us." Vivs waves her iPad.

"Where is she?" my mother and I ask at the same time.

"I guess we'll all find out together," I say. "Oh, Mom, guess what? I've raised almost three hundred dollars for the Holy Rollers."

"Who did you get to donate?"

"I held a raffle at school," I say proudly.

"As long as you didn't ask your aunt Barbara. She's on that fixed income, you know."

I'm saved from having to admit to my mother that I *did* ask her for money by Vivs's announcement that Laura is calling. She pushes a button and starts talking to her screen.

"Hey, Laurs. Perfect timing." She passes the iPad to my father. "Poppy, look who's calling!"

My father looks a bit confused, but when he sees Laura's face he lights up.

"Laura-belle!"

"Happy birthday, Poppy! Are you having fun?"

"Oh, sure. How are you?"

"I'm good. We're in Düsseldorf." Her hair has grown out another inch and she looks healthy.

"Are you eating lots of sausage?" my mother asks. Vivs snorts.

"You look a little fat," Kay continues. Clearly the gin has started to work its magic.

"I'm not fat, Grandma! Where's Max?"

"Hi, Sissy!" Max pokes his head in front of the iPad. "I miss you. When are you coming home?"

"Soon, I hope. How's school?"

"Good."

"Is Razzi still super fun?"

"Yup."

Knowing this is all the conversation she's going to get out of her brother, she turns back to my father.

"Poppy, what did you get for your birthday?"

"I got some nice balloons from your sister."

"Poppy, that's not your gift!" Vivs assures him.

"Oh, well, I don't need anything else."

"I wish I were there to give you a hug."

"Well, that would be nice. I haven't had one of those in a while."

"I just hugged you," Max reminds him.

"I mean from Laura."

Laura addresses me directly. "Hey, Mom, can I talk to you in private?"

"Sure." I take the iPad from my dad as everyone says goodbye to Laura, and walk toward the bathrooms. Luckily, it's still early and the restaurant is not too busy.

"What's up?"

"I want to come home."

My heart leaps with joy, but I play it cool.

"Okay, good. When do you want to come?"

"As soon as I can. I just need money to get to Amsterdam because that's where my return ticket takes off from."

"Okay. Is everything all right?" I'm thrilled by her news, but it just seems rushed. "Is Jeen coming too?"

"I . . . I'm not sure," she stammers. "Can you Venmo me the money tonight?"

"I'll do it right now," I promise her. "But, sweetie, tell me if there's something wrong."

"I'll tell you when I get home," she promises. "Oh, and I need to make an appointment with Dr. Dale as soon as I get back."

"Why?" I ask as nonchalantly as I can.

"I can't go into it now. I'll tell you when I see you."

"Okay. Well, I guess I'll see you in a couple of days."

"Can't wait to see you, Mommy!"

My heart melts. I'm such a sucker for that word.

"Can't wait to see you, too! Let me know what flight you're on."

"I will. Love you!"

"Love you too!"

I walk back to the table, a little dazed from our conversation. I see that dinner has arrived.

"Is she okay?" Ron asks with a mouthful of pasta. I'm sure the whole table is wondering the same thing.

"She's coming home!" I announce.

"When?"

"Later this week, I think." As I say it I get more and more excited. In fact, too excited to eat the chicken carbonara in front of me. My mind is working overtime trying to envision every scenario in which Laura's first stop after eight months away has to be Dr. Dale, our ob-gyn. Many ideas flutter by but the obvious one can't and won't be ignored.

She's pregnant.

To: Mrs. Randazzo's Class
From: JDixon
Re: Be My Valentine
Date: 02/06

Hello, Class!

Can you smell it? Love is in the air! The love for chocolate, that is. Which can only mean that Valentine's Day is but a week away and it's time to get ready for the class party.

    We will need some provisions, of course, so I've gone ahead and assigned you each something to bring. You're welcome. If you don't like what you've been assigned, be sure to bring it up with my co-class mom. Her name is Mandy Idon'tgiveacrap.

Aikinses—water
Lodys—napkins
Tuccis—cookies
Alexanders—cupcakes

Westmans—cups

Browns—plates

Cobbs—fruit

Burgesses—pretzels

Changs—apple juice

Dixons—Kisses (both kinds, for anyone interested ;)

The rest of you are off the hook this time around.

The plan is to play Valentine's Bingo, then Spin the Bottle. Only one of those things is true.

Please send your items with your child on the morning of February 14th.

Thanks, really. You guys do too much.

Jen

I hope they don't mind getting assignments. I just don't have time for the back-and-forth that picking and choosing entails. I'll be curious to see if I get any response from JJ after I left her hanging for lunch. In my defense, I had a crazy day that day and completely forgot that we were supposed to meet. I was at the hospital with my mother getting her blood work done (which took for freakin' ever) and there is absolutely no cell service there. When I walked out around 1:30, my phone started to buzz like an alarm clock. I had seven texts and four missed calls from JJ. The last few weren't pretty.

Hi. Just confirming lunch today. See you in half an hour.

Hi It's JJ. I'm here at SB. Want me to order for you?

I hope you're okay and nothing is wrong. I'll wait a little longer.

Okay. I've been here an hour. You have obviously forgotten, because if you remembered and something came up, you'd have texted me, right?

Why are you ignoring me? I just don't even know what to think of you.

This is why I never liked you in the first place. You really think you are just way better than everyone else.

And finally:

I hope you are dead in a ditch.

I felt terrible at first, but by the time I got to the ditch comment I was reminded why I have always given JJ a wide berth. But since it was uncool of me to forget our lunch completely, I sent her a very conciliatory text and an offer to reschedule any day next week. So far, she hasn't responded.

It's actually no surprise that I forgot about lunch. Things are at DEFCON 3 in the Dixon house these days, thanks in no small part to the return of Laura and Jeen.

They didn't actually come home until a week after my father's birthday. Laura went radio silent after I transferred her the money to get to Amsterdam, and I didn't hear from her until she sent me her flight info five days later.

Ron, Vivs, Max, and I gathered at the airport, outside International Arrivals, to meet her. I wasn't sure if Jeen was coming home with her until I saw Asami and her sister waiting as well. I waved to them, and Asami gave me a thumbs-up. Does she think I maneuvered this sudden return?

Ron held my hand tightly, a reassurance that we were okay after the previous evening's brief battle over, of all things, ice cream.

He's been tense about the business for months trying to figure out how to keep afloat while waiting for financing to come through. I really feel I have been doing my part to keep a tight ship, but when Ron opened the freezer after dinner last night and saw two pints of chocolate-chip Häagen-Dazs, he went postal.

"What the fuck is this?" he yelled. I can count on one hand the number of times I've heard him use the f-bomb, so I was immediately on high alert. So was Max.

"Dad said 'fuck,'" he whispered.

"Max, go in the living room. I'll bring you some ice cream."

He slinked away, and I gave Ron the best stink-eye I could muster.

"Was that necessary?" I asked.

"Do you have any idea how much this shit costs?" He shook a tub of ice cream at me. "Jesus, Jen, I'm busting my ass and all I ask is that you don't buy designer brands."

"Can you please just call them name brands? And calm down. My mother brought it over for Max."

"Oh, great, so now we're taking charity from your mother?"

"Um, no. She brought her grandson his favorite treat."

"Because *we* can't afford to give it to him."

"That's a very twisted way of looking at it." I had kept my voice calm until this point, but I don't take well to being yelled at for no reason, so I wasn't going to be able to keep a lid on it for much longer.

Ron's shoulders sank. He closed the freezer and handed me the Häagen-Dazs.

"They said no."

"Who?"

"The bank. They won't give me the full amount."

I frowned. "How much will they give?"

"Less than half." I can hear the stress in Ron's voice.

"Why not the whole amount?"

Ron shook his head. "Not a viable investment." He made air quotes.

After I delivered Max his bowl of chocolate-chip happiness, we spent the next hour talking through different financial strategies, but Ron kept coming back to his belief that Rolly Schrader will offer to invest.

"I feel like he's been sniffing around me this whole time, dropping hints but not saying anything."

"Well, if that's what you believe, then why don't you just call and ask him?"

Ron shook his head. "Because if I look like I need the money, he may not want to get into bed with me."

"Jesus, this is business, not the rules of dating."

"They aren't that different. One person is always more into it than the other."

We finally went to bed without resolving anything, and I could tell he felt bad about the way the whole discussion had come up in the first place. Ergo the strong hand-squeeze while we waited for Laura.

I hadn't seen my daughter in almost a year so when she and Jeen finally burst through the doors with their luggage piled on a cart I was so overwhelmed with maternal yearning, I swear I started lactating. My eyes blurred with tears and it was all I could do to stay behind the line.

Laura's body was hidden behind the luggage, so the first thing I noticed was that her hair was pink. *Oh Lordy, keep your mouth shut,* I said to myself. When she stepped around the cart to run to us, we had a full view of a much more zaftig Laura. The thin girl of yore had been replaced by a wide-hipped, fuller-busted woman. Still so beautiful, but decidedly changed. I looked at her belly area and it was definitely more rounded, but there was no obvious bun in the oven.

I hugged her with all my strength for a good thirty seconds before I would let go and share her. Max got the second hug, and then Vivs grabbed her and they immediately started whispering to each other like they used to when they were young. Finally, they broke free and Ron got to give her one of his famous bear hugs.

Out of the corner of my eye, I saw Jeen being fawned over by Asami and her sister. I thought about inviting them over—my parents were at my house waiting—but then I remembered that, God help us, my mother was cooking, so I decided not to expose them to it until they became part of the family. Laura and Jeen gave each other a quick kiss goodbye and we all piled into the minivan.

✦ ✦ ✦

On the drive home, we caught Laura up on all the gossip about her friends and our friends and even Max's friends. She gave us the broad strokes of the last few months of their trip. They had been traveling nonstop, basically driving from gig to gig in a crappy old van that Jeen bought for a thousand euros, and they never knew where they would land next. When I asked about her hair she proudly said, "I decided to do it yesterday!"

After dinner (salted lasagna with salted garlic bread, salt salad, and nine gallons of water) I waylaid Laura outside the upstairs bathroom and led her into my room.

"So, what's going on?" I asked as we flopped onto my king-size bed and effectively ruined the flocculence of the counterpane. (Not one but *two* word-a-day-calendar words!)

Laura rolled onto her side and propped her head on her hand. "It's good to be home."

"It's really good to have you home, sweetie. Is Jeen happy to be back too? Are you guys good?"

"I think so. I'll know more after I see Dr. Dale. When did you say the appointment was?"

"Tomorrow at two thirty. What's Dr. Dale got to do with it?"

She shook her head and sighed. "You are really going to kill me."

Stay calm, I say to myself, as my heart starts a staccato rhythm. *Just listen and don't judge.* "I'm not going to kill you," I say with what I'm sure is a strained smile. "Just tell me."

"I think I have an STD."

I had been waiting for the p-word, so I really didn't comprehend what she said to me. "What's an STD?"

"Mom! Seriously? You don't know what an STD is?"

I snapped to it. "Oh! An STD. Which one?"

She shrugged. "The one that makes you feel like you're peeing fire."

"Sounds like a urinary tract infection," I told her knowingly. God knows I had enough of those in my twenties.

"It's also kind of swollen down there too. And it smells bad. I've been uncomfortable for weeks."

Like many mothers, I like to think of myself as Jen Dixon, AAD (Almost A Doctor), but I'm going to leave this one for Dr. Dale.

"Does Jeen have symptoms, too?"

She rolled her eyes. "No. So he's wondering why I do. I'm hoping Dr. Dale can tell me it's something I picked up on a toilet seat."

"Because that happens."

"Mom, I'm kidding. I just need Jeen to know I wasn't with anyone else. He gets jealous sometimes."

"You know you don't need to prove anything to him, right? Your word should be good enough."

Laura closed her eyes and put her head on my legs.

"So . . . you're not pregnant?" I had to say it. Her head popped up immediately.

"Pregnant! God, Mommy, why would you even think that?"

"Oh, I don't know, maybe because you come home after eight months and the first person you want to see is the gynecologist?" There's no way I was going to mention the weight.

"That's not the only reason to go see the bush doctor."

"You're kidding!" I said sarcastically. "I had no idea."

"Pregnant." Laura snorted. "Can you imagine having two daughters knocked up at the same time?"

"What?" I gave Laura a puzzled glance.

"What, what?" She jumped to her feet and smoothed out her clothes.

"What did you just say?" I clarified.

"Nothing. I was just saying wouldn't it be funny if Vivs and I ever got pregnant at the same time. Boy, you'd have your hands full then, huh? I'm going to see if Nana needs help cleaning up."

She dashed out the bedroom door and left me baffled. *Vivs* pregnant? Not a chance. I'd know if she was, wouldn't I?

I debated storming downstairs and confronting her right then and there, but for once I kept a cool head and decided a private conversation was the smart play.

And that's why I convinced Vivs to meet me for lunch and shopping on this unseasonably warm Saturday afternoon. I haven't spent enough time with her lately to tell if she is hiding something. But one lap around Target and a pause by the women's exercise clothing area (which just happens to be right beside the baby stuff) will tell me everything I need to know.

✦ ✦ ✦

"Europe needs Target," Laura announces as we walk into our favorite store. For those of you who have never been, it is one-stop shopping for all your life needs. Where else can you get eyeglasses, a shovel, and a Starbucks venti iced green tea? I would live here if they'd let me.

When Ron looks at the credit card bills, he always asks me, "What did you buy at Target?" To which I always reply, "What *didn't* I buy at Target?"

I grab a shopping cart and we start walking through the women's clothing section. Laura wasn't originally supposed to come with Vivs and me, but I'm glad she did. Vivs was anything but chatty at lunch and has now settled into yet another mood.

Laura confided in me at breakfast that she thinks she may have gained a few pounds and needs some new clothes.

"Just some in-between clothes, until I lose the weight," she added. "It was the chocolate. I couldn't get enough of it."

She strolls over to the sweatpants while Vivs looks at the graphic T-shirts and I decide to try on a few bathing suits. I'm joking.

I can't wait to move on to the workout clothes. As I stroll ahead, I notice the maternity section. I totally forgot about this! They really have the cutest things these days. When I was pregnant with Vivs and Laura I basically wore sweatpants and an extra-large concert

T-shirt. I linger and wait for Vivs to catch up. I want to see if she gives it a glance.

Laura lopes toward me with an armful of colorful clothing. "I may as well get underwear, too," she says, dumping her new wardrobe in my shopping cart and moving on.

Vivs comes walking down the aisle with a blank expression on her face and nothing in her hands.

"Didn't find anything?" I ask.

She scrunches her nose and shakes her head. "I'm so stuffed from lunch, I feel disgusting."

"Are you sick?"

"I don't think so. I always overeat at Chili's." She pats her stomach, which gives me an opportunity to stare. It looks like . . . she overate at Chili's.

As we walk, Vivs asks what I think Laura is going to do now that she's back.

"Hopefully find a job in her field." I shrug, not sure what that field would be with a degree in art history. "Or she could work here. I'd love to get the employee discount."

Vivs ignores my rambling and walks past the maternity clothes without a second look.

"Do you think my boobs got bigger?" Laura yells from the lingerie section. I'd be embarrassed, but hey, it's Target. It's like being in your living room.

"Definitely," Vivs and I both holler back. We have arrived at the sportswear area and I like what I see, but Ron would kill me if I spent money on workout gear when I can get it for free at the store. Vivs is eyeing some colorful leggings.

"Those are cute," I offer.

She shrugs and moves on. The moment of truth is almost upon us. Ten more steps and Vivs will be out of sportswear and into the cribs-and-bibs section.

"I'm going back to shoes for a minute," Laura says, dropping a pile of bras and underwear in the cart.

"Did your feet get bigger too?" Vivs mumbles.

I walk ahead with my cart and linger by the baby area long enough for Vivs to catch up. I'm honestly surprised when she blows right by me and heads to the electronics section claiming to need new head-phones. If she *is* pregnant, she's doing a good job of hiding it. I feel like something would have come up either here or at lunch. I'm feel-ing lighter by the second. Thank God I didn't confront her.

We finish our tour through Target, where I pick up all the store-brand items I need, do the self-checkout with the girls' help, use the six coupons Ron left for me on the kitchen table, *and* get 5 percent off my purchase using my Target credit card. Boo-ya!

As we are walking out of the store, Vivs turns, gives me a funny look, then bolts toward the bathroom. She doesn't quite make it to the door before she throws up Chili's quesadillas all over the floor. As I run to her side, it's all I can do not to scream, "Fuuuuuck!"

18

I know I shouldn't be mentally bitching as I stand here on this freezing February afternoon watching Carlo and Abby perform their safety patrol duties with the enthusiasm of shift workers at the post office, but I can't help it. It's only been two weeks since the bake sale and this is my third stint honoring the raffle. Who knew I'd picked so many people whose assigned dates were for this month? *And* I have another one tomorrow! But I'm hoping against hope that the weatherman is right, and the storm of the century is coming later this evening. Lots of snow tonight means a possible snow day tomorrow, and that means no safety patrol!

The question is, am I feeling lucky? As I stamp my feet in an attempt to bring feeling back to them, I'd say the answer is . . . Not especially.

How did Shakespeare put it? "The sins of the father are to be laid upon the children." Well, he got that right. Vivs, my darling show pony of a daughter, is not only pregnant, she isn't sure who the father is. Sound familiar?

"Did I teach you nothing?" I lovingly screamed at her in the car on the way home from Target.

"Mom, stop!" both girls yelled back.

"No, I will not stop! Why did you guys hide this from me?"

"Gee, I can't imagine," Vivs drawled.

"You know this really hurts me, right?" I asked them.

"Why is this about you?" she snapped back.

Her lack of empathy is a very unattractive quality. I debated telling her this, but I was too upset.

"Because it is! I'm your mother." (*Oh God, I sound like Kay.*) "I don't understand why you wouldn't tell me *immediately.*"

Silence.

Then finally, "Mom, I wanted to tell you, but I knew how pissed off you'd be at me. I mean, you expect this stuff from Laura—"

"Hey!" comes a voice from the back seat.

"—but not from me. And I know that."

"Does Raj know?"

"I'm not sure he's the father."

This hits me like an anvil.

"Who else could it be?"

Silence.

We were at a stoplight, so I looked directly at her.

"Do I know him?"

She lowered her head and nodded.

"Who?" I demanded in my no-nonsense voice.

"Buddy Tucci."

The car behind me honked, but I couldn't move. I was frozen.

"Mom! I'm kidding!" Vivs yelled. "Cripes, move the car!" She started to laugh.

I went through the stoplight and pulled over to the side of the road. I could barely breathe.

"What kind of a sick joke is that?" I shrieked. I looked in the back seat and Laura was suppressing a grin. "Oh, you find this funny too?"

"Mom, I'm sorry. You should see your face."

"What the hell is wrong with the two of you? What could you possibly find funny about telling me you slept with my friend's husband?" I was near tears.

Vivs stopped laughing. "Look, I was trying to think of the worst thing you could hear, so that when I tell you the truth it won't seem so bad."

I gripped the steering wheel and tried to calm myself down.

"Saying it was Buddy was my idea," Laura chimed in.

"That's nothing to be proud of," I mumbled. But if I'm being honest, as diabolical ideas go it was kind of brilliant. The only thing worse would have been telling me it was Ron's.

"Who's the other possibility?" I asked, in a voice at least an octave lower than usual. I sounded like Gollum with a two-pack-a-day habit.

"There's more than one." She wasn't proud to admit this.

I'm not a stupid woman, but her answer didn't compute. "How is that even possible?"

"I've been dating around."

"You mean sleeping around." I hated the way I sounded but I couldn't stop myself.

"Like mother, like daughter," Vivs sniped.

"Hey."

Silence hung like mud in the car's atmosphere.

"How many possibilities are there?" My throat hurt from keeping my voice restrained.

"Four."

"Please tell me Raj is one of them."

"He is." She sighed.

"Who else?"

"A couple of guys I met on Tinder."

"Ew!" Laura chimed in from the back seat. "You didn't tell me that."

I swallowed a snarky comment and asked, "Anyone else?"

"TJ. From the gym."

My reaction was visceral, and I had no way of hiding it.

"You didn't use a condom with a sleaze like that?"

"I was drunk." She shrugged.

"Oh, my God. What is the one thing I have always told you girls?"

"Being drunk is never an excuse for anything," they answered in unison.

"Exactly. So please don't use that as an excuse. Arrgghh! I can't believe I have to see that guy at the gym."

"Don't say anything to him!" Vivs practically shattered my eardrums. I gave her my best dirty look.

"I mean it, Mom. Don't."

I closed my eyes and shook my head. Without saying another word, I put the minivan in drive and took us home all the while pondering where their empathy for me was.

✦ ✦ ✦

Today, as I shiver along with the patrollers, I still find it hard to believe. Vivs is twelve weeks pregnant and is thinking about going it alone. TJ and the Tinder guys were one-night stands, and she and Raj are broken up. I want to tell her that a baby brings you closer together, but who am I kidding? A child puts more stress on a marriage than money troubles and snoring combined.

Abby's voice pulls me out of my reverie. "We're done, Mrs. Dixon."

"Okay, let's get you guys some hot chocolate."

As we walk into the school, I notice the first snowflakes starting to fall. I take a breath and say a silent prayer to the weather gods. Mama needs a snow day.

✦ ✦ ✦

When the phone rings at four a.m., I assume it's the school's robocall letting me know my prayers have been answered. I pick it up on the first ring, hoping nobody else wakes up, and am surprised to hear an actual human on the other end.

"Jen, it's Sylvie." She is speaking very quickly. "They've called a snow day but the school's automatic alert system isn't working so I need all the class moms to call their classes and let them know."

My sleep-deprived brain catches only half of this. "Umm . . . okay. Now?"

"Yes, now. Thank you. I have other calls to make." She hangs up.

I lie down and close my eyes. All I want is to go back to sleep, but I force myself to roll out of bed and lumber down to the kitchen, wishing to God a house elf would magically appear and hand me a cup of coffee. I fire up the iMac and pull up the class list. Nineteen calls to make. If I'm lucky I'll be back at Club White Sheets in half an hour.

I decide to work in reverse alphabetical order. Why should those "A" people always be first? I dial the Zalis household. It rings five times before someone chokes out a "H'lo?"

"Hi, it's Jen Dixon calling to let you know the school is closed today for a snow day," I say with what I think is just the right amount of enthusiasm for 4:15 a.m.

"What?"

"It's a snow day today." I stifle a yawn. "School is closed. Let Rachel sleep in."

"Why did you call?"

"To let you know."

Click.

Okey-dokey. That went as expected. Next on the list is the Wolff house. The call goes straight to voicemail, so I leave a message there and on both their cell phones and hope they get it. May they all be this easy.

Mostly I get mumbled acknowledgments, but a few responses are quite exciting, like when I call the Westman house and Jackie's husband growls, "Stop fucking calling me, Lorraine."

"Sorry, it's Jen Dixon from school. There's a snow day today. Thanks, bye." I get off as quick as I can. I don't know who Lorraine is, but I feel bad for her.

When I call the Batons' house, Jean-Luc picks up on the third ring.

"'Allo?"

"Hi. It's Jen Dixon calling to let you know the school is closed today for a snow day."

What follows is a polemic (word-a-day-calendar word!) *en fran-çais* that I imagine is telling me exactly where I can shove my snow day, followed by several graphic curse words and a slamming down of the phone. It sounds like Mary Jo has a little Ike Turner on her hands.

I'm surprised when Ravi picks up on the first ring. She answers the phone saying, "What's wrong?"

"Hi. Nothing. Just wanted to let you know it's a snow day. Why are you up?"

"I'm always up at four thirty."

"Why?"

"Zach has early ice time three days a week."

"Oh, right." I silently thank God for the millionth time that Max doesn't play hockey. "Well, hopefully you don't have to go out today. Gotta go. Six more people to wake up."

"K. Bye."

Two rings at the Cobb house and then Graydon picks up and screams out an ear-splitting *"Snow day!"*

"Hi," breathes one of Hunter's moms on the second ring.

"Hi, it's Jen Dixon calling to let you know the school is closed for a snow day."

Nothing.

"Hello?"

Silence.

"Kim? Carol?"

Again, silence. And then, light snoring. Oh my God, she fell back to sleep! I'm not sure what to do. If I call back, I will only get a busy signal. I hang up and try both their cell phones, but they go directly to voicemail.

My last phone call turns out to be my favorite, for both its substance and its brevity. After four rings, JJ Aikins picks up. "Hello?"

"Hi, it's Jen. The school is closed today because of the snow."

A long pause and then JJ says simply, "No shit, Sherlock."

I hang up and smile. My work here is done. I grab a glass of water and head back upstairs to hopefully get a few z's.

✦ ✦ ✦

"Are you okay?" That seems to be the question on everyone's lips now that the news about Vivs is out. And it's the first question my best friend asks when I pick up the phone this morning.

"Peachy. How are you?"

"Uh, worried about you. What's the latest?"

I sigh and cradle the phone in my neck while I butter my toast.

"Nothing much to report. She's a healthy fourteen weeks along. Still not really showing."

"Huh. Any news on the father?"

"She says it doesn't matter because he won't be in her life."

"Well, it might matter to him!" Nina exclaims.

I take my toast and coffee and sit down at my kitchen-counter office.

"I agree. But she can't actually know whose baby it is until it's born, so she figures why put somebody through that for no reason."

"What about an amnio?" Nina asks.

"Too risky," I say with a mouthful of toast.

"Has she talked about where she's going to live?"

"I mean, I assume she's going to stay here where she has a support system."

Nina starts to laugh. "Grandma Jen!"

"I know!" I groan. "I can't believe it. What's up with you?"

"All good here. Chyna's going to try out for the lacrosse team. Most of her volleyball friends play, so she wants to do it with them."

"That's a tough sport."

"I have a tough girl."

"That you do. Any boyfriends?"

"None that I'm aware of. Although a kid named Kyle seems to text her a lot. She says they're just friends."

"How's Garth?"

"He's good. Starting to love his work, which is a nice change from hating it. He decided to create a city-wide school fitness competition. The winning school gets the Big Kahuna for a day."

"Do I want to know what that is?"

"It's a big blow-up water slide."

"What do they have to do to get it?"

"They have to complete a bunch of school-wide fitness challenges like running around the track three times and going back and forth on the monkey bars for two minutes straight. There are twenty-five different challenges and all the able-bodied students in each school have to complete them."

"What if you aren't able-bodied?"

"You know Garth—everyone's included. Special challenges will be designed for whatever a kid can do."

"Well, that sounds pretty genius. Go, Garth."

"Yeah, he's psyched."

I look at the clock on the wall.

"Shit! I've gotta run. Carmen awaits."

I can't see her, but I know she just rolled her eyes.

"Don't be a hater." I grab my sneakers and start putting them on.

"Not a hater. Just . . . mystified. So not like you to be a groupie. Actually, I take that back. It's just like you."

"Exactly. What can I say? It's my happy place."

"Well, I'm glad you have one. I'll talk to you in a few days."

"Love you."

"You too. Bye."

✛ ✛ ✛

I swear it's as though my own words jinxed me. I actually had an "incident" at spin class today. I still don't think I did anything wrong but apparently hair-pulling is a big no-no.

They have had to add a lot of bikes to the spin room because Carmen's class has become so popular. As a result, the bikes are closer together than they used to be, so you have to be very aware of personal space. I had a bike right behind a tall millennial with super long hair, almost down to her butt. When the class started, she put it up in a high ponytail, which would have been fine if she wasn't a head whipper. I was enjoying the class, so I didn't say anything the first two times her ponytail hit me in the face during Bryan Adams's "Summer of '69." The third time she whipped her head around, her hair flew into my mouth. This is not a pleasant experience when you are gasping for every breath and singing your heart out at the same time. So I grabbed her ponytail and gave it a yank.

Well, you'd think I'd tried to scalp her by the scream she gave.

"Oh my God! What are you doing?" she screeched loud enough to be heard above the music.

"Your hair keeps hitting my face!" I yelled back.

"Well, just let me know. You don't have to pull my hair out!"

"I just pulled it a bit to get it out of my mouth."

"What's all the chatter, ladies?" Carmen asked through her microphone. Neither of us answered her, but we stopped arguing.

She got the class back on track, but, for the first time ever, I didn't enjoy myself. After the stretch, the head whipper scurried over to Carmen and started whispering and pointing at me. Really? Are we in fifth grade? I walked up to them and halfheartedly apologized for the earlier disruption.

"Jen, do you know Beth?" Carmen asked.

"No, but I'm well acquainted with her hair."

"See?" Beth whined.

"Did you really pull her hair?" Carmen was all business.

"Her ponytail kept hitting my face."

"You didn't have to yank it out of my head!" Beth exclaimed with a level of exaggeration that I usually associate with Max.

"I gave it a tiny tug," I said to Carmen.

"Well, it hurt," Beth informed me.

"Well, if it did, I'm sorry. Next time you might want to put it in a bun." At this I turned and strode out of the room as gracefully as one can with cycling shoes on.

I was still brooding when I caught sight of TJ over by the dumb-bells (how ironic). Vivs's shrill warning to not say anything to him was loud and clear in my mind, but I headed in his direction any-way. The adrenaline was still pumping from my smackdown with Beth and I was raring for a confrontation. Besides, I just wanted to see how he would react to me. I still had my spin shoes on, which made me look like a lumbering ogre as I made my way to him.

"Hey, TJ." I interrupted his biceps reps. He looked surprised but not ashamed of himself which is what I had been expecting to see. Just the fact that he'd slept with my daughter should have made him uncomfortable, but he smiled without a care in the world.

"What's up, Jen? Haven't seen you here in a while."

"Well, maybe you're just not looking for me."

I let that linger in the air just long enough for him to feel uncom-fortable.

Eventually he broke the silence. "*Should* I be looking for you?"

"I don't know; should you?"

He looked genuinely confused at this point and I realized that what I was saying might be misconstrued as flirting. Big whoops.

"Well, I'll start looking for you if you like." He smiled and started pumping again.

This had become a very unsatisfying conversation, so I cut bait before I said something I regretted.

"Uh, that's okay," I mumbled and continued my graceless pro-gress to the locker room.

19

To: Mrs. Randazzo's Class
From: JDixon
Re: This and that
Date: 3/12

Hello, my lovelies,

Just wanted to get a bit of business out of the way before we all head off to parts unknown for spring break.

I need all permission forms for the class trip to Fort Osage in before March 15th. Many of you have already obliged, but the slowpokes are holding up the process. (I'm talking to you, Jackie Westman.) The trip happens the Tuesday we get back from break, so Razzi needs those forms. Ali Burgess, Mary Jo Baton, and the always popular Asami Chang are the lucky winners of a day with the kids, learning all about the olden days of the pioneers (or as Razzi calls it, high school).

Have a wonderful break! I know I will as I head to Sin City for a few days of complete debauchery (more like a lot of time at Circus Circus and the indoor amusement park).

Let it ride!
Jen

As I type the last lines I can't help but think again about the night we finally told Max where we were going for spring break.

It was about a week ago. He had gone twelve whole days without saying or doing anything too obnoxious, so we decided to put him out of his misery. He had been asking endlessly why we weren't going skiing for spring break like we always do. The main excuse I gave was that we couldn't go anywhere because Sissy was having a baby. (That was a whole *other* conversation that had us trying to explain how there can be a mommy but not a daddy. Thank God I had Hunter's two moms as my go-to example.)

We knew that telling Max we were going to Las Vegas wouldn't really send him into a tizzy, so we worked on our presentation. We dressed up in *American Ninja Warrior* gear (well, workout clothes) and Ron created a mini obstacle course in the basement using a jump rope, the sofa cushions, and the treadmill. Laura, who has a bit of a 'tude about not being asked to go to Vegas with us, put her feelings aside to help. She blindfolded her brother, brought him downstairs, and uncovered his eyes to reveal the whole setup.

"Guess where we're going for spring break?" I prompted him.

He looked around incredibly confused.

"Skiing?" he asked hopefully.

"Nope. Guess again."

"Maxi, it's somewhere I would love to go," Laura hinted unhelpfully.

He looked at her and shrugged. "The gym?"

"Hey!" Laura gave his arm a light punch.

"I told you we should have put a sign up," I said to Ron.

"Where are we going?" Max was getting frustrated.

"Watch me, buddy." Ron started going through the "obstacle course" and Max gave it one more try.

"Camping?" he guessed with very little enthusiasm.

"Oh, just tell him!" Laura shouted. Ron jumped off the couch and yelled, "We're going to see *American Ninja Warrior*!"

We all looked at Max expectantly and after two seconds of stunned silence he screamed *"What?"* and ran around in circles making incoherent noises. Anyone watching from the outside would have thought we had just set his bum on fire. He launched himself toward both of us with so much force he knocked me down.

"Thank you thank you thank you! Wait, where is it? Who's going to be there? Will the California Kids be there? Are we going today?"

Ron tried to answer the barrage of questions—"It's the semifinals in Las Vegas"—but Max wasn't even listening.

"Will Drew Dreschel be there? Can I bring Draper? I gotta tell Zach T." At this he ran upstairs and left us in sudden silence.

"Well, if he doesn't want to go, I will," Laura deadpanned.

She's been a bit down in the dumps since she got home. Dr. Dale assured her that her UTI was not sexually transmitted, but Jeen suggested they take a break anyway. Since then she has been moping around the house making passive-aggressive comments about Vegas. I finally told her that, one, she had done enough traveling for the year and, two, I really needed her to stay and look after Vivs. The pregnancy is going well but I'm having anxiety about leaving her alone. With Laura checking in on her, I can relax a little. Laura grudgingly accepts this but still gets in a shot every now and then.

It certainly doesn't help that Max has spent every meal filibustering about all the things he's going to see and do, most of which fall under the category In Your Dreams.

"Graydon says you can try on Iron Man's suit in Vegas. And Zach B. told me you can jump off the top of a really high building with a bungee cord."

Laura rolls her eyes. "What a waste."

"I think you have to be a little older for those things," I tell him.

"Draper says he's *been* to Vegas with his dad and there are girls who show their boobs all over the place."

"Not the places we're going, buddy," Ron assures him.

"Good. Ain't nobody got time for that," Max informs us. Man, I really need to block YouTube on his iPad.

After dinner, Laura and I are in the kitchen cleaning up when she hits me with her latest random thought. "I think I'm going to find my own place."

Don't react, don't react don't react, I chant to myself.

"Oh really, sweetie? Why?"

She folds the dish towel she has been using and puts it on the counter.

"I think it's time. You guys are great, but I kind of got used to being on my own in Europe. I'm feeling a bit under the microscope here."

I have to tell you that this is laughable. She comes and goes as she pleases and she eats whatever she wants. I have not said word one about the fact that she hasn't even looked for a job. Something occurs to me.

"Are you going to move in with Jeen?"

She snorts. It's an incredibly unattractive sound.

"No. Definitely not. We've barely seen each other."

"Do you have a place yet?" I'm continuing with the calm questions because at this point she clearly doesn't have a plan, just a thought.

"No. I've been looking but everything around here is really expensive."

No shit. I can't believe she thinks she'll get her first apartment in Overland Park. *Try HUD housing, sweetheart.*

"Well, let me know if I can do anything to help." I fill my water glass and head into the living room to watch God knows what on Nickelodeon with Max. It's clear to me she'll be here for a while.

"Thanks, Mom." Laura's smile is so genuine, I feel guilty.

✦ ✦ ✦

Today I have a checklist of about six billion things I need to do before we leave for Vegas. First on the list: stop exaggerating.

It's a rainy, cold day so I pull my bright-yellow Gore-Tex rain jacket over my sweater and hustle out to the minivan. Kay and Ray top the list of people to see, so I drive to my old neighborhood.

Everything about my parents' house says home to me. It's not the house I grew up in, but it is the house I brought Vivs and Laura to when we came back from Europe and started living the normal years. As I pull into the driveway, I shake my head at the pig-shaped pink mailbox that my mother insisted on buying at the church craft fair a dozen years ago because Margaret Dugan's "special" son made it. It's actually pretty cute, even though the pig's butt faces the road and you have to pull the tail to open it. It's the only one of its kind in fancy Overland Park, if you can believe it! The house is a sharp-looking traditional two-story, painted dark gray with white trim. My father has always kept meticulous care of the lawn. "Just try to find a dandelion," he is fond of saying to pretty much anyone.

I knock and then immediately use my key to get in. As I step into the foyer my nose flares in recognition. Kay and Ray's house has always smelled like a combination of burnt toast, bleach, and Shalimar, my mother's favorite perfume.

"Hello?" I yell, because yes, they are getting hard of hearing but also to preempt any potential embarrassing encounters.

"In here, sweetheart!" my mom yells back. I follow her voice to the kitchen. She and my father are sitting at the table eating something that looks like it might be shredded cardboard.

"Hi, guys. What's for breakfast?"

"Muesli," my father says, still chewing. Bits of cereal land like spittle on his lips and chin.

"For the fiber," my mom adds as she hands him a napkin. "It doesn't taste half bad with soy milk. Want some?" She lifts her bowl toward me.

"I'm good, thanks. I just came by to see if you need anything. Remember I leave tomorrow for spring break."

"Vegas, baby!" For some reason my mom is very excited about this trip. "Jennifer, I'm going to give you one hundred dollars and I want you to go to the roulette wheel at the Mirage and bet the whole thing on black 22."

I don't know why I'm surprised. My mother has basically abandoned most of her previously held beliefs, including "No good ever comes from spending time in a casino."

"Mom, I don't know if I'm going to get to the Mirage."

"Well, of course you will. Aren't you going to take Max to see Siegfried and Ray?"

"It's Roy, and they don't do that act anymore since Roy got attacked by one of the white tigers."

My father nods and Kay looks shocked. "Oh, that's terrible! Is he all right?"

"I think he made a full recovery. Can't I make your bet at another roulette table? Maybe the one in my hotel?"

"I suppose so." She sighs. "I just always heard the Mirage is so elegant."

"We're staying at the Venetian, and it's very elegant too."

"Well, okay, I guess." Defeated, she hands me a hundred-dollar bill. "Remember, black 22."

I consider asking why this specific number, but I've got places to go, so I give them both a hug and remind them that Laura will be checking in every day.

"Will Vivs check in too? You know we haven't seen her since the night Laura got home, remember, Ray?"

My father nods again.

We haven't told my parents about Vivs's pregnancy yet. I'm not sure how the news will be received.

"She's been working crazy hours at Jenny Craig," I fib. "I'm not sure she'll have time. Love you guys!" I beat a hasty retreat out of the kitchen and ultimately the front door. I can't wait until all this is out in the open.

✦ ✦ ✦

After stopping at the dry cleaner to pick up my favorite summer dress, and the shoe repair guy to get my newly soled silver sandals—both of which I'm taking to Vegas—I pull into Peetsa's driveway. I'm borrowing the sunhat her mother brought her from Italy that I have admired for years.

"Hey, come on in." She answers the door in jeans and a cute blue sweater. I follow her to the kitchen, where she has a bunch of papers spread out around her laptop.

"Whatcha working on?" I help myself to a cup of coffee from her half-full pot.

"Ugh, my résumé. I'm going to try to find a job."

"Huh. What are you thinking about?"

"Something in sales again." Peetsa's last job was selling cell phones, and Buddy always said she was really good at it.

"Can you go back to Verizon?"

"I'm hoping to try something new . . . maybe cars."

"Cars! Do you know anything about them?"

She shrugs. "What's to know? You read up on the product and sell the strengths."

I try to imagine a beautiful, knowledgeable woman trying to sell me a car, and I find it doesn't appeal to me. I picture that same woman selling to Ron, and I'm guessing he'd buy two.

"You're going to be great."

"I need an interview first."

"I have no doubt you'll get one. What's going on with Buddy?"

She lets out a sigh and sits down at her table. I do the same.

"He's living his life. I think he's dating." She shrugs, but the casualness of the gesture doesn't reflect in her face. "We're on this stupid schedule with the kids where we pass them back and forth twice a week. We all hate it, but what else can we do?"

"I read somewhere that the new trend in divorce is for the kids to stay in the family home and the parents move in and out."

"Yeah, that's not happening. Buddy wants to sell the house. That was this week's bombshell."

"What? Why?"

"He wants the money to buy a condo down by the Plaza, like where TJ lives."

The mention of TJ makes my stomach turn. It also makes me debate telling her Vivs's daddy dilemma. I figure what the hell. Misery loves company.

"Vivs's baby might not be Raj's."

Peetsa starts to laugh, then stops. "Wait, seriously?"

I nod.

"Who else?"

"Well, apparently there are a few possibilities, including TJ."

She gives me a blank look. "TJ who?"

"T-J." I emphasize the initials.

"TJ! Eww . . . she slept with him? That guy sleeps with everyone!"

Hearing him described that way makes me want to throw up. I lean my head into my hands.

"Yuck," Peetsa says to punctuate her feelings.

"You're understating it," I tell her.

"I know. I just don't want to make you feel any worse."

"She won't know whose the baby is until it's born. She says it doesn't matter because she doesn't want any of the guys in her life. She wants to raise it on her own."

Peetsa shakes her head. "I knew Raj was on shaky ground, but wow. Are you okay?"

There's that question again.

"I guess. As okay as can be expected."

"When is she due?"

"September." I see the clock on the microwave and realize I have to go. I stand and grab Peetsa's hat off the counter.

"Hey, thanks for this."

"No problem. Grandma! That's some pretty big news you're leaving me with."

"Yeah, well, I like to light up the room before I leave."

"Mission accomplished." She stands and gives me a hug. "Try to have a good time. When are you back?"

"Wednesday. I'll call you."

"Okay." She walks me to the door and waves until I get in the car.

✦ ✦ ✦

Vivs is next on the errand train. I'm having lunch with her at her desk. She has to try some new foods that Jenny Craig is pushing, so she asked me to join her for a free low-cal meal.

While I'm waiting for her to finish up with a client I check my email on my phone and find one from Razzi.

To: JDixon
From: WRandazzo
Re: Class Birthday Parties
Date: 3/15

Hi, Jen,

Something has been on my mind for quite a while and I wanted to share it with you. It's about classroom birthday celebrations. Can you please ask the parents to use a little more restraint? I so appreciated that when we celebrated Max's birthday this week you just brought a snack, a candle, and a book. That's all it should be. This fad of hiring a balloon clown or a juggler to help the festivities along is getting to be too much for me. The petting zoo left a smelly mess in my classroom, not to mention the goat almost bit me. So tell them to take it down a notch, and that it doesn't mean you love your kid less.

Thanks, and have a great break.

Winnie

She's right. The one-upmanship that has been going on is ridiculous. I'm about to shoot off a stern email to the class when Vivs tells me she's ready and leads me back to her cubicle, where an impressive spread of diet food is laid out.

"How are you feeling, sweetie?" I ask her as we sit down to sensible portions of stuffed pizza bites and egg, cheese, and turkey sausage burritos.

"Hungry and tired all the freaking time." This is her stock answer these days. Ever since she told me about her pregnancy all her animosity has gone away and we're back to talking every day.

"At least you don't have morning sickness."

"True," she says as she stuffs a pizza bite into her mouth. I do the same and am pleasantly surprised.

"Wow. That's actually not terrible!"

"Say it louder, Mom, I don't think Caroline out front heard you."

I ignore this. "So, you know we leave tomorrow. Will you be okay?"

"I'll be fine! I got through the first ten weeks without you. I think I can get through the next five days."

"Why are you snapping at me today?" I take a bite of the turkey sausage burrito but keep my thoughts to myself.

"Sorry. I'm just . . . arrrrgh! There's too much going on."

"I know," I tell her, and I really do. Pregnancy is a bitch at any time, but going through it without a partner is brutal. "I really wish you knew who the father is."

"Again, it doesn't matter. I'm not going to be with him anyway."

"I saw TJ at the gym," I tell her.

She stops chewing. "You didn't say anything to him, did you?"

"I thought about it, but no. I just said hello."

She scowls, and her voice rises several decibels. "Why would you even do *that*?"

"I wanted to see if he'd at least act uncomfortable with me, but he was just doing his arm workout as though he hadn't slept with my daughter."

"Cripes, Mom, just stay away from him, okay?" Vivs is disproportionately annoyed, in my opinion.

"Got any of the cheesecake?" I ask as a way to change the subject.

"God, I hope so." She walks to the fridge at the back of the office.

✦ ✦ ✦

After stopping at UPS to drop off three returns to Amazon, I head to school to pick up Max. Thank God, it's finally stopped raining, but the wind has picked up so I wrap my arms around myself as I walk from the parking lot. March has most definitely come in like a lion. I'm happy to see the Chloes are at their safety patrol post and a parent I do not recognize is with them. A small glow of satisfaction flows through me. We're in the home stretch for the school year and there have been very few patrol incidents. Go, me!

I approach Ravi, Peetsa, Alison, and Asami, huddled together against the biting breeze.

"Jen, you're so lucky to be getting out of this weather," Ravi greets me.

"I know, I can't wait." I spy Jackie Westman in my peripheral vision and excuse myself from my friends to make a beeline toward her.

"Jackie! Permission slip!" I bellow in a fruitless effort to embarrass her. I secretly admire her ability to not give a crap if she's the worst at handing things in. There is a quiet dignity to her laziness.

"I'll give it to Razzi," she yells back, and I turn before I even reach her. I've done all I can do.

The bell rings as I head back to my group and the kids come streaming out. I spot Max holding onto his baseball hat so it won't blow away.

"Mom, can I go to Draper's?"

I shake my head.

"Not today, babe. We have lots to do before we leave. We need to find your bathing suit."

They all groan at me.

"Sorry! Am I the only one going somewhere warm?"

"I think you are!" Peetsa laughs. "Lucky duck."

20

To: Mrs. Randazzo's Class
From: JDixon
Re: I love you guys . . .
Date: 3/18

Dear best, best, best, best friends,

I realize we are all on vacation, but I want you to know I am still here for you. And believe me, it's not always easy to be me being here for you. I don't like being the bad guy. I'm not the bad guy. I'm the good guy. I try to be a good person, I really do. But it's been a tough year and I'm tired of cutting coupons. I am. I hate it. But I do it because we are going broke and my husband says saving twenty cents on paper towels is going to keep us going and who am I to argue? I'm old and flabby and he's not. We'll need money for the baby, not to mention my parents aren't getting any younger. And let's face it, I'm no spring chicken, although some guy by the bathroom did ask me to kiss him, so there's that. Do you think I put out a loose vibe? I don't think I do, but you never know what people pick up on.

    Oh yeah: Razzi wants me to tell you to stop bringing your kids

> *things on their birthday. The goat poop was just too much. She's a party*
> *pooper! Actually, the goat was the party pooper. "Pooper" is a weird word.*
> *I love you all.*
>
> *Jennifer Rose Howard Dixon, class mom forever and ever. Amen.*

Yup. I actually sent that. As God is my witness, I don't remember even writing it. But apparently, I did. And now the world knows just a little too much about me.

Oh, I was drunk, no question about it. And that would be my excuse, except I believe I have mentioned that being drunk isn't an excuse for anything. Damn my words of wisdom for coming back to bite me in the ass.

How I came to write such an email is kind of a weird tale, so bear with me. We got to Las Vegas without much fuss. Only one drama marred the trip—when I realized at the airport that I had left my phone on the kitchen table. Mild panic flooded my system as it registered that I wouldn't be one hundred percent available for Vivs. I was going to go home and scrap the trip until Ron, my trusty voice of reason, told me I could carry his phone. I immediately texted Vivs and Laura and asked that one of them FedEx me the phone to the Venetian ASAP, to which Laura replied, "Chill, Mom," and Vivs replied, "Who is this?"

On the airplane, Max got to meet the pilot and they made him an honorary co-pilot. The fact that he was one of seventeen honorary co-pilots on board that day didn't make it any less special for him. You'd think we were headed to Disney, with the number of kids on the plane.

We were picked up at the airport by one of Rolly's employees—a short brown-haired guy in his late twenties named Steve. He whisked us to the hotel in the longest, whitest limousine I have ever seen. Max was rendered speechless for a good five seconds and then basically dove into the car and started pushing every button he could find. I would have stopped him, but he was only doing what I would have done if it was acceptable adult behavior. I settled for pretending I was Celine Dion when we pulled up to the Venetian . . . and Ron was my bodyguard.

Ron and I had been to this hotel before, but obviously Max was a first-timer. The grand painted ceilings, enormous archways, and polished tile in the lobby alone had him convinced that royalty must live here. The Venetian really is spectacular; books have been written on its art and architecture. But when all is said and done, you turn the corner and you're in a casino, complete with old ladies on oxygen playing the slots, and people drinking scotch at ten a.m. No amount of marble can mask that.

Our room was great—actually a bedroom and an open sunken living room with a pullout sofa for Max and a terrific view of the Strip. The décor was sufficiently decadent, in keeping with the rest of the hotel.

The phone rang almost as soon as we got in the room. It was Rolly welcoming us and letting us know that dinner was at eight at Canaletto Ristorante in the hotel . . . nothing fancy, he insisted. He also informed us that he had hired a babysitter to stay with Max.

I felt bad leaving my eight-year-old with a stranger on our first night in Las Vegas, but he couldn't have cared less. Unlimited TV and a chance to order room service are apparently all it takes for him to happily kick us to the curb. And it certainly didn't hurt that Cassie was a blond, very pretty twenty-two-year-old who told us she has three younger brothers. She's the daughter of one of Rolly's employees and was brought to Las Vegas for the sole purpose of taking care of Max. I'm guessing this was Janine's idea, and that she thought she was doing us a favor. As it happens, I like spending time with my kid on vacation, but I think in Janine's world that's considered something akin to waterboarding.

I remember being so happy to see the Schraders that night. The maître d' led us to a great table near the back of the very lively restaurant, where our friends were already half a bottle of wine in. It took absolutely no time at all to fall into our routine of booze and banter.

At some point Rolly laid out the plans for the weekend, including a company trip to the Hoover Dam that we were welcome to join in on, tickets to see David Copperfield's magic show with Max, and, of course, the big event, the reason for the season, going to see *American Ninja Warrior* live. It all sounded perfect, and the more I drank, the more perfect it sounded. We were discussing the fact that this trip is Max's birthday present this year—no party necessary—and after that things get a little fuzzy . . . like trying to see through stained glass. I don't even remember getting back to the room, let alone firing up my laptop and sending an email to the class. Asking Ron for clarification was like asking the blind man what he saw. We're such idiots. It was so irresponsible to drink that much when we were in a strange environment and Max was with us.

The next day, I remember with brutal clarity. I woke up to a world-class headache and a note from Ron saying he'd taken our son out for breakfast. I hadn't even heard them leave.

After a two-minute pee, a gallon of water, and three extra-strength Tylenol I started to feel a bit more human. I looked around our messy room and noticed my laptop was open on the desk. I figured Cassie had used it and Max had given her the password. I closed it and put it in the safe.

My mojo really cranked up after Ron and Max came back with a large coffee and a breakfast burrito filled with scrambled eggs and bacon.

"Did you have fun with Cassie, sweetie?" I asked as I shoveled the food into my mouth. I felt myself coming alive with every bite.

"Yeah. She taught me how to play blackjack. With betting chips and everything."

I raised an eyebrow at Ron. He started to laugh.

"Don't look at me; I didn't teach him. But when you think about it, it's a great way to perfect your addition and subtraction."

"Then we should have taught him two years ago, when he was learning those skills."

"Can I play *real* blackjack?" Max interjected.

"Sure. In about thirteen years." Ron ruffled his hair.

Our bus to the Hoover Dam wasn't leaving until eleven, so we spent the first part of the morning walking around the hotel, checking out the pool, and taking a gondola ride along the Grand Canal.

We bumped into Janine in the lobby, wearing workout gear (of course) and looking like she had broken a good sweat. She kissed my cheek and hugged Ron as if she were seeing him for the first time. "Hey, guys! Are you just getting up?"

"No, no. We've been taking in the sights," Ron assured her. "Have you met our son—" He was interrupted by Janine turning and addressing me.

"They have a spin bike in the gym! You should try to work yourself out later."

"Are you going to the Hoover Dam?"

The look she gave me screamed, "Are you out of your mind?"

"Been there, done that. I went in tenth grade on a field trip. I doubt it's changed."

"Oh, too bad. I was looking forward to spending some time with sober Janine," I joked.

She lit up. "Good luck finding her!"

"Are we seeing you tonight?" Ron asked. We had tickets to David Copperfield.

"Magic show? Pass. But I'll definitely see you tomorrow for the ninja thing." She winked and sashayed away. I tried very hard not to let it bother me that she didn't even acknowledge Max during that whole exchange. I chalked it up to her not being a kid person and moved on.

The Hoover Dam was well worth the forty-five-minute bus ride and hour-long tour if for no other reason than Max walked away with five fun facts that he couldn't wait to share with Razzi. Unlike his wife, Rolly, whose grandchildren were not on this trip, wouldn't leave Max's side and made sure he got the best view of everything. He even bought him a T-shirt that said, "Keep Your Hands Off My Dam Shirt."

The nice thing about *not* seeing the Schraders that night was we didn't drink, and we went to bed at a reasonable hour. We took Max to New York–New York for an early dinner, then just made it to the MGM Grand for the seven o'clock Copperfield show. It was a little campy, in my opinion, but the man made a car appear onstage out of nowhere! That is some talent. Max was convinced it was the best thing he had ever seen, and he was probably right. It definitely had more of a wow factor than *Bubble Guppies Live,* which is the only other show he has ever seen.

Afterward, Ron went to the blackjack tables. We had budgeted $50 a night for him to gamble, so I took Max back to our room and expected to see him in ten minutes. Apparently, I was asleep when he got in.

✦ ✦ ✦

Sunday at five was the taping of *American Ninja Warrior,* so naturally Max was up at the crack of dawn in anticipation. I wasn't sure what I was going to do with him all day, but the amazing Cassie called and offered to take him to Circus Circus. I wasn't going to say no to that. It gave Ron and me a few hours of Mommy-Daddy time which included a quickie and a relaxing afternoon by the pool. It wasn't as warm as I had anticipated, but hey, when you've been in 20-degree weather for months, 72 feels pretty damn good, plus I got a little sun on my pasty-white skin. Ron was in an amazing mood, having turned his $50 into $600 the night before, and it was nice to see him relax for a while.

At four o'clock, Rolly had that same super white limo take us all over to the show, which was taped in an empty lot across from the Luxor Hotel. The group included our family, the Schraders, Steve, our guy from the airport, and Cassie, who confessed her life goal is to be a contestant. I wanted to tell her to aim higher, but thought I'd leave that for her own mother to say.

We were met by an official-looking guy dressed all in black, with a clipboard and a headset on.

"Mr. Schrader? I'm Luke. This way, sir." We followed him through a labyrinth of trailers and trucks until we emerged, quite suddenly, at the obstacle course.

"Holy crap!" screamed Max, and I had to agree with him. The set of *American Ninja Warrior* was truly a sight to behold. Astonishing in its size, the course was all red, white, and blue, surrounded by chrome and lights, and built over a large rectangular pool. It was inspiring and terrifying all at the same time.

"Can I go on there?" Max asked Rolly.

"Unfortunately, no. You can't even touch it."

He looked at me and shrugged. "I asked them earlier."

"Being here is more than enough," I assured him.

I think Max could have stood there all evening just looking at the course, but Luke had other plans for us.

"Want to meet the hosts?" He directed the question to Max.

"Yes please!" I was shocked by Max's politeness and really, how sad is that? My expectations have been so drastically lowered by his behavior this year that basic common courtesy has become a surprise.

Luke took us to the platform where the hosts do their play-by-play, and Max was in heaven. They were having some kind of meeting but immediately jumped up when we got close. Two guys and a girl all walked over and greeted Rolly like an old friend, which made me wonder if he was a part owner in the show. I mean, we were really getting the VIP treatment.

"This is the young man I was telling you about." Rolly presented Max to them, and for the first time in recent memory, he was speechless. They took pictures and told Max he could sit on the platform with them for part of the show if he wanted. I hung back to avoid saying anything painfully stupid or embarrassing as I am wont to do when celebrities are involved. I once met the weatherman from channel four and told him I never watch his show. What?

We then went to meet the competitors. Miraculously, Max's voice came back to him and he spent the next fifteen minutes discussing the challenges of the course with them. It sounded like gibberish to me—I mean, is there really something called a Daytona Beach wing nut? Since this was a new season of the show, Max didn't know any of the athletes, but it didn't seem to matter. He took pictures with all of them—even the girls!—and wished them luck.

Luke said the taping was going to start soon and took us all to our seats. Front row center, of course. I could seriously get used to this. Max went up to the booth to spend the first part of the show with his new buddies, and the adults were left to fend for themselves. I had to admit I was having a good time. I mean, I couldn't imagine any other circumstance under which I would actually choose to be there, but my boy was happy, the weather was nice, it was relatively interesting, and Janine had just handed me a glass of wine!

"How does everyone know Rolly?" I asked her.

She shrugged. "He supplies the merch." I'm assuming she meant the merchandise. A bag of it was delivered to our hotel room this morning.

"So that's why we're all getting the VIP treatment."

"Well, that and the fact that he bought a VIP experience at a charity auction we went to a few months ago. He couldn't wait to have you guys come and enjoy it."

"He did that for Max?"

"For you." She punctuated her answer by pointing at me.

I honestly didn't know how to respond to that, and thankfully I didn't have to, because the taping had started. I looked to see if Ron had been listening, but he was talking to Steve from the limo.

The show itself was loud and crazy and exciting. Seeing people give their all, in feats of unimaginable physical difficulty, only to be denied victory by something called the Psycho Chainsaw, was truly heart-stopping. Only four guys made it to the end; the rest took a bath, literally, falling into the pool below the obstacle course. Max, who spent the second half of the show sitting between Ron and me, seemed to feel every victory and every defeat as deeply as the athletes. When the show finally ended (three hours to tape a one-hour show!) he turned to us with tears in his eyes.

"Thank you so much for bringing me here," he choked out. "This is the best day of my life." Then he hugged us and buried his head in my chest like he used to when he was little.

"Thank Mr. Schrader too, buddy." Ron cleared his throat and I could tell he was choked up, too.

"Let's get the hell out of here, shall we?" Janine effectively broke the sentiment of the moment. "I'm starving. Where's that babysitter?"

Cassie had spent most of the show backstage, talking to the competitors and taking notes on their training regimens. I thought about telling her I had trained for a mud run a couple of years ago, but it would have been like telling a chef training at the Cordon Bleu that I once made toaster strudel.

"Steve is going to take Max and Cassie back to the hotel in a taxi and the rest of us will take the limo to Caesars," Rolly announced to our group, and we reluctantly parted from our son on the happiest day of his life.

Once in the limo, Janine popped the cork on a bottle of Veuve Clicquot for the ten-minute drive up Frank Sinatra Boulevard to Caesars Palace and our reservation at Gordon Ramsay's restaurant Hell's Kitchen. "Now the fun begins," she exclaimed, and I kind of felt sorry for her. I'd been having fun for hours.

Caesars Palace resides, in my opinion, at the corner of elegant and tacky. Think Donald Trump's house and, well, Donald Trump. Fifty years ago, Caesars was the crown jewel of Las Vegas—the opulence was stupefying and you just had to see it to believe it. These days the one-upmanship between hoteliers in Sin City is so fierce that Caesars looks not so much amazing as average and a little dated.

Hell's Kitchen has pride of place at the front of the hotel and looks like a larger version of the set the TV show is shot on. Lots of red and blue, big glass windows, and not one but two chef's tables. I thought for sure we would be led to one of them, because that's just how Rolly rolls. But we were escorted to a corner table by the window with a view of the Strip.

As we settled into our seats, I grabbed Rolly's arm.

"I don't know how we can ever thank you enough for today. You made our son the happiest kid in the world."

"It was my pleasure." He beamed and firmly placed his hand over mine.

"And Janine told me you bought the VIP experience at an auction? Why didn't you take your grandkids?"

"Believe it or not, none of them are big fans. And I knew Max was from the first time we all had dinner and you told me about his Halloween costume."

"Well, it meant the world to us." I pulled my hand away and turned to Ron. "Didn't it, sweetie?"

"It really did." He was looking at Rolly's hand and mine.

"You owe us big-time!" Janine laughed and signaled the waiter to come over.

"Can we have a bottle of the Cakebread chardonnay?" Turning back to us, she clapped her hands together and said, "Can we talk about that show?"

We spent the next couple of hours laughing over some of the epic falls from the show and sharing gambling war stories, most of which came from Rolly. The food was delicious and, as always, we were having a great time. I did get weird vibes from this couple every now and then, but for the most part they were a blast.

After the second bottle of wine, Janine took my hand in one of hers, Ron's in the other, and made what was most definitely an alcohol-induced declaration.

"We really love you guys."

I didn't want to leave Rolly out of the admiration circle, so I grabbed his hand. Ron said, "The feeling's mutual."

Janine grinned and raised an eyebrow to her husband. "We also think you are, like, the hottest couple we know."

"Sorry?" I was sure I had heard that wrong.

"You're hot! You're both really attractive."

I didn't respond to this, but I guess Ron felt the need to say something.

"Well, you guys are great-looking, too."

For your age, I finished for him in my head.

Janine grinned at her husband.

"See, Rolly? I told you."

Rolly was an almost purple shade of red at this point and I'm not sure whether it was because of the alcohol or this conversation. Janine continued.

"So, what are we going to do about it, we four attractive people?"

"Let's get a picture!" Ron suggested, holding up his phone.

"Great idea!" Janine enthused and jumped up to move closer to my husband. "Jen, why don't you just squeeze in on Rolly's lap?"

I took her suggestion, but as we posed for the waiter—Janine wrapped around Ron like a boa constrictor, and me on Rolly's lap—I got a very strong *Bob and Carol and Ted and Alice* vibe, and not in an "Oh, I love that movie!" way. It was more like "Holy shit, are we being propositioned?" I jumped off Rolly's lap the second the waiter took the shot and grabbed for my water.

Janine uncoiled herself from my husband and signaled for the check.

"Shall we move this party back to our hotel room?"

This did *not* sound like a good idea to me, and I was trying to figure out a polite way to say so.

"Are you okay?" I thought Ron was talking to me, but when I looked up, his eyes were on Rolly, who was half leaning on the table and shaking his head. He looked like he was trying to breathe. Ron was at his side in an instant.

"Oh my God, Rolly!" Janine cried out.

"Jen, call 911." Ron laid Rolly on the floor of the restaurant and loosened his collar. As I reached for my phone, our waiter told me someone was already calling.

I always knew Ron was a good guy to have around in an emergency, but he blew me away with his calm control over the situation. He had already started CPR when the paramedics arrived four minutes later (response time noted!), and they took over. I had my arm around Janine and we watched along with everyone else in the restaurant as they worked on the man whose lap I had been sitting on five minutes ago. Is that what gave him the heart attack?

I called Cassie and told her what had happened. She assured me she could stay as long as we needed her.

Janine went in the ambulance with Rolly, and Ron and I followed in a cab to University Medical Center. By the time we got there and found Janine, Rolly was stable, but the doctor was still examining him.

"He may need an angioplasty," Janine told us through tears. "My dad had one and he was fine." The word "fine" was almost lost in a fresh round of sobs. I hugged her and led her to a chair in the waiting room while Ron went to get us water.

This may sound glib, but if you want to do some serious people-watching, hang out in a Vegas ER for a couple of hours. After Janine went to sit with Rolly, Ron and I had front-row seats to quite a procession of misfits and weirdos walking through the door with either drug- or alcohol-related injuries or bizarre objects inserted where they shouldn't be. That's not to say UMC doesn't see its share of major emergencies like gunshot wounds, car accidents, heart attacks, and strokes, but in the few hours we were there the most serious thing I saw was a very drunk college kid with a $25 poker chip stuck in his nose.

I was still trying to process what had happened that evening prior to Rolly's heart attack. I was stone cold sober by then and thinking about whether Janine's remarks about how "hot we are" and "taking it back to their hotel room" still had the same salacious undertone, and you know what? They did. No matter how you sliced it, there had been a proposition on the table that night, and it wasn't the one Ron had been hoping for.

He was sitting beside me, leaning back with his eyes closed, so I nudged him awake.

"Hmm? What? Any news?" He kept his eyes closed.

"No, but we never talked about what happened tonight."

"What do you mean?" He cracked one eye open to look at me.

"I mean how Janine propositioned us."

Now both his eyes were open. "What? No, she didn't!"

"Uh, yes she did." I was keeping my voice to a whisper.

"You're drunk."

"No. I *was* drunk, but now I'm not and I know what I heard."

"Which was what exactly?" I couldn't believe he was asking me this.

"She told us how hot we were and asked us to go back to their hotel room."

He was fully awake now and looking at me like I was insane. "They told us how much they enjoyed us and suggested we all go back to our hotel. To go to sleep."

We stared at each other, and then Ron hit me with a curveball.

"You were the one flirting with Rolly all night. Taking his hand, sitting in his lap, and laughing at everything that came out of his mouth." He didn't sound angry, just matter-of-fact. "I figured you were trying to help me close the deal."

I was stunned. I started to argue, but he hadn't said one thing that wasn't true. I had taken Rolly's hand and laughed at all his jokes and even sat in his lap. Holy crap. Was that what it looked like to the Schraders, too? I was so confused.

Ron had closed his eyes again, so I decided to check my email on his phone. I hadn't done it since we got here, and my iPhone still hadn't shown up. I was alarmed to see emails from almost every parent in Max's class. Shit! Something must have happened. Every subject line read "I love you guys . . ." What the heck?

Ravi's was the first one I'd received, so I clicked on it and then scrolled up to see what the original message said. You can imagine how thrilled I was to see that it was none other than me myself and I who had professed my love for Mrs. Randazzo's class at 2:20 a.m. Vegas time two nights earlier and then proceeded to overshare every piece of personal information in my life. It was like reading something someone else had written and being embarrassed for them. I started in on the responses.

To: JDixon
From: RBrown
Re: I love you guys . . .
Date: 3/19

Jen,

Did you mean to send this? Are you all right?

Ravi

To: JDixon
From: CAlexander
Re: I love you guys . . .
Date: 3/19

Hey Jen,

Well, someone's having a good time in Vegas! I'll have what you're
having!

Love,
Carol

To: JDixon
From: AChang
Re: I love you guys . . .
Date: 3/19

Jennifer,

What does this mean? What baby? Is Laura pregnant? Please explain
yourself when you sober up.

Asami

To: JDixon
From: PTucci
Re: I love you guys . . .
Date: 3/19

Jen,

Holy shit! Did you send this to everyone? Are you okay? I'm going to call you.

Xo P

And of course, I still didn't have my phone, so I never got that call.

To: JDixon
From: SCobb
Re: I love you guys . . .
Date: 3/19

Jennifer

Still celebrating St. Patrick's Day are you?
There's no shame in clipping coupons! I do it all the time and it saves us tons of money.

Shirleen

The rest were pretty much the same . . . except for one.

To: JDixon

From: JJAikins

Re: I love you guys . . .

Date: 3/17

How DARE you single me out in your email! Everyone has been doing fun class birthday party things. The petting zoo was a big hit with the kids. BTW, animals poop, that's what they do.

JJ

I started out mortified, but by the time I finished reading the responses all I could do was laugh. No email from Sylvie Pike, so she hadn't seen it yet. I anticipated a big powwow when she did.

Janine came out to let us know that Rolly was resting comfortably and no immediate surgery was required.

"But he needs to see his doctor when we get back. Thank God we're flying home tomorrow."

"Today." It was now 3:30 in the morning.

"Oh my God, I didn't even realize. You guys, please go home and get some sleep. You are such good friends to stay this long."

"Are you sure?" Ron asked. "We don't mind hanging around in case you need something."

"Positive. Get the hell out of here." She gave Ron a dramatic hug then pulled me close and whispered, "Remember, what happens in Vegas stays in Vegas." With that she passionately kissed my cheek and walked back to the patient area.

I knew it!

✦ ✦ ✦

Rolly and Janine were gone, as were most of the people from their company retreat—including Cassie and Steve—but Ron and I stayed two more days with Max. We did a lot of the touristy stuff like

Madame Tussaud's and indoor skydiving and spent as much time as we could at the pool.

My cell phone finally arrived the day before we were leaving. For reasons unknown, Laura had sent it FedEx ground instead of overnight. I was happy to get it until I turned it on and had to endure it buzzing for the next ten minutes with updates and messages.

As we were waiting for a taxi to take us to the airport, Ron mentioned how glad he was that he'd never gone back to the tables after his big win, even though he really wanted to. He felt good about bringing his winnings home.

"Oh shit . . . shoot!" I said with a sideways glance at Max.

"What?"

"My mother gave me a hundred dollars to bet at the roulette table. I totally forgot."

"Well, it's too late now."

I grabbed the hundred out of my purse, put my phone in my back pocket, and threw my bags at Ron. "I'll be back in five minutes."

I dashed through the lobby to the casino and was out of breath by the time I found a roulette table that was active at nine in the morning. No one was playing, so I ran right up, pulled out my mother's hundred-dollar bill, tossed it on the table, and blurted, "Black twenty-two."

Apparently this is not standard protocol at the roulette table, if you can believe it. I got the stink eye from the croupier and the pit boss walked over with a security guard to see what the hell was going on.

"Please settle down, ma'am."

"I'm sorry! I have to make this bet. And my cab is waiting."

"Maybe you should just get in your cab, miss," the pit boss—who bore a striking resemblance to Vin Diesel—strongly suggested.

I realized I probably looked like a crazy person and was getting myself into trouble. The last place I wanted to end up was as someone's bitch in casino jail, so I took a breath and tried to act normal.

"I'm sorry. It's just my mother, who is a cancer survivor"—oh yes, I did play that card—"asked me to place this bet for her while I was here, and I completely forgot until right this minute and our cab is waiting to take us to the airport, but I just need to place this bet because I promised her. Please, I'm not some nutty gambler."

The croupier looked at Vin Diesel, who gave a slight nod. The dealer then turned to me.

"Do you want to bet the whole hundred?"

I sighed with relief. "Yes, please, on black 22."

She gave me two $50 chips, which I put on the 22 square; then she spun the wheel and dropped the little white ball.

I immediately felt relief. At least I'd done what I promised. My phone rang.

"Where are you?" Ron asked when I picked up.

"Sorry. I just placed the bet. I thought I was going to get arrested because I guess I looked like an insane person when I ran up to the table—"

"The cab is loaded up, so hurry," he interrupted me.

"Okay." I hung up and had started walking away when I heard a voice say, "Black 22!" I turned back, and the croupier lady was smiling at me.

"We have a winner!" she enthused. I was dumbfounded.

"You're kidding! Holy shit! I can't believe it." I was so happy that I was bringing home some winnings for Kay. I figured that I had probably doubled her money, but then the dealer shoved a large stack of chips at me.

"Is this mine?"

She nodded. "Would you like to place another bet?"

"How much did I win?" Adrenaline was flowing through me so quickly I was light-headed.

"Thirty-five hundred dollars."

"*What?*" I guess I said that a little too loudly because Vin Diesel was back giving me a dirty look.

"Ma'am, would you like to place another bet?" the dealer repeated.

I wanted to with every ounce of my being. I finally understood the gambler's high. I wanted to bet it all on every number all day long, so I could feel that pure bliss again and again. And honest to God, I think I might have if my phone hadn't buzzed at that moment with a text from my husband asking what the hell was taking so long.

I cashed out my chips and put thirty-five crisp hundred-dollar bills in my wallet. I couldn't wait to give them to my mother.

On the plane ride home, I crafted a conciliatory letter to my class. I mean, I hadn't said anything derogatory about anyone except myself, but I still felt I owed them some kind of explanation.

To: WRandazzo's Class
From: JDixon
Re: What Can I Say?
Date: 3/21

Hello my apparent besties,

What's that old saying? Some guys just can't handle Vegas. And I would be one of them.

My most sincere apologies for that free-form slam poetry over-share I sent you all a few days ago. I wish I had a better reason than "too much wine," but I don't. I'm sorry to have burdened you with my silly problems when I'm sure you have enough of your own. I do, however, still stand by my assertion that "pooper" is a funny word.

I should mention that the heart of the email—regarding class birthday parties—was not a drunken illusion, so please keep that in mind until the end of the year.

Onward,

Jen

21

It's two days until my birthday and I don't know whether to laugh or cry. I'm turning fifty-two and I'm going to be a grandmother.

"At least you'll be a hot grandma." Nina is trying to cheer me up this morning. "You'll be a GMILF!"

"You just wait. It's all a big joke until you turn forty-nine. What have you got, three years?"

"Uh, five, but thanks for knowing me so well. Sorry I can't be there for your birthday, but Chyna has a lacrosse tournament in Chattanooga."

"Oh please! It's not even a big birthday. I'm not planning on doing anything special, trust me."

My call waiting beeps in and I put Nina on hold.

"Hi, Mom, anything wrong?"

"No, sweetheart, but I was wondering if you could pick your father up at the club at one thirty? I would, but I promised Mary Minnis I would take her to her follow-up."

"Sure. You said one thirty?"

"Yes. Thanks, sweetheart, I'll call you later." She hangs up and I click back over to Nina.

"Sorry about that. It was Kay."

"Everything okay?"

"As far as I know."

"Speaking of Kay, I guess I won't see you until the walk."

"Have you raised your five hundred dollars?" I'm hoping she says no.

"I actually ended up with seven hundred and forty-five. And people are still donating."

"Show-off. I've only got the safety patrol money and a hundred from Ron's store. Oh, and twenty from my aunt Barbara."

"The cancan girl came through! So, what's the total?"

"Three hundred and sixty-five."

"Better get at it!"

"I know, I know."

"Listen, I gotta run, but give the girls and Max a hug for me. I can't wait to see Vivs with a bun in the oven!"

"She looks great, like she swallowed a small volleyball."

"God, I wish I had carried like that. I looked like I'd swallowed the whole volleyball team." She hangs up, cackling.

I hightail it upstairs to get dressed. I'm having an emergency pow-wow with guess who? But not about what you think. I'm convinced Sylvie Pike never saw my Vegas email, because it's been a month since I sent it and she has never said a word. But she did text me this morning that Sherlay DeJones had some kind of meltdown at safety patrol and we needed to meet with her.

It's a beautiful April morning and all I need is a light jacket. I love this time of year in KC so much. The trees and flowers are starting to bud, and everyone is out walking or on their bikes after months of hibernation. I'm in a great mood as I pull into the school parking lot with Billy Joel telling me to say goodbye to Hollywood.

As I'm walking around to the front of the school I'm startled by the sight of Homeless Mitch painting the trim on the outside windows. A few months ago, seeing him would have sent me into a mild panic attack but I've come leaps and bounds since then. Ever since I gave him the leftover bake-sale cookies and told him to have fun at the shelter, we have kind of a running joke. When I see him I always ask, "Hey, Mitch, having fun?" and he always has a snappy reply. Some of the highlights have been "It's better than taking a shower in a car wash" and "Better than trying to climb a tree in roller skates." Today is no different.

"Hey, Mitch, having fun?"

"It's better than getting slapped in the stomach with a wet fish." He grins.

"Are you working for the school?"

"Just odd jobs here and there. Didn't your mom tell you? She set it up for me."

Of course, she did. My mother is a tireless advocate for others. She even gave her roulette winnings to a battered-women's shelter. When I presented her with the thirty-five hundred-dollar bills, she was like a kid on Christmas morning.

"Oh yippee! Ray, look at this!" She fanned out the money in front of my dad.

"What are you going to do with it?" I asked them.

They looked at each other and said in unison, "Donate it."

And that's exactly what they did. I thought of about sixteen other things I would have done with it, but I'm sure the Friends of Yates Emergency Shelter for abused women is putting it to good use. I mean, who needs lipo?

"She didn't tell me, but I'm so glad she hooked you up," I tell Mitch, and head into the school. I meet Sylvie outside Principal Jackowski's office.

"She's in with him now" is how she greets me. Sylvie has her hair pulled into a messy bun today, so she looks all business.

"What happened?" What I really want to ask is "Why am I here?" I mean, am I supposed to be on Sherlay's disciplinary committee?

"All I know is she was at her post and around eight twenty-five she threw her vest and stop sign on the ground, sat down on the curb, and started hysterically crying. Thank God most of the kids were already in school. Mitch, the homeless guy that's always around, found her and brought her inside."

Huh, Homeless Mitch to the rescue again.

We sit in the chairs usually reserved for kids who have been sent to the principal's office and try to speculate what could be going on. My first guess is PMS.

Sylvie pooh-poohs the suggestion. "I think it's a little more serious than that."

"Really? On my worst day I could have Lizzie Bordened an entire town. A little crying is nothing."

Principal Jackowski's door opens and he asks us to join them.

Sherlay is slumped in one of the two chairs in front of his battered oak desk. Her blond hair looks like it hasn't seen a brush in a good long while. Sylvie takes the other chair and I lean against the wall like the bad cop in an interrogation room.

"Miss DeJones has tendered her resignation." Jackowski sounds so formal.

"Oh no! Sherlay, why?"

She just shakes her head. Jackowski answers for her.

"She just thinks it's time. She wants to get a fresh start."

Fresh start? She's twenty-three. How much fresher could she be?

"What about your grandmother?" I ask.

"She thinks it's a good idea too." Sherlay's eyes are swollen from crying.

"So we need to think about who is going to cover the morning shift for safety patrol till June." The always practical Sylvie states the obvious.

"Why don't you ladies take some time to discuss your options," Jackowski suggests as he stands up and points to the door (the universally acknowledged sign for "Get the hell out of my office").

We find a table in the cafeteria, which is thankfully empty this time of day.

"What happened?" Sylvie asks Sherlay kindly.

"Scott broke up with me." She sighs shakily.

"Were you guys serious?" I have to ask, because I know they dated a few times, but I didn't know they were in a relationship.

"I thought we were. He introduced me to his mother."

"Did he, though?" Sylvie says gently. "I thought you told me that you just showed up at his house when you knew she'd be there for Sunday dinner."

I can't believe how much Sylvie knows about their relationship. Sherlay wipes her nose on her sleeve and looks sheepishly at us.

"Well, he has dinner with her every week, and he never once invited me!"

A picture is beginning to take shape for me—a potentially over-eager Sherlay trying to close the deal too quickly on cute bachelor Scott Green.

"Is that why he broke up with you?" I ask, and am rewarded with a swift kick under the table from Sylvie. Who does she think she is, my husband?

"It doesn't matter," Sylvie says. "What matters now is what you're going to do. Any ideas?"

"My mom lives in Joplin. I thought I might go there."

"What about work?" I lob in.

She shrugs. "I only did this job to be close to Scott."

Well, that's nice to hear.

"I used to do hair. Maybe I'll find a job in a salon."

"You can always go back to school, sweetie. You might want to give that some thought," Sylvie suggests.

She shakes her head as she tears up. "School will just remind me of my Scott-man."

Oh God. My patience is running out. I draw the line at cute nick-names. I try to get the conversation back on point.

"So, when is your last day?"

"Today."

"Today? Can't you finish out the week?"

For this I get another kick under the table. Clearly, I don't know what an appropriate question is.

"We'll be fine. Don't worry. Just take care of yourself."

Sylvie gives Sherlay a one-armed hug and sends her on her way, toward an exciting future as a beautician in Joplin.

I turn to her. "Kick me again. See what happens."

"I know, sorry. I just didn't want you to say anything that might convince her to stay."

"You wanted her gone?" I'm surprised.

"God, yes! She's a little bit nuts, in case you didn't notice. We never vetted her properly before we gave her the job."

"Well, why would you have to? She's Marge's granddaughter. And she went to school here, didn't she?"

"Yeah, but we didn't know about her stalker tendencies."

"Why, because she showed up at Scott Green's house to meet his mother?"

"That wasn't even the half of it. They'd gone on a handful of dates—always dinner and a movie and nothing else. He liked her, but she wouldn't leave him alone. She would stop by his classroom every day and bring him hot chocolate."

"That bitch."

"Seriously, it was every single day, and half the time she'd be interrupting his class. He asked her to stop, but then she would just wait outside the classroom until first period was over."

"I can see how that would be annoying, but hardly stalker material."

"That was just the beginning. She would wait by his car after school, show up at his basketball games—"

"He plays basketball?"

"Some pickup game at the Y on Saturdays." She shrugs. "Anyway, she just kept showing up everywhere. He was getting a really bad feeling about her."

"Wait, how do you know so much about this?" I know Sylvie's the PTA president, but this seems to fall outside her job description.

"He goes to my church. And that's the other thing! Sherlay started coming to church just to see him. She isn't even Catholic," she added in a whisper. "He told her in March that he didn't want to see her anymore, but apparently she didn't get the hint until he went ape shit when she showed up for Sunday dinner last week."

"Was he going to report her?"

"I guess he could have, but technically she wasn't doing anything illegal. She didn't threaten him, she was just . . . ubiquitous." I want to tell her that was yesterday's word-a-day-calendar word, but I don't.

"I can't believe all this has been going on and you never said a word." I think back to Ladies' Night at TGI Friday's and realize that Sylvie's lips only loosen under the influence of alcohol.

"Well, now it's done, and we need to figure out what to do in the mornings for the rest of the year."

Oh, crap! We need two and a half months covered.

"The kids can do the mornings," I say with a confidence I don't feel.

"But we need an adult supervisor. Maybe you can make a parent schedule."

The thought of finding parents to cover the morning shift makes me want to join Sherlay in Joplin.

"You and I can cover it until you get a schedule in place." At that, Sylvie stands up. "I'll do tomorrow and you can do Friday."

Great. Safety patrol for my birthday.

✦ ✦ ✦

I have about an hour to kill before I need to pick my dad up from his monthly meeting at the Kiwanis Club, so I decide to pop into the nail salon across from school for a manicure.

I have never been to Cathy's Nails, mainly because I have a terrible biting habit. My mother has told me for years that if I get a manicure once a week my hands will look so nice that I won't want to bite them. Oh, Mom, you can't possibly understand the siren's call of a nail tip. It's like having a snack at the ready anytime, day or night.

So I rarely get manicures, but hey, it's birthday week and I have some time on my hands, so what the hell.

Cathy's Nails is small and cheerful and smells like acetone. There are two manicure stations and two foot baths in the back.

"Can I get a manicure?" I ask the only person in the room—a thin African American woman, probably around my age, sitting at the first station, flipping through *US Weekly*.

"Do you have an appointment?"

"No."

"Well, pick your color." She gestures to a kaleidoscopic row of polishes. In keeping with my personality, I choose a pinky beige.

"I've never been here before." For some reason I feel the need to share this with her.

"I can see that," she replies, looking at my hands. I look, too, and for the first time I see my mother's hands looking back at me. Just one more reason to hate getting older.

"Are you Cathy?" I ask as she attacks my nail beds.

"Yes" is all I get back.

"Not much of a chatty Cathy, are you?" I say to amuse myself.

She sighs and continues her assault on my cuticles. The silence is deafening.

"How long have you had this place?" Never let it be said that I don't know how to annoy someone.

"Twenty-two years."

"Wow, that's a long time."

She nods at my inane comment. I look around. The walls are painted a light yellow and adorned with pictures of beautiful women with great-looking nails. Right behind Cathy is the price list for services, from which I find out I will be paying $14 for my manicure and the pleasure of Cathy's company. A bargain at twice the price!

I also notice a homemade sign advertising an apartment for rent above the salon.

"How much are you renting the apartment for?" I ask as Cathy mercilessly digs dirt out from under my nails.

"Four hundred."

"What's it like?" I'm thinking Laura may want to check it out.

"Small," she replies. What a saleswoman!

"How small?"

She stops and looks at me. I can tell she was beautiful at one time, but life has clearly given her an ass-kicking and now she just looks tired.

"You want to see it?"

"I might bring my daughter back to look at it." She nods like she's heard that one before.

We're on to polish now and I have to say that, despite her lack of any notable social skills, Cathy really knows what she's doing. Even my crappy hands look great when she's done. I sit under the dryer for a few minutes and take the time to count my blessings, as my mother would say. I'm not very good at personal reflection, but today I take a stab at taking stock. Wonderful husband who's trying like crazy to make life better for us, three great kids in varying stages of annoying me, a mother on the mend, a father in love, good friends to count on, and of course the love of my life . . . Carmen. All in all, I have it pretty damn good.

And then I remember safety patrol.

✦ ✦ ✦

"I can do a day if you want," Saint Ron offers after my thirty-minute tirade while we're getting ready for bed.

"Want to do my birthday?"

"Sure. When is it?"

I punch his arm.

"Ouch! Okay, Friday it is. Anything I should know?"

"Don't let anyone get hit by a car."

"Check. Oh! I talked to Rolly today."

"How is he?"

"He sounds good. I think he really had a wake-up call."

"I think we all did," I say. Ron has been much less of a workaholic since Vegas and he's home for dinner almost every night.

"You know, he stopped drinking. And so did Janine."

"And it took you until nine thirty at night to tell me this? That's front-page news."

"Sorry. I didn't want to say anything in front of Max."

"Wow. I wonder how it's affecting them."

Ron shrugs. "It's not like they had to go into rehab or anything."

"Did you guys talk about anything else?" My question is leading but not specific, because I promised Ron I'd stop asking about the business. He said if there was any news he'd tell me and asking was just annoying the crap out of him.

"We did. They're coming to town this weekend and want to have dinner Saturday night."

I'm not sure how I feel about this. We haven't seen them since Las Vegas. Ron and I have discussed the alleged proposition many times. He swears he didn't hear the same thing I did. It's so frustrating. It reminds me of the time I had jury duty. Three days of testimony and when I sat down with my fellow jurors I couldn't believe we had been sitting at the same trial. Now I understand why juries have things read back to them. We could have used a stenographer in Vegas.

"Okay. Do you know where we're going?"

"Not yet. He's going to let me know. And before your head explodes, let me just tell you we didn't talk business."

"Who's asking?" I slide into bed and thank God he said something. Otherwise I would have been brooding for the next hour.

There's a knock at the door and Laura's voice saying, "Can I come in?"

"Sure, sweetie." I sit up and put a pillow behind my back.

"I just got off the phone with Jeen."

Now that's a name we haven't heard in a few weeks.

"How's he doing?" I ask.

She shrugs. "Good. His band is going back out on the road and—"

"No," I say as emphatically as I can.

"No, what?"

"No, you're not going out on the road with them." I look at Ron for backup, but he's pretending to read his emails.

"Who says I want to go back on the road with them?" Laura is genuinely affronted by my suggestion. "And by the way, Mom, I'm twenty-two. I can go anywhere I want."

"Then why are you telling us if you're not planning to go?"

"I was going to ask you if I could have them over for a good-bye dinner next Friday, but jeez, I don't know if I want to anymore."

"So, are you guys together?"

"No." She sighs. "Everything feels different now that we're home."

"So, why do you want to have a dinner for him?"

"It's not just for him, it's for the whole band. I got really close with them on the road. And Jeen and I still want to be friends."

I feel bad about jumping to conclusions, so I make it easy on her.

"Well then, of course you can. If you want, Ron and I will take Max out for the night, so you can have the place to yourselves."

Ron finally looks up and raises one eyebrow at me.

"She's not fifteen anymore," I tell him, because I know he's thinking about the party Laura threw for herself when we went away one weekend and left Vivs in charge. Ron looks at her.

"I don't want to see any empty Kahlúa bottles or vanilla milkshake cups. And this time *you* clean up the vomit."

Laura rolls her eyes. "Am I ever going to live that down?"

"Not a chance. It's already in the speech I'm giving at your wedding."

22

To: Safety Patrol People
From: JDixon
Re: Morning Patrol
Date: 5/15

Hello, fellow sufferers!

I have glad tidings on this rainy morning. After a considerable (some would say over-the-top) vetting process we have hired a full-time crossing guard.

Mitch Jones will be donning the neon orange first thing tomorrow morning. We are so happy to have him.

The fifth-grade patrollers will finish out the year with Mr. Jones supervising, and starting in September he will be the official patrol patroller.

For the lucky parents still on the schedule to supervise, you are off the hook. Go buy a lottery ticket, 'cause this is your lucky day.

If you have any questions, by all means direct them to PTA president Sylvie Pike. My work here is done.

Jen

I'm so happy to be writing this email and to have the safety patrol monkey off my back. I actually have Ron to thank for the whole thing, although he hates to be reminded.

The night before my birthday, we ate leftovers at home. Max and I had the remains of skillet tacos from the night before and Ron had the rest of the chicken souvlaki he'd had for lunch at the Greek place near his store earlier in the week.

The next morning, while I slept in, he got Max to school and supervised the morning shift of patrollers. Or should I say, he tried. Apparently just after Ron got to his post, he had what he described as a bathroom emergency. "Urgent diarrhea," he called it. Is there any other kind? He didn't want to leave the one safety patrol kid who showed up (Chloe's mom later informed me that she'd let her sleep in after a grueling evening of rehearsing for her dance recital) so he asked Mitch, who was painting the posts on the school entrance, to keep an eye on things until he got back.

He never got back.

A fourth-grader found him passed out in the boys' bathroom with his pants around his ankles and a huge mess in front of and behind him. Poor kid. He can never un-see that. The school called an ambulance and then called me. Long story short, Ron had food poisoning (most likely the chicken) and we spent the day in the ER.

I didn't find out about Homeless Mitch's involvement until I got an urgent text from Sylvie Pike.

Where are you? And why did Mitch do safety patrol with Chloe? Please text me back!!

So I did.

I'm in the hospital with Ron.

Could I have been more specific? Probably. Did I give a royal rip in that moment? Nope. Ron couldn't move his head without throwing up. And when there was nothing left to throw up, he violently dry-heaved. He was on one IV for hydration and another for antibiotics.

Of course, this little detour canceled my birthday plans and the dinner we had on the books with Rolly and Janine. It took Ron a good three days at home to get fully back on his feet.

So tonight, almost a month later, is do-over night. Ron is taking us to my favorite BBQ place, Q39, and my mouth is already watering for their short ribs.

Vivs, Laura, and Max are with us as we settle around a table. Vivs is in the best months of pregnancy—she's past the exhausted stage and is now in the cute-pregnant-girl stage. She looks so healthy.

"Do they have garlic bread?" Max asks as he looks at the menu.

"I don't think so, buddy," Laura answers, ruffling his hair. Max has loved having his sister home. His obnoxious behavior has all but disappeared and he is so much more pleasant to be around. I never realized what a stabilizing force Laura is in our household.

"We have some news," Vivs announces after we order.

"Oh? What's that?" I ask.

"Laura and I are moving in together!"

"What?" There goes my stabilizing force. "Please tell me you're kidding."

"We're not kidding," Vivs assures me.

"But you two fight like cats in a bag. How are you going to live together without a referee?"

"That was when we were younger," Laura protests. "It's going to be great. I'm going to help Vivs raise the baby."

"Can I live with you too?" Max asks.

"Okay, stop the bus." I have too many thoughts running through my head and I need a minute to reboot.

Ron starts with the basics. "Have you found a place?"

"We found an apartment at the Arcadia and it's perfect, but we're going to need one of you to cosign the lease. If you do, we can move in at the end of the month."

"The Arcadia is nice. Can you afford it?" Ron continues the questions calmly while I try to find my voice.

"The rent is a thousand dollars a month, so five hundred each," Vivs answers.

"Mom, can I live there too?" Max asks again.

"No," I answer harshly.

"You can come see us anytime you want," Laura assures him.

"You don't even have a job," I sputter out to her, then turn to Vivs. "And you! You'll be going on maternity leave. How do you expect to pay the rent?"

Our BBQ feast arrives at this moment and the table is silent while our waiter puts our food down.

"Can I get you guys anything else?" he asks.

"More water, please," Vivs tells him and he turns away.

"Mom, we've got it worked out. Jenny Craig pays for maternity leave. When I go back I'll work days, and Laura got a job at J. Gilbert's in the evenings, so we'll have it covered. And we're hoping you'll look after the baby a few days a week, too."

A few days a week?

"What's the job?" I direct to Laura.

"In the kitchen. I'll be training to sous chef. You know how much I love cooking."

I remain silent, so Laura adds, "I need this, Mommy. I can't live at home. I want my own place."

"With your sister and a baby," I point out. "You guys don't have any idea how hard life is with an infant."

"Yes, we do! We were there for Max, remember?"

And they were. The girls were teenagers when Max came on the scene and they used to fight over who got to do everything for him . . . except change poopy diapers. It was like having two full-time mother's helpers. How could I have forgotten that? I had imagined that Vivs would move back home and we would all be one big happy family. I should have realized that my independent spirit would have her own ideas.

"So, I guess it's a done deal," I say, defeated.

"As long as you cosign our lease." It comes out as a plea from Vivs.

"Of course we will," Ron answers.

After an awkward silence I sigh loudly. "Well, you're going to need some furniture."

✦ ✦ ✦

"Having fun?" I ask No Longer Homeless Mitch as he puts on his safety patrol vest and grabs the walkie-talkie.

"Why yes, I am." He smiles, giving me the first ever straight answer to that question.

"I'm so glad this worked out."

"Me too," he says. "Didn't think it was going to, for a while there."

He ain't kidding. The background check he went through was something akin to a colonoscopy. I totally understand why the school wanted to be thorough, but really, was the lie-detector test necessary?

After Mitch came to Ron's rescue that day, I got royally chewed out by Sylvie and Principal Jackowski for circumstances that were beyond my control. I countered their ire with a suggestion that they consider making Mitch the full-time patrol patroller. At first, they rejected the suggestion outright and I was going to give up, but then I thought, *Jennifer Rose, what would your mother do?* At that, I pushed harder and countered every argument they had. He was already doing odd jobs at the school, and yes, he was homeless, but if we paid him he could rent the room above Cathy's Nail Salon across the street. I really sounded like Kay in that room and it felt so good. They finally agreed to do a strong background check.

What they found was the not uncommon tale of a forty-five-year-old veteran who had done two tours in Afghanistan and received a Purple Heart for taking shrapnel in his left knee—hence the limp. He came home on leave to take care of his father, Carl, who had been diagnosed with liver cancer, but never went back so he was considered AWOL and given a dishonorable discharge.

With no health insurance, Mitch took care of his father the best he could, but they were evicted from their apartment when they were four months behind on the rent. Carl died in the emergency room of Osawatomie State Hospital three days later. Mitch fell into a huge depression and spent four months in a psychiatric hospital. All his identification was stolen while he was there, and he has spent the last couple of years trying to get it back. He sleeps at the shelter run by the church my parents go to and is known as a problem solver within that community. He doesn't panhandle and he started hanging out on the park bench across from William Taft because he sometimes does odd jobs for the lady who runs the nail salon (our friend Cathy!). He loves kids, and kids seem to gravitate toward him. These days that isn't necessarily a plus, what with increased awareness of sexual abuse, but they decided to give him a shot on a trial basis and today is day one.

I'm supposed to hang out with him for the first two days and show him the ropes. I can't imagine what I could possibly tell him that he doesn't already know, but it's a nice day, so what the heck.

The Chloes, who are on morning duty as well, cheerfully put on their vests and grab their new stop signs. My team is looking good.

"How are the new digs?" I ask Mitch as we all head out to the corner of 12th and Hayward.

"Big improvement from my last place."

"Is Cathy cool?"

"Cool?" He laughs. "More like ice cold. But it's okay. I've known her for a while—I painted that salon two times. She knows I'm no trouble. But now that I live there, she thinks she has a free handyman." His big smile tells me he doesn't mind.

As I'm watching Mitch and the Chloes, I see Ron and Max in Bruce Willis pulling into the parking lot, so I walk over. Max jumps out the second the car stops and dodges my attempt to give him a hug.

"Bye, Mom!" he yells as he sprints toward his friends. I turn to Ron on the driver's side.

"What's up, good-lookin'?"

"He's full of beans this morning. I couldn't get him to eat breakfast."

"Spring fever," I say knowingly. "The kids are all nuts this time of year." I can't believe that we are but a month away from summer vacation. This year Max is going to a sleep-away camp with Draper and Zach T. I still don't know how Alison Lody talked me into it, but it seems my son can't wait to get away from me. He's so excited. Ron thinks he's going to have the best two weeks of his life. I think we'll be lucky if he changes his underwear even once.

"Don't forget we have early dinner plans," I remind my husband.

"Yup. I'm looking forward to seeing them."

"Me too." I kiss Ron and he drives off. But am I? We haven't seen Rolly and Janine since Las Vegas. I'm still not convinced I'm wrong about what happened there. I guess I'll know in a few hours. I'm meeting Janine for a spin class at four, and we are meeting the boys for pizza at six. And here's the big news . . . even Max is invited! Something has definitely shifted in the Schraders' world.

✦ ✦ ✦

Carmen has brought her A game today as usual. We are doing a medium jog off the saddle to "American Pie" by Don McLean, adding in tap-backs and push-ups during the chorus. I was a bit late for the class, so I sneaked in the back and haven't seen Janine yet.

As we cool down and stretch to Bruno Mars's "It Will Rain," Carmen randomly gives me a shout-out.

"Where's my girl Jen Dixon?"

I raise my hand from the back row.

"Well, happy belated birthday, woman!" At this she plays Stevie Wonder's "Happy Birthday" and a very sweaty Janine walks over with a cupcake and a candle. The whole class applauds me as I make a wish, blow it out, and hug my friend. I generally don't like surprises, but this one is so unexpectedly great that all I can do is smile ear to ear.

"Oh my God. I really didn't see that coming," I tell Janine as we walk out of the spin room, still toweling off.

"I knew you'd never tell anyone it was your birthday and I think it's nice to have people celebrate you."

"I wouldn't want it every day, but it was kind of cool to get a shout-out!"

We walk to the juice bar at the front of the gym and grab our usual green juice.

"It's so good to see you," I tell Janine once we're sitting down. "You look great."

She rolls her eyes. "Well, thank God there are *some* benefits to clean living. Most of it sucks."

"Ron told me you guys stopped drinking. I finally found sober Janine!"

"She's no fun, trust me."

"I'll be the judge of that. It's nice of you to quit in solidarity with Rolly."

She shakes her head while she's guzzling her juice. "I didn't do it for him. I did it for me! After his heart attack, our doctor insisted I get a checkup. My blood test came back with some kind of early indicator that my liver was having problems. I had to fess up about how much we enjoy a glass of wine, and he strongly suggested I cut way back. Since Rolly can't drink, I figured misery loves company, so I stopped."

I'm fascinated. "Just like that?"

"It wasn't easy, believe me."

I feel like there's a lot she isn't saying.

"Thank you again for my cupcake."

"Well, I figured I owed you after Vegas."

Here it comes! I play it cool. "What do you mean?"

"My God, you guys were great when Rolly collapsed. I don't know what would have happened if you hadn't been there."

"Oh, that." I'm trying hard to hide my disappointment.

"Yes, *that*. What else would it be?"

Screw it. I have suffered long enough.

"Janine, we're women of the world, so I'm going to ask you something straight up."

"Okay." She smirks. I'm sure I sound like an idiot.

"In Vegas, were you trying to get us to swing with you and Rolly?"

"What?" She bursts out laughing.

"Oh . . . I'm . . . I'm sorry . . ." I stumble.

Then she continues: "You have to ask? Of course, we were." She can't stop howling.

While she's having a good old cackle about it, I feel less than satisfied. This should be my "I knew it" victory lap.

"So, wait, stop laughing. Tell me what was going on. Did you really think we'd do it?"

"Oh, who knows? This new, sober me is having a hard time processing the whole idea to begin with."

"So, it was more of an alcohol-induced notion?"

"Uh, yeah." She shakes her head and wipes the lingering sweat off her face. "Well, mostly. I'd be lying if I said I didn't think about it sober, but Rolly was a really hard sell. I think me talking about it that night at the restaurant is what gave him his heart attack."

"Do you think me sitting on his lap pushed him over the edge?"

"Probably," Janine deadpanned, then smiled when she saw the look on my face. "Jen, I'm kidding. His valves were clogging up for months. The doctor said it was just a matter of time."

The hum of the gym is all around us, but I feel like I'm alone in a cocoon with her.

"What does Ron think?" Janine asks.

"It never even occurred to him. He thinks I'm crazy."

"I figured." She considers me for a moment. "Since we're asking tough questions, I have one for you."

"Fire away."

"Are you guys only friends with us so Rolly will invest in your business?"

"Oh my God, no! We love you guys."

She raises an eyebrow at me, so I backtrack a bit.

"I mean, at first we thought, *Hey, maybe they'd be good people to invest,* but when that didn't happen, we still loved spending time with you guys."

"And what about now that we're not drinking?"

I shrug. "I guess we'll find out at dinner tonight. If it's boring, you may have to consider going back on the booze."

"Definitely. To hell with my liver. Keeping you amused is priority numero uno."

We shower at the gym and head over to Minsky's, our favorite pizza joint. I'm surprised when I first see Rolly—he's much thinner and seems a bit frail. But his smile when he sees me shows the old Rolly is still there.

"You look good, old man." I give him a big hug.

He blushes. "Thanks. You too."

They both hug Max warmly and insist that he sit between them. He's happy to oblige.

"So, what brings you guys to town—business?" I ask after we have ordered a couple of summer salads, a BBQ chicken pizza (low-sodium for Rolly), and a Papa Minsky.

"Nope. We really just came to see you guys. I'm cutting way back on the business. Nate and Katie are taking over a lot of my duties, so I can lower my stress level."

Nate and Katie are two of his three kids. His third, Grant, is a lawyer.

"I'm glad they're stepping up for you."

"Oh, they've wanted to for quite a while. I'm still not ready to be put out to pasture, but I'm glad to hand some of the day-to-day headaches over to them."

"Isn't your walk for breast cancer coming up?" Janine asks me. I can't believe she remembers. It's a good bet we were drunk when I told her about it.

"Yes! Oh, God. It's in less than two weeks. I still need to get sponsors. Anyone have twenty bucks they can spare?" I say this half jokingly, but I'm not at all surprised when Rolly takes up the torch.

"I'd love to sponsor you! How about two hundred dollars?"

"Oh, Rolly, that's way too much. Really." I can't help but think that if he comes through, my fund-raising worries will be over.

"Nonsense. It's for a great cause. Where's your donation page?"

I text him the information and he nods to Janine. "Can you take care of this tomorrow, Tootsie?"

"You bet."

"Thank you so much!" I'm always amazed by people who can just give this amount of money away without even thinking about it. Must be nice.

My eyes meet Ron's and I see a little sadness in them. I'm guessing he's finally giving up on the idea of Rolly rescuing his business. I reach for his hand and give it a squeeze. I wish I could make it all right for him.

✦ ✦ ✦

"So, are we in financial ruin?" I ask half joking as we drive home. Max has his headphones on, so it's okay to talk.

"Not quite. But my dream of being a yoga studio titan is fading fast."

"I'm sorry, babe."

"I still think it's a good idea."

"Do you think he was ever considering investing?"

"I really don't know. He was so interested every time I talked about it, and he had great advice. But I called him the day the bank rejected me. If he wanted to invest, that would have been the time. I should have seen it then, but I wasn't ready to give up hope."

"Maybe it's for the best. No chance of ruining a good friendship."

23

To: Mrs. Randazzo's Class
From: JDixon
Re: Bowling
Date: 5/22

Hey there, parents of almost fourth-graders!

I wanted to give you a heads-up before we scatter for Memorial Day weekend that the third grade (yup, all of them) will be going bowling on Wednesday, May 26th. Why, you ask? Well, my best guess is that by then, Razzi will have run out of things to teach them and they'll need something to do to kill time until the last day of school.

Thanks to the Wolffs, who have connections at the bowling alley (I find it's better not to ask), our babies will be able to bowl to their hearts' content for the bargain basement price of $5 . . . shoes and snack included! They should bring the money with them on the morning of the trip and yes, Jackie, I will remind you again before the big day.

So . . . who's up for a nice quiet morning of bowling? I will be taking a hard pass on this one because this particular activity really isn't up my *alley. (Thank you, I'm here all week.) But we'll need three volunteers and I'd like to see a dad or two step up to the plate for this final outing.*

While I have you, the end-of-year gift for Razzi is going to be unbreakable. Could you please ask your child to write down two things they loved the most about being in her class this year. They can feel free to get creative and draw a picture as well. Please have them do it on an 8½-by-11 piece of paper in portrait mode (aka the tall way, not the wide way). I need these ASAP. I know I should have asked a couple of weeks ago but truthfully, I forgot. So, for once my lack of planning becomes your urgent problem. Welcome to my world.

Find me at pickup before the holiday weekend, and once I have them all, I will go to Staples and make some kind of book that she will no doubt treasure for the rest of her life.

As always, response times blah blah blah . . .

Jen

I can tell my enthusiasm for class mom-ing is waning in these final days of school. But I don't feel too guilty. I'm whistling into the wind most of the time anyway.

Big weekend ahead! The Susan G. Komen is this Sunday and, as luck would have it, Vivs and Laura are moving in together on Monday.

"I can't believe you found movers to work on Memorial Day," I said when they told me.

"We didn't. We figured you guys would help, and maybe a couple of guys from the store."

I sighed and silently wished I lived on whatever planet my daughters do.

"Ron would have to pay his guys time and a half to work a holiday, so you might want to hit up some of your guy friends to help with the heavy stuff." They don't really have that much to move, thank God.

The phone rings and I see it's my mother. My heart sinks. We finally told her about Vivs, and she has been calling me nonstop for days with all her "thoughts." I brace myself for another fulmination (word-a-day-calendar word!).

"Hi, Mom."

"Oh, Jennifer, I'm so glad you're home." Her voice sounds strained. "I have some terrible news."

"What is it?" I've gone from zero to full panic in record time.

"Your aunt Barbara died."

"Oh!" I'm a little ashamed to admit that I'm relieved it isn't my father. "How? When?"

"Yesterday. She was coming out of a grocery store and just dropped dead. They said she had a brain hemorrhage."

"Oh my God, that's awful. I'm so sorry. How did you find out?"

"Her lawyer called your father. He's listed as the next of kin. He's very upset."

"I'm sure he is. Will there be a funeral?"

"According to the lawyer, she didn't want one. She probably didn't want to spend the money. She's being cremated and wants her ashes thrown into some volcano on Maui."

"Haleakala?"

"That's the one."

I decide not to share with my mother that Number 6 on my bucket list is to go to the top of Haleakala, before sunrise, and ride down on a bike. I read about it on a travel website years ago and it sounded amazing. Aunt Barbara sure knew how to go out in style.

"So, the lawyer is going to call you. I guess Barb left you a little something in her will."

"Oh God, you don't think it's her cats, do you?"

This actually makes my mother laugh. "I hope not, for your sake! No, it's probably an old piece of jewelry or something."

"It doesn't matter. I can't believe she even thought of me. Hey, give my love to Dad and tell him I'll call him later."

"I'm sure he'd like that. Bye."

✦ ✦ ✦

Sunday morning, I have a good carbo-loaded breakfast because I've decided to attempt the 5K run before I walk the mile with the Holy Rollers. Sign-in starts at two o'clock down at the Black & Veatch headquarters, so I spend my morning doing light stretches and getting my head in the game, as Garth would say. He, Nina, and Chyna arrived yesterday morning and it feels like old times. Nina and the suddenly tall and gorgeous Chyna have raised a combined total of $1,638. They'll be doing the walk; Garth is going to run with me.

We all head over to the registration table on Lemar and are greeted by a sea of pink. People from all over KC are sporting vibrant pink T-shirts with various logos on them—a team name or some kind of F U to cancer. Tears spring to my eyes at the sight of so many women and men coming out in support of ending this horrible disease that nearly took my mom.

It's warmer than usual for this time of year so I peel off my favorite Lululemon jacket to reveal the light-pink team T-shirt my mother had made for all of us. On the front, "Holy Rollers" is superimposed in white over a dark-pink awareness ribbon. On the back it says, "Even the Hand of God Is Giving Cancer the Finger."

After we register, we find our group and there are a ton of hugs, mostly for Nina and Chyna. We have quite an impressive group. With my crew, plus Peetsa, Ravi, Asami, and Alison from school and all of mom's chemo-sabes and church friends, the Holy Rollers are twenty-five strong and have raised almost $16,000. The power of kindness never ceases to amaze me. Fresh tears start streaming down my face.

"Are you okay?" Laura puts her arm around me.

"Yes, baby, thank you. It's just all a little overwhelming, isn't it?"

"I can't believe how many people are still affected by breast cancer. You'd think they'd find a cure."

"They're trying."

"Ready to do this?" Garth approaches me, decked out in his running shorts and pink T-shirt. He looks like he's gained a bit of weight. I guess the desk job doesn't give him as much time to exercise.

"Let's go." I kiss Laura. "See you at the walk."

"Don't let me slow you down," I tell Garth as we join everyone at the starting line.

"I'm here to run with you, not make the time trials. Having any mud run flashbacks?"

"You and me at the starting line . . . absolutely. Good times."

Over the loudspeaker, the announcer says that the timed runners should get to the front.

"No thank you," I tell no one in particular. Garth laughs.

Soon enough the untimed runners are encouraged to get under way. To my surprise, Alison shows up by my side, with tears in her eyes.

"There was a time I couldn't imagine I'd be running anywhere, let alone something like this."

I take her hand. "I'm so glad you are."

"Are you guys ready?" Garth asks. He taps his Fitbit and off we go!

I haven't run since I started spinning and I quickly remember why, because my left knee starts to twinge after the first kilometer. Damn it! I say nothing and work through the pain. The good news is my cardio is strong. At least I'm not out of breath. But by the fourth kilometer Alison has pulled ahead, so I tell Garth my knee is hurting, and he makes me walk the last part of the run. I'm not alone. Lots of ambitious souls are taking it easy on the final stretch; however, I think most of them are survivors. I have no such excuse.

I suck it up long enough to jog across the finish line and give

Garth a high five. He hasn't even broken a sweat. The Holy Rollers are waiting for us.

"Good job, guys!" Nina enthuses.

I start my excuses before anyone even asks. "My knee gave out."

Max and Ron come over and hand me water. The walk is about to begin, and hundreds of people are gathering to listen to instructions and get some inspiration.

As the sea of pink starts to move, I find myself beside Peetsa. I haven't seen much of her since she started her new job selling Hyundais. I put my arm through hers and thank her for coming.

"Are you kidding? I'd do anything for you. And who knows, I might meet a guy here."

"Yes, a breast cancer walk really is the place. Good thinking."

"Did I tell you I had a date?"

"What? No, you did not!! What the hell?"

She laughs. "I love telling you things. You are the best audience in the world."

"Well, tell me about this, please!" I practically shout.

"I can tell you it was epically bad. And if this is what dating is like these days, I'm going to die alone."

"What happened?"

She lets out a frustrated growl. "I met him when I went to get an outdoor light fixture at Home Depot. I thought he worked there because he was so helpful, but it turned out he was just picking up mulch and I caught his eye."

"Continue," I encourage her.

"We had a good laugh about me thinking he was a salesman and ended up having a soda at the little snack shack. His name is Dave; he's divorced and has two sons, both in high school."

"So far so good."

"That's what I thought, but then—"

At this moment women all around us start chanting, "Cancel Cancer! Cancel Cancer!" so loudly that we have to stop talking. I'm dying to hear about her date, but it can wait. We raise our voices and

join in. I catch up to my mother and settle in beside her. She is glowing. This is Kay in her element. Not only helping people, but leading others to help as well.

I put my mouth right to her ear. "Congratulations, Mom. This is
a big hit!"

"Thank you for all your help, sweetheart. I'm really proud of you.
Between this and what you did for Mitch, I feel like you're really getting the hang of it."

"Of what?" I yell.

"Of caring," she says simply, and squeezes my hand.

✦ ✦ ✦

The after-party, if you will, is at my house. Everyone has chipped in
and we're having a big barbecue, with Ron as grill master. People
are eating the dogs and burgers as fast as he can crank them out.

I finally corner Peetsa and ask her to finish her story.

"So, he asks me out for the next Friday—two days ago," she continues as we settle into lawn chairs. "I didn't want him to know where
I live yet, so I said I'd meet him at the restaurant."

"Where?"

"Outback Steakhouse."

"Okay, not bad."

"He's thirty minutes late."

"Okay, bad. Did he say why?"

"He blamed the traffic." She shrugs.

"Could be true."

"Right, so I don't give him any attitude. I'd already ordered a
glass of wine and I was relaxed, so whatever, right?"

"Good," I tell her.

"He asks me if I have a drinking problem."

"Excuse me?"

"Ya. He's like"—she lowers her voice—"'You couldn't wait for
me before you ordered a drink?' I told him I waited fifteen minutes
and then felt like an idiot sitting at the table alone."

"Right. Of course you ordered a drink."

"Then he was like, 'My ex-wife is an alcoholic, so if you've got any of that going on the date ends now.'"

"You're lying." My eyes are about to pop out of my head.

"I wish I were. I threw my wine in his face and walked out."

"You did not!"

"No, I didn't, but I thought about it."

We are both laughing when Ron interrupts us and hands me my phone. "It's ringing," he tells me.

"Shit! Sorry." Annoyed, I look at the phone and some weird number is on the screen.

"Hello?" I stick my finger in my ear, so I can hear properly.

"Jennifer Dixon?"

"Yes."

"My name is Kale Ho. I'm the executor for Barbara Howard's estate." He sounds like a radio announcer for a funeral home.

"Oh! Hello." I move toward a quiet corner of the backyard. "My mother said you'd be calling."

"I'm sorry to bother you on a long weekend, but I just wanted to touch base. I'm very sorry for your loss."

"Thank you. Truthfully, I didn't know her very well. We were more pen pals than anything."

"Well, that's surprising, considering that you were one of only two people she mentioned in her will."

"I'm surprised, too," I assure him.

"It was your aunt's final wish to have her ashes thrown into Haleakala."

"Yes, my mother mentioned that."

"Did she mention that Ms. Howard wanted you to be the person to throw her ashes in?"

My heart leaps. I'm going to Hawaii!

"No, she didn't. I'm honored." I pause, wondering if Aunt Barb left money for a plane ticket. If she didn't, my chances of going were slim to none, and slim just left town. I ask the lawyer.

"Not that I know of. I believe she expected you to use the money that she has left you."

"Oh. Okay." I'm silently hoping it will be enough. I don't even want to imagine the look on Ron's face when I tell him I need to go to Hawaii.

"She left part of her estate to the animal shelter in Maui that is now taking care of her cats for as long as they live."

"I'm so glad they're being taken care of." I quietly thank God she didn't leave them to me. I'm gazing at my backyard and admiring the view. I can see Max trying to get Ron to let him turn the hamburgers. Vivs is sitting with my father, sharing a joke. And people are just enjoying the beauty of the evening. I realize for the first time in a while that I am perfectly content.

"What she left *you* is a one-time stipend of seven hundred dollars."

"That's so nice," I say absently, wondering if there's any rosé left.

"Yes, it's very nice."

"I'm sorry, what?"

"I said it *is* very nice. That's a life-changing amount of money."

Well, that's a bit of an exaggeration, I think. "I'm pretty sure I'll be spending the whole seven hundred just to get to Hawaii."

"Ms. Howard left you seven hundred *thousand* dollars."

"What?" I must be hallucinating. "That's not possible. My aunt was on a fixed income."

"That is true. But she also owned five thousand shares of Apple stock."

I look for some place to sit down. There isn't a chair nearby, so I sink to the grass.

"Mrs. Dixon?"

"Yes?" I'm crying as I look across my backyard and focus on my husband. "How did she come to have that much stock?"

"I believe she started buying it back in 1980. I wish I had. I'm going to send you some papers to fill out. This isn't a complicated estate, so we should be able to close it out within a few months."

"Thank you, Mr. . . ." I've forgotten his name.

"Ho. Kale Ho. I'll be in touch soon."

I sit with my phone in my lap for a good five minutes before Nina comes over and asks if I'm okay. I don't even know how to answer her.

24

To: Mrs. Randazzo's Class
From: JDixon
Re: As they say in Hollywood, that's a wrap.
Date: 6/04

Greetings, fellow parents,

And just like that, it's over. We are on to fourth grade. Kudos to all of you for making it through another year of elementary school. It was touch and go last week when we had to calculate radius and diameter in the math homework, but I got through it . . . barely.

Razzi has asked me to remind you to turn in all textbooks. I believe she's still missing five math and twelve science books, so get your little nerds to hand them over.

Congratulations to Ali Burgess for taking the top spot in email response times this year. A Starbucks gift card is waiting for you on Razzi's desk.

Don't forget, tomorrow is the third-grade swan song. The last dance. The final jam, if you will. We have been assigned the left half of

> *the field beside the parking lot as the site of our shindig. I know, not the best location, especially since we'll be playing softball. My suggestion is to park on the street if you don't want your car dented.*
>
> *And that, my friends, is that. Thanks for another interesting year. (Most of) you helped make it much less annoying than usual.*
>
> *Aloha!*
>
> *Jen Dixon, Class Mom*

I always have mixed feelings when I write my final letter. There is relief, of course, but there is also something close to pure joy. I'm fine with both.

I send the email, then run upstairs to continue packing. We're taking off for Maui the day after tomorrow and I've changed my mind a dozen times about what I'm going to wear when I throw Aunt Barbara into Haleakala. I want to look nice, but I'm also planning for us to bike down the volcano afterward. I think I'm going to go with Peetsa's idea of bike shorts and tank under a loose-fitting dress. That way I can throw the dress into my backpack after the ceremony. I've written a little speech that I'll give before I sprinkle her ashes.

I still can't believe I'm going with Ron and Max. Without the inheritance there's no way we would ever be able to take a trip like this. I think my parents would have wanted to come, too, but my dad has really slowed down this past year and there is no way Kay would go without him. He asked me to take lots of pictures, so he can see everything when we get back.

Ron was still standing at the grill when I got off the phone with Mr. Ho, so I walked over to him and whispered in his ear, "Aunt Barbara left me seven hundred thousand dollars." After his initial responses of "Yeah, right" and "That's not funny," he kept asking me over and over if I was sure.

"I mean, are you *really* sure?" he whispered for the fourth time. "No offense, but sometimes your hearing isn't the best."

"What?" I said. (That joke never gets old.)

As we were intensely whispering, I noticed we were getting some curious looks from our guests.

"What are you two plotting?" my mother demanded.

I needed a distraction, so I blurted out the first thing that came into my head.

"Karaoke!" I announced excitedly. I was met with unmistakable groans. Undeterred, I dragged out Max's karaoke machine and diverted everyone with a good old sing-along. It was a slow start but once I busted out my go-to song, "Tik Tok" by Kesha, the tide definitely turned. And let me just say there wasn't a dry eye in the house when my mother and her chemo-sabes sang the post-cancer anthem "Fight Song." It was a great party.

My parents stayed to help clean up, meaning that they sat on the couch apologizing for not helping. I told them what the lawyer had said, and Kay's response was classic:

"Well, good for Barb, that little minx. But she should have spent it, for heaven's sake."

Nina had an entirely different reaction. She told me to be careful what I do with money that I didn't actually earn, because it will always follow me. I know she was thinking about the inheritance she got when her parents were killed and how she squandered a lot of it on Chyna's skeezy baby daddy, Sid.

I happen to agree with my mother. I think Aunt Barbara should have lived a little higher on the hog—maybe not waited until pineapples were on sale to make that soup—but as my dad is fond of saying, you can't spend other people's money. I don't think I ever really knew what he meant until now.

✦ ✦ ✦

The mystery of why Aunt Barbara left me the money was partially solved via FedEx a few days after the party. I had just come from the girls' new apartment, where I reorganized the kitchen and refereed their umpteenth squabble, this one about shelf space in their bathroom. I keep promising myself that I'm going to stay out of it, but the petty side of me loves watching them bicker (as I predicted they would) until I swoop in and turn chaos into order. It's quite the heady power trip. All in all though, I'd say they are managing pretty well. If they weren't, there's no way I'd be going to Hawaii for two weeks. But Laura has taken on the role of birth partner with gusto. And Vivs is in the salad days of her pregnancy . . . sixteen weeks and counting! She's back to working out and she is really glowing.

Anyway, I found a large FedEx envelope leaning against the front door when I got home. I assumed it was from Mr. Ho, and I was right. After grabbing a coconut water from the fridge, I sat down at the kitchen table and ripped it open. There were some documents to sign and a quick note from Mr. Ho telling me where to send them back. There was also a thick manila envelope with my name written in the same handwriting I recognized from Christmas and birthday cards. Aha! A note from Aunt Barbara! A message from the great beyond. And hopefully an explanation.

But the envelope held none of those things. Inside I found a stack of carefully preserved original pieces of artwork created by a young Jennifer Howard, lovingly bound together with a paperclip shaped like a cat's face.

"Oh, wow," I said to no one as I leafed through the pages. There were drawings of proportionally questionable humans and oddly shaped animals, and other colorful scribbles you'd associate with a child's artwork. One picture stopped me—a large, bold pink and purple flower in the middle of the page. Some immature handwriting across the bottom read *Aunt Barbara you are the prettiest flower in the field love Jenny.* At least I think that's what it said. Between the penmanship and the spelling, it was hard to be sure.

It's an interesting moment when you realize the impact you've had on someone's life without ever knowing it. The fact that Aunt Barbara had kept every crappy piece of artwork my mother made me send her was incredibly touching. I suddenly felt guilty for not making more of an effort.

With tears in my eyes, I called my mother.

"Am I a bad person?" I asked after telling her about the manila envelope.

"Jennifer, don't be silly. You were always kind to Aunt Barbara. She didn't expect much from any of us."

"But she kept those pictures for all these years." I sniffled.

"I know. That lawyer sent your father a bunch of photographs she'd saved from when they were kids."

"He must have loved that."

"He did. Look, she was in our lives as much as she wanted to be. You have nothing to feel bad about . . . except maybe not donating more of your money to charity."

I should have seen that one coming. Ever since we told my parents our plans for Aunt Barbara's $700,000, I have been receiving regular jabs about our decision.

"Mom, I think five percent is enough. We're investing the rest in the business."

"Ten percent would be better."

"I'm hanging up. I love you."

✦ ✦ ✦

It's a cloudy and cool last day of school, the kind you sometimes get in June for no particular reason, but that doesn't keep the kids from having a great time. We end up playing wiffle ball instead of softball, so that no cars will be harmed. As you can imagine, Bruce Willis is very relieved. Actually, I'm kidding. Ron couldn't make it to the picnic, so his beloved BMW was never in harm's way.

The kids are enjoying grilled hot dogs and chips courtesy of Jackie Westman's husband, who, I discovered, had recently purchased EJ's deli. The jig is up, Jackie! No more just bringing cups for you!

I'm just about to grab a garbage bag and start the clean-up process when I see Alison Lody has beaten me to it.

"What are you looking at?" Peetsa comes to stand beside me. She has mustard on her lip; I motion for her to wipe it away.

"Just Alison doing my job for me. Maybe she can be class mom next year."

"She really changed this year."

"Did she?" I wonder. "Maybe we changed."

Peetsa face-farts. "I know I did. I'm a single mother and I sell cars!"

She starts to tell me about her first sale, but we're interrupted when Sylvie Pike comes flowing by in a bright blue peasant skirt and white pullover sweater. She gives me a high five.

"Good job," she tells me.

"You too." I smile. "Even if you did trick me into leading safety patrol."

"I have no idea what you're talking about!" she says with fake indignation. "But while I have you, can I put you down for class mom next year?"

"Uh, that would be a 'Hell no.'" She turns to Peetsa, who shakes her head immediately.

"I have a full-time job."

The look Sylvie gives us says this isn't the last we'll be hearing from her.

Something tells me I've already been volunteered.

Acknowledgments

I have no one to thank. I did it all myself.

Who am I kidding? It takes a freaking village to get this done.

First on the list . . . thank *you* for reading my first book! You took a chance on an unknown author and made me feel like a rock star just for writing it. And thanks for sharing your nightmare class mom stories! They were as horrifying as they were inspirational.

A special thanks to Robert Folsom, KC resident and an invaluable resource to me on all things Native American. You're the best!

A big thanks to the whole crew at Henry Holt and Company for even wanting a second book. Serena, Maggie, Pat, Jessica, and Maddie, you are a dream team to work with. My writing is always a bit sharper after a meeting with you guys.

And while I'm thanking the suits, I need to give a shout-out to the groovy folks at Raincoast Books who are my Canadian distributor. Fleur, I've never met you, but your emails are extremely thorough!

Thanks to super-agent Paul "Lefty" Fedorko for negotiating a much better deal than I deserved, and for being my one-man fan club.

Kelly Ripa, your support and encouragement meant everything to me. Thank you!

Shout-out to my sister, Wendy, who, between gardening and golf, somehow squeezed in the time to read a few drafts of this story and give me some very helpful insights.

She's going to think I'm nuts, but I have to thank Ali Wentworth, who tirelessly answered (and continues to answer) every stupid new guy question I had about being an author . . . including the all-important "What page do I sign the book on?"

And finally, thank you to my husband, Michael, and my daughters, Jamie and Misha, for being in my corner. You guys are the reason for everything.

About the Author

Laurie Gelman was born and raised in the Great White North. She spent twenty-five years as a broadcaster in both Canada and the United States before trying her hand at writing novels. The author of *Class Mom*, Laurie has appeared on *Live with Kelly and Ryan*, *Watch What Happens Live*, and *The Talk*, among others. She lives in New York City with her husband, Michael Gelman, and two teenage daughters.